Summer
at the
Castle
Cafe

Donna Ashcroft

Summer at the Castle Cafe

bookouture

Published by Bookouture in 2018

An imprint of StoryFire Ltd.

Carmelite House
50 Victoria Embankment
London EC4Y 0DZ

www.bookouture.com

ISBN: 978-1-78681-371-8
eBook ISBN: 978-1-78681-370-1

This book is a work of fiction. Names, characters, businesses,
organizations, places and events other than those clearly in the
public domain, are either the product of the author's imagination
or are used fictitiously. Any resemblance to actual persons, living or
dead, events or locales is entirely coincidental.

To Jules Wake,
I couldn't have done it without you x

Chapter One

Alice Appleton glanced out of Castle Café's front windows as she assembled a chocolate and strawberry gelato that would rival any from Sicily, despite being made in a small seaside town near Dorset.

Bright sunshine shone onto the café's patio outside and sparkled on the sea beyond. Alice skimmed the stunning view and her eyes caught on a blue rowing boat bobbing on the water. Her stomach rolled so she looked away, adding a layer of chocolate sprinkles to her scrumptious creation and wiping down the work-surfaces. She polished the fingerprints off the cappuccino machine so it gleamed, before heading out from behind the counter.

Alice had worked in the Castle Café since she moved to the area four months before, and the sunny room still made her smile. The walls had recently been painted a fresh cream and were decorated with an eclectic mixture of art from the local gallery; vases filled with pink geraniums sat on the tables; and Ella Fitzgerald played on a record player perched on the corner of a counter that displayed a mouth-watering selection of cakes.

The café had been built inside the ground floor of one of the castle's original turrets and a cosy extension provided plenty of space for holidaymakers to sit. The upper levels of Cove Castle housed a restored chapel, a gift shop and the owner's offices and living quarters, including a large library that tourists came from far and wide to visit. A few years earlier, the previous owner had added a restaurant that opened in the afternoons and evenings for those who wanted more than hot drinks and cakes. On colder days, the locals and tourists headed for the restaurant, but today the sun shone, so the café had filled before midday and the room buzzed with voices.

On her usual mission to serve as many customers in as little time as possible, Alice sped between the tables, heading for the back of the café where the tourist she'd named 'Sir Crankster' sat reading a newspaper. She gripped her tray tightly as she dodged a toddler playing with a doll on the floor. As she did so, her foot caught on someone's handbag and she tripped, hands flailing as the ice cream on her tray leapt off with a flip worthy of an Olympic gymnast.

'Perfect,' she groaned as the dessert somersaulted and landed in a nil-point mess on the floor, firing an impressive splat onto Sir Crankster's jacket. The man rose slowly from the chair and stared at the mess, watching the milky gloop drip to the floor.

'You idiot!' he squawked, making everyone in the small café fall silent. Even the flower in the vase on his table seemed to wilt.

'I'm so sorry.' Alice went red, and frowned at the floor, which now looked reminiscent of a child's finger-painting. 'I tripped.'

She wiped her suddenly damp hands on her white frilly apron, avoiding looking at the crimson-faced man as she knelt to pick up the pieces of broken glass, feeling her entire body flush. Six months ago, she'd have served a dozen customers, balancing a tray of desserts in one hand and pirouetting her way around the tables. These days her grace seemed to have deserted her.

'Excuses!' spat the man. 'This isn't what I expect from a reputable café, you'd be better suited to a truck stop on the M5.'

'I… ' Alice tried to smile as she framed an apology.

'Don't you flutter those eyelashes at me young woman, a pretty face isn't going to get you out of this mess. This jacket is new and you've ruined it. I'm going to complain to the management.'

Alice nodded her agreement as her boss, Cath Lacey, appeared from the back with a dustpan and a mop. Cath's red curls shone in the afternoon sunlight and her permanent smile had moved up a couple of watts.

'I'm so sorry,' Cath said, reaching down to pull Alice up from the floor with one hand before placing herself between the two of them. The gesture was sweet but embarrassing. At twenty-eight, Cath was only two years her senior, yet she behaved like her mother.

'If you come into the kitchen, we'll sort out your jacket.' Cath pushed Alice further behind her, handing her the mop and bucket as she manoeuvred the customer efficiently towards the back of the café. Cath wore the same black-and-white uniform as Alice, but her straight back and determined air made her look more like a sergeant major than a café manager.

Alice stifled a sigh. Had it really only been six months since she'd been running the restaurant in London? Now she was here, trying to change her life and making a big mess of it.

'Alice will clear up while I serve you another ice cream, and you can have a lovely slice of cake on the house to go with it. I'd recommend the Death by Chocolate if you've got a sweet tooth. If we don't get the stains out of your jacket, you can let me know how much we owe you for dry cleaning.'

Their conversation faded and Alice knelt down and mopped the last of the dessert from the oak floor. The hum of conversation from the other customers had resumed but she didn't look up. Instead she continued to sweep and mop without catching anyone's eye, but her stomach was in knots.

When she had finished, Alice stood quickly, making a beeline for the kitchen. On her way, she saw one of their regulars, Ted Abbott, who always popped in for a drink and chat after finishing his postal round. He gave Alice a kind grin and mouthed *don't worry love*. She nodded, holding her tears at bay and marched into the kitchen, picking up a bag of newly ironed tea towels and tablecloths that Cath had dumped on the floor.

Alice switched on the lights, illuminating the bright yellow walls. A blue Aga sat to the left of the room, next to a butler sink filled with soapy water. Alice took out the plug, then rinsed the sink while the water disappeared. Next, she put the linen away, folding every item carefully.

Alice stopped to rest her head against the cool wood of one of the large oak cabinets that loomed over the kitchen counter. She closed her eyes and took a few deep breaths. Even the slightest things could set her off now, things that would never have scratched the surface before.

Exhaling noisily, Alice opened the heavy cupboard door and grimaced at the mess. There were tall cups mixed with teacups, mismatched glasses of varying sizes scattered across the dusty surface, mugs and… was that cutlery? *In a cupboard?* She began to pull everything out, blowing dust from the china and glass, arranging everything on the kitchen counter below, feeling her pulse slow from a speedy hammer to a soft patter as she worked.

Alice knew she needed to get back to the front, but Cath was there and her colleague had proved herself to be much better with the customers.

Wiping everything down, Alice arranged the glasses, cups and mugs in height order and put the cutlery in a drawer with other members of the same family. There were still three shelves to sort, did she have time? It wouldn't take long but she'd need a chair to reach them – five foot five didn't get you far. She hopped onto a chair and leaned an arm on the bottom shelf, reaching up to pull down – *oh dear god* – herbs and bowls. She shook her head as the shelf shifted under her arm, followed quickly by a sharp crack and an ominous snap. The chair wobbled as she eased back to see what had happened.

'*No, no, no,*' Alice moaned as the cupboard tilted and dropped down the wall, spewing shards of white plaster over the worktops and newly arranged kitchenware. The cupboard jerked and stopped where it was, hanging in mid-air like a drunken trapeze artist. Then, as if part of a synchronised routine, the rest of the contents of the top shelves began to slide forward.

Alice froze as a teapot and three cups tumbled out, crashing onto the worktop, barely missing the glasses she'd organised, scattering across the room in tiny pieces. Instinct alone made her lean forwards and grab the cupboard door, slamming it shut and probably smashing more crockery in her attempt to save it. The chair wobbled and she almost lost her balance again before righting herself. Turning backwards, Alice held the door closed with her head, fighting tears.

What was she doing? She'd never done anything this stupid when she'd been working at the restaurant in London.

'What's going on?' Cath stumbled into the kitchen, almost tripping over the chair Alice was standing on.

'I…' Alice opened her eyes, taking in Cath's horrified expression. 'I was reorganising the cupboard.' Somehow the explanation made her feel worse. 'I'm an idiot.'

Cath shook her bouncy red curls and smiled. 'You're a gem Alice, you've just been working too hard since you moved to Castle Cove and spending too much time training for the triathlon you're doing instead of having fun.' She tiptoed her way over the broken bits of crockery and put a hand out to hold the cupboard door shut. 'I knew this would happen eventually, my boyfriend put it up, but he did it in a hurry. Can you see if you can find something to keep it shut, a nail perhaps? Don't fancy my chances trying to catch this stuff if we open the door, and I know a friendly carpenter we can call on to get it upright again.'

Alice hopped off the chair, looking around at the wonky cupboard balancing against the wall, and the smashed glasses, china and plaster scattered across the worktops and floor. 'The mess!' Her heart began to palpitate.

'Nothing a sweep won't fix.' Cath fixed Alice with a stern expression. 'Don't go crying over spilt ice creams and cupboards, Alice, there are far worse things on heaven and earth.'

'I'm not sure I can do this…'

'You need to stop beating yourself up. That man out there,' Cath bounced her curls in the direction of the café, 'has complained every time he's been here this week. If it's not the Cuban art hurting his eyes, it's the temperature of his green tea. He even said the chocolate cake I gave him was too sweet! I ask you, who needs that kind of negativity in their life?'

'Not me.' Alice frowned. 'It was an accident.'

'Never doubted it, but if he comes in again, perhaps you could try using an extra scoop of ice cream?' Cath grinned, her green eyes dancing. 'And I'll give you a list of all the other customers I'd like you to see off, if you like?'

Alice relaxed as tears pricked her eyes. 'I'll clear it all up and replace everything that's broken.'

Cath pursed her lips, erasing her sunny expression for a couple of seconds until it flashed back again. 'No chance, I'm actually relieved to find out you do things wrong.'

'What do you mean?'

'You're so efficient, I was beginning to wonder if you were one of those Stepford women.' She grinned.

'Should I be offended?'

Cath laughed. 'Absolutely not. You're the most organised colleague anyone could ever want, it's just intimidating having someone do everything right all the time. I've never met anyone as methodical as you.'

'I'm sorry.'

'Don't be silly.' Cath squeezed her shoulder. 'I'm joking Alice, you're an absolute godsend. With Lily King, my right-hand woman, covering a maternity leave in the castle restaurant, I don't know what I'd have done without you. Come on, you can help me clear up after we shut. I don't think anyone will notice a few missing cups, it's all forgotten.'

She lifted a hand before thumping it back down on the cupboard. 'Can you find me a nail and hammer before we go back out front please, my hand's starting to cramp.'

'Sure.'

'And shall we finally go for that drink tonight, there's a quiz at the Anglers and you'll get to meet more of the locals?' Cath's smile was infectious.

'I can't, I'm sorry, I've still got to swim.' Alice went to find the small toolbox, swallowing down the huge bubbles of panic.

'Maybe you'll have time afterwards?'

'I might…' Alice lied. Shuffling through the toolbox, she found a hammer and nail and handed it to her boss.

'You want to see how the customers are doing?' Cath asked. 'I think Ted's almost ready to pay. He'll make you feel better, he might even have some gossip to share.'

'You think he's been steaming envelopes open again?' Alice joked as she headed for the café. When she got to the kitchen door Alice's eyes lingered on the customers catching up over hot drinks and huge slabs of cake. Beyond them the horizon beckoned and the sea glittered in the radiant sunshine.

After her shift, Alice would have to face her biggest fear again – she wasn't ready, but she wouldn't give up. Over the past sixteen weeks, she'd been absorbed into the Castle Cove community – that and working in the café had made her feel like she belonged, and despite being at her lowest ebb, they had given her the strength to carry on.

Chapter Two

The sea might look calm but Jay O'Donnell knew better than to trust appearances: like women, what you saw wasn't always what you got. Glancing at his watch – *damn, was it already that late?* – he steered the lifeboat west, which was apparently the direction the teenagers had been heading in when they'd set off.

If Jay had a pound for every idiot who went to sea in a rowing boat without a freaking lifejacket, he'd be rich enough to buy his own yacht.

He grimaced, checking the sky, squinting his blue eyes at the sultry late-afternoon sunshine. Good job it was the end of May because otherwise it would've been dark by now. At least they had a few hours of daylight to search and the weather was good. The coastguard had called them and were looking too, so hopefully it wouldn't take long to locate the kids, but he still didn't like it. Surely they should have seen them by now?

Jay's stomach churned just as his best friend Shaun Wright thumped him on the back. Shaun was a big man, not as tall as Jay, but broader-set and the force made Jay cough.

'You look happy.'

Jay let out a short hiss between his teeth. 'Mel's flight to Dubai.' He checked his watch again. 'Takes off in twenty minutes.'

'And you're here?'

Jay kept his eyes on the horizon. 'She wasn't happy.'

'Mate.' Shaun thumped him on the back again, this time harder. 'You're not even on call today, you know you're an idiot?'

Jay shrugged. 'These kids are only seventeen, God knows what they were thinking.'

'I imagine hormones got in the way of actual thought.'

'Yes, but who goes for a nice little row on the sea at four in the afternoon without taking any lifejackets or phones?'

'I've always wanted to ask, were you ever young or did you hatch from an egg middle-aged?'

Jay sighed. 'Twenty-seven isn't middle-aged, and since I've lived in Castle Cove for most of those years, and have known you for all of them, you know the answer to that.'

'Have I known you that long?' Shaun grimaced. 'Wow I feel old.' He turned his face to check to the left of them. He had a small bump on his nose from an old rugby injury. That, and his intense green eyes and boyish face, had made him popular with the girls at school. Still did, only now those girls were women.

'She really gone for good?' Shaun changed the subject.

'So she says.' Jay answered frowning. He'd been seeing Mel for eight months, ever since he'd helped fish her out of Castle Cove one afternoon when she'd been learning to surf after consuming half a bottle of prosecco. They'd had fun; the simple, have lots of sex without too many strings kind, but she'd been studying for a hotel management degree and had landed herself an amazing placement in Dubai, and now she wanted more.

'Did you even consider joining her?'

Jay swept his eyes across the horizon, at the dark water, and took in a deep breath of salty air. 'Nope.'

'Think you'll wait?'

'For what?' Jay sighed. Shaun had always been a romantic, ever since he'd set eyes on his first love in sixth form.

'Her,' his friend grunted.

'I don't think that would be a good idea for either of us. She asked me if I saw her in my future last night, I just… what does that even mean?' His eyes flickered over the sea again and he stopped. 'See that?' He pointed, then turned to clue in Mark and Jenny, the other lifeboat volunteers in the back of the boat.

'What?' Shaun asked.

'Something red, over there.'

Shaun lifted the binoculars secured around his neck and angled them towards the spot. It might have been thirty seconds before he said, 'Looks like an oar.'

'Shit.' Jay shook his head as he turned the boat and headed towards it. You never knew what you were going to find on a rescue. Like Shaun, he'd been volunteering on the lifeboats for nine years. Shaun had followed in his uncle's footsteps, while Jay had volunteered at the age of eighteen, after he'd watched a lifeboat launch a rescue.

Despite the years, he'd never come to terms with the unhappy endings. And you never knew, that was the worst of it. Sometimes you'd find someone who had been in the water for three hours and they'd be fine; sometimes a short swim, a few minutes of trouble and a person wouldn't make it. He tensed his hands and let them go, no point in going there.

'See anything?'

'No,' Mark shouted from behind him.

Shaun was still searching the water. His friend had eagle eyes, the best in the business. If there was a thread of cotton surfing a wave, Shaun would find it.

'Not yet.' The tension in his voice matched Jay's.

Why did he do this to himself? He could be sipping a beer in an airport lounge right now, having a last, slow goodbye kiss with Mel. Trouble is, they both knew he'd rather be here – maybe that had been the problem all along.

'Yes, maybe.' Shaun paused, giving the boat time to eat up some distance. They passed by the oar, Jenny picked it up, and they carried on.

'There's a shape, I can't make it out.' Shaun stopped talking again. Jay squeezed his eyes but still couldn't see anything, just waves, waves and more waves.

Despite the danger he loved it, loved the rise and fall of sea spray, how the horizontal slice of water at the horizon welded itself to the sky. He loved the feeling he got when they saved a life, getting there just in time. He'd lost count of the number of people they'd rescued, but refused to put a number to those they'd lost.

'Got it, something, looks like a boat, and it's blue.' Shaun's voice lifted and Jay cranked the speed up a notch. They needed to hurry, sometimes seconds meant the difference between life and death.

'They're both lying down.' Shaun sounded confused. 'Maybe hurt, I can't see from here.'

He shifted to the edge and signalled Jenny and Mark to ready themselves. 'Oh… okay, I see.' Shaun's voice tilted and dropped as he peered through the binoculars. 'I think they might be okay.' His shoulders relaxed as they pulled closer to the boat and he leaned over the side. 'I noticed you lost your oar, sir, I'm just wondering what happened to your trousers?'

Ten minutes later a red-faced couple were walking towards their parents, wrapped in towels while the crew watched.

'They didn't realise the time apparently, and they didn't even notice that they'd knocked one of the oars out of the boat.' Shaun chuckled, slapping Jay on the back. 'Oh, to be young again.'

'You're hardly ancient, and they ought to be billed for wasting our time.'

'I'll take that ending over any other.'

Jay ground his teeth. Of course he was pleased, it just rankled how many perfectly healthy people were happy to put themselves in harm's way for no good reason. He saw it at least twice a week. Death, when it came, was swift and unfair and sometimes you had no choice over it, but for many it could be avoided if they'd just used a bit of sense.

Unfortunately, like the couple in the rowing boat, most people didn't think about the danger until it was too late.

Chapter Three

Alice squeezed her feet into the sand, doing a Mexican wave with her toes. The wetsuit dug into every crease and crevice of her body, moulding itself to her like a second skin. How did people wear these things?

She wriggled her hips to see if the suit would dislodge. But it didn't help. Warm rain tumbled into her eyes, dripping down her face, and she swiped it with the back of her hand. She already looked like she'd been swimming.

The sun was barely visible but Alice could just make out a shimmer high in the sky behind the clouds. Dawn had well and truly arrived, complete with a flock of diving seagulls that were taking an annoying interest in the bag she'd perched by the edge of the promenade. She watched the waves roll in and out, focusing on the pretty white foam, instead of the heave and sway in her stomach.

The sky looked dark but the sea seemed calm, although it wasn't always easy to tell what lay beneath the surface.

Alice wouldn't go far but perhaps she could dip her toes in today? Maybe she'd be able to get up to her knees this time? Just the thought had her stomach somersaulting.

'Come on,' she said to herself. She needed to hurry, there weren't many people about, but if she didn't get a move on she might attract an audience. Plenty of people walked their dogs along this beach in the mornings.

Biting her lip, she dropped her towel on the sand and walked forwards.

Bump, bump, bump. The few steps it took to get to the edge of the water had her heart accelerating. Her muscles joined in, making her limbs heavy and uncooperative. The waves rolled in and out, over and over and she stood for a few moments watching. Funny how quickly they reshaped the surface of the sand; if only life's memories could be erased so easily.

Could she dip her toes in the sea this time? Her heart thumped and blood rushed to her ears making her lightheaded as she moved closer. There was a training schedule to stick to for the triathlon and she only had eleven weeks and two days to conquer this, or every change she'd made over the last few months would be pointless.

Ignoring her chattering teeth, Alice forced herself forwards and dipped one toe into the water, absorbing the cold like a punch. Even at the beginning of June, the temperature of the sea barely hit fifteen degrees. But, nothing felt as bad as the first step, at least that's what her mum always said. She eased the rest of her foot into the water forcing herself to leave it there, and shivered uncontrollably when a wave hit her ankle.

'C-c-c-cold... ' Something dark fluttered in her solar plexus making her breathing tight. She hadn't had breakfast but felt like throwing up, maybe she should sit? But what if a freak wave came and dragged her out, sucked her under the waves and held her down?

She stepped back out of the water. Her foot tingled from the chill but her heartbeat slowed down a notch. Alice bit her lip and stared at the sand. How many times would it take before she could do this? This must be her hundredth attempt in the last twelve weeks, since she'd been training for the triathlon, and the recurring nightmare about drowning was getting worse each time.

Her heart hammered as she forced herself to step forwards again and her breathing became shallow as the icy water enveloped her feet.

She'd written a plan. Had revised it again last night, had to stick to it no matter what, time was running out.

Alice forced herself to take another step and she felt the sea slither up her ankles. When the next wave came, it covered her calves and her breath caught in her throat. She swallowed the panic even as her breath shortened and she began to gasp.

Five minutes, five minutes more was all. In the battle between fear and schedule, the schedule had to win.

Had to.

Sharp fingernails bit into soft palms as she continued to stand, absorbing each wave as it hit, counting down.

'Sixty, fifty-nine, fifty-eight, fifty-seven.' She'd do each minute, one second at a time and build on it. 'Fifty-six… '

'What the hell are you doing?'

The voice made Alice jump and she half turned, determined not to move her feet from the water. The beach looked empty apart from a golden lab snuffling a wet stick and to his right, a glaring man.

'Me?' The word shot out on a squeak, was she standing on something important? She checked underneath her, there was nothing obvious. Maybe Mr Grumpy had a special space on the beach that she'd somehow strayed over?

'Haven't you looked at the sky? You shouldn't be swimming.'

'I… 'Alice blushed. 'I'm—' A wave thumped her legs and her toes sunk into the sand sending her off balance. She wobbled but managed to regain her footing. Her heart hammered as the man drew closer, but she didn't move. Despite the tension in her chest, she was determined to stay where she was.

'Only an idiot would swim in this. If you get yourself stuck out there, it'll be me and my team who has to get you.'

Who was this guy?

Alice watched her toes sink into the water again. Why couldn't the water stand still just for a moment?

'For your information, I wasn't—'

'I've already been out this week rescuing people who should know better,' he snapped.

Her face flushed and she bunched her fists. Didn't he understand? 'I never intended—'

'No-one ever intends to get in trouble.'

The man's eyes narrowed. He wore a grey waterproof jacket and dark jeans that were soaked, like his hair. Water dribbled down his face and she almost lost her breath, seriously, because – forgetting the crappy attitude – this man was unbelievably hot. Tall, over six foot, he was broad like a rugby player with gorgeous blue eyes, and a mouth designed to send a sane women crazy.

'They just do,' he continued.

What was he talking about?

'I've picked up twelve swimmers since January, they've usually got the kit, too.' His eyes rolled over her wetsuit, making frozen nerve endings zing.

Did he have a hearing problem? 'I haven't been in.'

'You're wet.'

'It's raining.' Why was she defending herself?

'Your feet are in the water, even your towel's soaked.' He pointed to the discarded bundle on the beach.

'I— look, it's raining. I didn't swim, I couldn't swim in that if it looked like a mirror, let alone now.' She waved a finger at the horizon, zipping it around as if she were writing in the sky. 'I'm not stupid, I wanted to get a feel for it, not that it's got anything to do with you.'

'Seriously—'

'Who are you anyway, the *swimming police?*' Now it was her turn to interrupt in her loudest, most irritated tone.

He wasn't smiling, but his face changed as she ranted, transforming from red-faced to wide-eyed.

'It's a public beach, is there a law against paddling? Because if there is, you'll have a busy summer arresting half the toddlers in the country.'

'It looked... ' He swept a hand downwards, pointing at her wetsuit.

'Maybe I have a thing for rubber.' She enjoyed the flash of shock on his face. 'Besides, it's a lot more practical than jeans.' She gestured to his wet clothes.

'I—' He held up a hand again. 'I thought... it looked like you were going in and it's dangerous, the currents can be strong when the weather changes. It creates rips, not everyone understands how changeable they are. We rescued a man yesterday who swam too far out, but it's not always such a happy ending.'

'Well thanks for the advice, I'll be sure to save that little gem of positivity for the next time I go in.' Bubbles of anger caught in her throat.

'Paddling's fine, I have no problem with that if it's really what you were planning all along.' His tone suggested otherwise. 'The toddlers of the world are safe.'

She rolled her eyes and shivered, feeling cold but strangely fired up. How long had they been standing in the rain while her feet morphed into iced prunes? She'd lost count.

She'd. Lost. Count.

Alice looked at her feet: she was still standing in the water. Her heartbeat sped up.

'I'm just looking out for you.' Mr Grumpy said in a gentler tone.

Panic fired her temper again. 'Not everyone appreciates being told off when they've done nothing to deserve it,' she shot back.

A wave rolled over her toes bringing with it another shock of cold. She fought to ignore it but her shoulders started to shake.

The man shrugged as the dog nudged his leg with a stick before dropping it. Alice watched as he bent to pick it up, trying to ignore the way the wet material moulded to his legs and behind. Muscles bunched across his shoulders as he threw the stick and he turned, almost catching her watching. Her face flamed.

'I don't think I've ever seen anyone dress like that to just watch the sea and paddle.'

'Then I guess it's time you broadened your horizons.' Alice finally snapped, jerking her feet from the water and marching across the sand, before stomping past him. 'If it's all the same to you, next time can you please just walk away and mind your own business?'

He shook his head, a half smile forming on his mouth. 'I'm afraid there's absolutely zero chance of that. I'm the coxswain on the local lifeboat, which means if anything happens to you out there, I'll be coming, whether you want me to or not.'

Alice rolled her eyes, irritated by the man's arrogance, even as she wondered if she might see him again.

'So, stay safe – or I'll see you again soon.' The man called his dog and headed towards the promenade without looking back. Alice shivered and dragged her eyes to the sand to stop herself from watching the mystery man as he walked away.

Chapter Four

Jay tried knocking before he opened the front door, but he knew from experience his mother wouldn't answer. She was probably too busy talking to her spirits.

'Mum.' He tripped over the black-and-white cat in the hallway, almost landing face-first in a pile of shopping. He picked up the bags and headed for the kitchen, putting the apples, carrots, milk, and teabags away before going into the sitting room.

It felt like time had stood still. There were pictures of him and Steve everywhere: on the mantle, on walls, on random tables and underneath lamps. He tried not to look, but his eyes were drawn to the one of them standing side-by-side on the beach, bikes strewn behind them in the sand, their matching blue eyes lit as the ball hovered frozen in mid-air between them.

Even now he could remember Steve catching it straight afterwards, his expression glowing with the excitement of having beaten his big brother, a tumble of emotions shining from his face. Steve had never been one to hide his feelings, and he hadn't reached the age when he'd learned he should.

Gayle O'Donnell sat on the sofa looking half asleep, her long fingernails sliding across a large pack of Tarot cards.

'Jay?' She asked without opening her eyes and he wondered briefly what she'd do if he said no.

'I've been calling.' Why did he sound so angry when he was with her?

She sighed. 'I'm not sure where my phone is.'

'Probably in your handbag.' He didn't bother looking, it was always in the same place. 'Have you charged it recently?'

'Not this week.' She stood and examined him closely, revealing startling blue eyes. The same colour he saw every day in the mirror. 'I don't need a phone, I'd know if something was wrong.' She tapped a finger on the cards. 'You look tired.'

Jay shrugged. 'Rough night.'

Her skirts swished as she moved closer, then she slid a hand across his cheek. 'Shall I read your cards, find out if what's bothering you is important?'

'No.' He stepped backwards, almost tripping over another cat. She only had two, but they seemed to stalk him. 'That won't be necessary,' he murmured. 'Shall we have some tea?'

She didn't keep coffee in the house, or anything stronger, although it was a little too early for that anyway.

'I wanted to talk about July.' He wandered into the kitchen, knowing from the quiet rustle of skirts and beads that his mother had followed.

'What about July?' Her voice rasped and he heard her drag out a chair. Despite the small size of the kitchen, she'd managed to fill it with an assortment of clutter, including a large crystal ball, white table and four chairs, one of which wobbled. He usually tried to avoid it, but could never remember which of the chairs it was. He put the kettle on and noticed two empty cups in the sink.

'You had a visitor?' She'd shunned her friends after the loss of Steve, and he wasn't aware of any new ones.

'Let me do that for you, dear.' His mother stood and pulled down a couple of pink china cups from one of the cupboards, indicating he should sit. He sat down and immediately realised he'd ended up in the wobbly chair again. Maybe it was just him, he always felt off balance when he was with his mother.

'It's ten years in a couple of months, Mum.' The words dropped into the silence and Jay saw her tense. 'Don't you think we should talk about it?'

'I can never remember if you take sugar.'

'No.' Jay felt a familiar knot form between his shoulder blades. 'I thought we could go to the beach together, maybe have lunch.'

'I might have run out of milk.' His mum pulled the fridge open. There were two pints in the door – Jay knew because he'd just put them there – but he wasn't surprised when she closed it. 'Sorry love, we've run out.'

'You want me to get some?'

She turned, avoiding his eyes. 'I'll use my special tea, you don't need milk with that, if you don't mind.'

Jay didn't bother to answer because it wasn't a question, she did the same thing to him every time he came to the house. She finished making the tea and put it in front of him and he stared at the black liquid. He'd have to drink it, she'd be upset if he didn't and he wasn't here to upset her. He picked up the delicate china cup and sipped the hot tea, trying to avoid swallowing the floating leaves.

A few years ago, he'd swallowed all of them and had almost choked as they slid down his throat, then after gently patting him on the back, his mother had made him drink a whole new cup. That had taught him a lesson he wouldn't forget.

'How's that girl you were seeing?' She squeezed her eyes shut as she tried to remember, revealing a hint of crow's feet. They were the only sign his mum was ageing, and at fifty-five she could still pass for late thirties. He'd often wondered if her youth was the result of moisturiser or magic, maybe there was something to this spiritualisation lark? 'Mel, wasn't it?'

'She's in Dubai.' Jay sipped his tea, avoiding the leaves as best as he could. It tasted bitter but drinkable.

'Long way.' She put down her cup, her blue eyes assessing him carefully and he knew what was coming next. 'You miss her?'

'No.' The word came out on a half laugh. He'd known the relationship was casual from the start. Mel had wanted to leave Castle Cove and he didn't, it was as black and white as that.

'You sad?'

Jay thought about the girl on the beach, about how she'd looked in that wetsuit. 'No.' He took a long sip, feeling the leaves play with the edges of his lips. He finished and put the cup down. As soon as he did so, his mother snatched it to her and swirled the cup in one hand.

'I worry you get lonely.'

Jay laughed. 'I've got plenty of friends.'

And female company if he felt like it, but he wasn't about to share that with his mum. She raised her head and met his eyes as if she'd read his mind.

'I see changes coming,' she whispered looking into the cup again and he braced himself for the inevitable. He used to joke with her about the readings, asking her to stop, but he'd soon learned it was easier just to let her get on with it. 'A girl.'

Jay ground his teeth. There was always a girl.

'This one's different.' She met his eyes again and he looked away. The last one had been different too, only Mel hadn't turned out to be any different from the rest of them.

'There's a new adventure, but I can't make out anything else.' His mother put the cup down. 'We'll check again next week, maybe there'll be more.'

Jay sighed. 'We still haven't talked about going to the beach, remember? About having a walk and lunch, for Steve.' He caught the hint of emotion in her eyes before she looked away. She stood and took both of their cups to the sink, humming as she washed them, along with the other mystery cups. He couldn't bring himself to push her any more. He'd organise the whole thing and then just come early to pick her up.

It had been ten years since his younger brother died and he wasn't going to let his mother avoid it any longer. It was time for both of them to move on.

Chapter Five

Rain hammered down on Alice's helmet and dripped down her face, and the long hill and angle of the wind made the icy water blow straight into her eyes, making it hard to see. She pushed herself and pedalled harder. The trip from Alice's house to the Castle Café clocked in at around three miles normally, but she'd taken an extra-long route this morning, following the outside of the town so she could work up to the six and a half miles she'd need to do for the triathlon. But the steep hills made it hard going.

When she'd first tried the same journey three months before, her legs had screamed like banshees, now they weren't screaming so much as freezing and her shorts were cutting into her skin. Lycra worked well for mobility but wasn't so good for an unpredictable British summer.

Usually at seven thirty in the morning it was light enough to see, but the bad weather had come in a quarter of the way through the journey and now the road looked like something a mole could happily live in. Large green fields and leafy trees framed the road, creating a gloom and dimming visibility even further.

Alice reached out and bashed her bike lights for about the twelfth time. They flickered, but instead of firing up, went out immediately. She bashed them again, but this time they didn't even flicker.

'Dammit.'

Alice would see if she could fix them when she got to the café. The kit in her backpack should have all the equipment, otherwise it would be another grim cycle home if the weather didn't cheer up.

She squinted, concentrating on the tarmac, determined not to accidently ride over a rock and go flying over her handlebars.

Harsh lights shone in front of the bike indicating a car or truck approaching from behind and Alice grimaced through the unexpected rain. The narrow roads sometimes made it difficult for people to pass. She sped up and approached a curve in the road, after this the driver would have space to accelerate, as she couldn't see anyone coming from the other direction.

'Go,' she grumbled, but instead he seemed to drive closer. It had to be a man, a woman would hang back, not drive right up her...

Surely, he'd move soon, take the opportunity to shoot past? Still, she'd miss the headlights, it was amazing how dark it got when the clouds covered the sky.

The bike bumped over something and Alice heard a clatter; she swayed but managed to straighten up. She pedalled faster, whizzing through a puddle, splashing icy water on her trainers and ankles.

Maybe she could pull over? No, that wouldn't work, there was nowhere safe to stop. The roads were narrow and there weren't any pavements until she got back into town, nearer Cove Castle. She'd have to put up with it.

Unless...

Alice approached a patch of good road, so took a chance and waved her arm back and forth. 'Go.'

The driver didn't get the hint, maybe he was blind?

Lordy, she hoped not.

Starting to feel nervous, Alice skidded a little as she rounded a corner. She'd travelled over three quarters of the way, but didn't give herself time to appreciate the view. She hardly registered the dark spots near the cliffs as they flashed past, determined not to count the places you could hide a body.

Her thighs screamed as she pedalled, and her wrists tensed as she forced herself not to touch the brakes.

Was the driver a murderer or convict escaped from prison? His lights were shining directly on her and hadn't moved position at all. Did he enjoy terrorising cyclists, or was this just a horrible joke?

She needed to move faster and get out of this situation.

Alice's calves ached and her breathing got heavier but she didn't give in. The road leading to the main street and castle looked closer already and she could almost imagine the café. At least the lights from the vehicle behind made cycling easier because she could see everything in her path.

Alice pulled onto Cliff Hill and into the castle car park a few minutes later and jumped off the bike, bending to hold onto her knees, breathing deeply to stop the cramps.

In out. In out.

Sweat mixed with rain dripped down her forehead and her legs shook, but strangely she felt good. More alive than she had in months, aside from when she'd had that ridiculous argument on the beach.

A flicker of light flashed across her body and the bike, as a truck curled into a space nearby. Could it be the same one that had been following her?

Alice turned to see if anyone was around but the car park looked empty. Her heart sped up, even though she knew it was stupid. This was Castle Cove for God's sake, not the middle of London. Still, as she locked her bike her fingers fumbled with the numbers on the combination.

A door opened, making her whirl round. A pair of large feet hit the ground with a bump, followed by a tall, broad body. Alice squeezed her eyes to see better in the darkness and then shot them towards the sky.

'Seriously?' She shook her head as the guy from the beach strode over.

'You need to get your lights fixed.'

His voice sounded rough, like he had a cold starting but didn't know what to do with it. She knew his type, they'd never let something as trivial as a bug stop them from doing what needed to be done.

'You!' He moved closer and squeezed his eyes together, trying to make her out. 'The girl from the beach.' He didn't sound happy that he'd recognised her. 'Have you got a death wish?'

She blew out an irritated breath. 'You nearly forced me off the road driving right up behind me. Do you get points for knocking cyclists off their bikes?'

'Only the annoying ones,' he grumbled.

'What?'

He put his hands on his hips, which emphasised how narrow they were compared to the broadness of his shoulders, and she shivered as tingles appeared in parts of her body they had no business being.

'It's dark.' He tapped a finger at the sky as if she needed it pointing out. 'Or do you still have a problem reading the sky?'

'It started raining during the journey and I didn't know about the lights until it was too late.' Alice admitted. 'Besides, you scared the living daylights out of me, driving up my bum the whole way. Why didn't you just pass, there was plenty of room?'

'I stayed behind you and lit the way. If I hadn't, someone might have come and knocked you off your bike and onto that bum you're so worried about.' His eyes dipped to scan her feet and legs travelling upwards, but then he seemed to realise what he was doing and raised them. Cheek, he didn't even have the decency to look embarrassed.

'I was fine.' Alice turned to pick up her backpack ready to march to work, but he blocked her path. Despite that, and his height, she wasn't afraid, and wasn't that stupid? 'Until I almost fell off my bike trying to stay ahead of you.'

'I slowed.' His forehead creased. 'Dimmed my lights, stayed back. You must have known I was trying to help.'

Alice shook her head. 'How could I know? Your superhero costume was hidden inside your car.' She squeezed her hands into tight fists, feeling the adrenaline in her body fading. 'All I knew was a truck was following me ready to do who knows what.' Her heart juddered as the memory lashed through her. 'You scared me stupid.'

'I'm sorry.' He put his hands in his pockets. 'That wasn't my intention.'

'Look.' Alice drew her eyebrows together. 'I get it. You obviously like to… help people.' She chose her words carefully, substituting 'help' for 'annoy' in her head. 'It's great, honestly, I'm sure the world needs more people like you.'

He narrowed his eyes. Okay, so she probably hadn't sounded like she meant it. 'But I don't.'

'Everyone needs a little help now and then.'

'If I do, I'll be sure to let you know. In the meantime, I'd just like it if you left me alone.'

With any luck, their paths would never cross again. Despite that face and, *mmmmn*, that body, it would be better for her, much better if he left her alone to get on with her adventures.

He rocked back on his heels. 'You'll fix the lights?'

Alice wouldn't risk another ride like the one she'd just had. 'Scouts honour, I've got a toolkit in my backpack.' She pulled it off her shoulders and knelt, the zip had come partly undone at the side so she slid it closed.

'I don't think you were ever a scout.'

'What makes you say that?'

He smiled properly this time, flashing perfect white teeth – of course they were bloody perfect – and her hormones did a triple somersault. 'Because a scout wouldn't have been cycling in the dark with broken lights.'

'You got me.' Alice nodded. 'I wasn't a scout, but I will get the lights fixed. So... ' She checked her watch, making it obvious she was keen to get away. 'If we're done, can I go?'

He looked irritated. 'I didn't realise our conversation was keeping you.'

He stepped to one side and she marched past. It was only a short walk up the hill to work. Alice looked up as the grey stone building came into view. Like a palace in a childhood fairy tale, Cove Castle had turrets at each edge and a huge staircase at the entrance leading to a large wooden doorway.

Alice didn't go up the stairs, instead she stayed on the pavement and headed to the right of the building, towards the café which was located in the bottom of one of the turrets. The back of her neck prickled as she walked, sensing the man was still behind her. Hadn't he seen enough when he'd been following in the truck? It was only when she heard footsteps that she stopped and turned.

'Are you following me?'

'Nope,' he said as he swept past, leaving her standing in the middle of the pavement feeling ridiculous.

'Oh.' Now it was her turn to walk behind him. Her eyes followed the path of the denim of his jeans from his feet upwards to his bum. It only seemed fair that she check it out, given that he'd had ample opportunity to do the same.

His jeans were faded, she could tell even in the half-light and they curved across skin as he walked, giving away just enough to tell her he must work out.

Alice dragged her eyes up and fixed them on the sign above the café. Almost there. Then she'd be able to change, have a cup of tea and a chat with Cath. She'd tell her about the strange man who'd been following her, they'd laugh and that would be that.

Alice nodded to herself, then stopped dead as the mystery man walked up to the café door, opened it and strode in.

Chapter Six

Alice opened the door to the café a crack and peered through it to see the man giving Cath a hug and a kiss on the cheek. He looked taller next to her friend, so big his body dwarfed her. She could just see a flash of Cath's red curls, along with the profile of her smiling face and a couple of small hands hugging him back. She stopped in the doorway and watched her colleague blush. Lover, friend, who was this guy?

'Um, hello.' Alice moved inside and let the door close behind her, feeling oddly deflated.

'Alice, meet Jay, he's the carpenter I told you about. He's come to fix your cupboard. Just one of his many talents, or so I've heard.' Cath winked as Jay turned and Alice watched his expression change as he saw her.

Okay, maybe he hadn't been following her. Carpenter? She was surprised he hadn't made a career out of rescuing people.

'You work here?' Jay frowned.

'I—'

'She's the one who broke the cupboard, almost pulled it off the wall doing her OCD thing.'

'I probably should have worked that out,' Jay murmured. 'I get the feeling you can be trouble.'

'The shelves looked dusty,' Alice grumbled. Okay so she liked keeping busy, and what was wrong with making things neat and tidy? Plenty, judging by her would-be rescuer's expression.

'We wondered if you could take a look, hang it back on the wall and maybe check the door and all the bits that broke. Also, Alice has been on about better shelving in the larder.' Cath looked back and forth between them and her expression changed. 'You know each other?'

'We've… met,' Jay murmured.

'Not really.' Alice tossed her backpack over her shoulder. 'I'd better change, I got wet on my way here because I had to peddle so fast.' She hit Jay with her sternest expression.

'You sure you need my help with the cupboard?' Jay asked, watching her through narrowed eyes as she moved across the café. 'I wouldn't want to… interfere.'

'It's fine,' she said, more sharply than she'd intended.

'No really.' He put his hands on his hips. 'I wouldn't want to get in the way by trying to… *help*.'

Alice stopped and turned to face him, not sure whether to feel annoyed or guilty for giving him such a hard time in the car park. 'I'm sorry about getting mad, but it's mostly your fault.'

'My fault? I'm not sure what happens wherever you come from, but down here we look out for each other. In my book swimming when the weather's bad, or cycling in the dark with no lights is dangerous. I'm not going to apologise for commenting on either, you'll either hurt yourself or someone else, and I'm not a fan of either scenario.'

Alice bristled. 'You're the one who almost made me fall off my bike.'

'Now kids.' Cath put her hands in the air. 'I'm not sure what's going on, but my guess is you both need a dose of caffeine before continuing this conversation. Jay, why don't you set up in the kitchen? Alice, why don't you get changed while I fish out my referee outfit?'

'I'll get changed and make some coffee.' Alice muttered.

'I need to pick up some tools from my truck,' Jay explained. 'Yes, to coffee thank you, so long as you promise not to spit it in.'

Alice raised an eyebrow.

'I like it strong.'

'Same way I like my men,' Cath said in her sing-song voice, grinning and following Alice to the café counter as the bell on the front door tinkled, signalling Jay had left. 'You never told me you'd met our local carpenter.'

'I bumped into him on the beach about a week ago,' Alice admitted.

'I've never seen anyone irritate him, he's generally very placid, he must have the hots for you, girl.' Cath looked delighted.

'Even if that were true, I'm not interested,' Alice said. 'I'm leaving in September remember, besides he keeps telling me off. *Don't swim, don't cycle.*' She made a yappy mouth with her hand. 'He'll be telling me not to breathe next.'

'If you're not interested, why didn't you mention him?'

'Because he didn't make enough of an impression on me to remember,' she lied. 'He thought I was swimming when the sea was rough.'

'I'll bet he gave you a hard time about it.' Cath laughed, putting on the water heater and coffee machine. 'You know he volunteers on the lifeboats?' Alice nodded. 'He's lovely, but he gets very serious if you suggest doing anything even slightly risky, especially on the water. He could do with someone in his life to lighten him up.'

'I'm not exactly a lightening up kind of girl.'

'Maybe he'll lighten you up, then?'

'Not listening.' Checking the door, Alice took off her jacket, then unzipped her backpack and started to pull everything out. There was her crisp black-and-white uniform, a small towel, first aid kit, torch, water bottle, mobile, keys and purse. She mentally ticked them off as she arranged them on the counter. 'Something's missing.'

'What?'

'Can't see my fix-all kit.' She frowned.

'What's a fix-all kit?'

'Puncture repair, spanner, tools to fix things on the bike, I always take it with me.' She turned the bag upside down and shook it. 'It's in a little waterproof bag, I wanted to see if I could fix my lights on my break.'

'Did you pack it?' Cath asked.

Alice raised an eyebrow.

'Stupid question, what was I thinking?'

'It was near the top.' She shut her eyes. 'I remember clearly putting it in last so I could get to it easily.' She paused, remembering. 'The bag was unzipped at the side when I got here, I went over a few bumps and I was going really fast, it could have fallen out.'

'You could find it later?'

'Not without lights, and I'd have to walk to search properly,' she tutted. 'I'll be fine to cycle tonight, the weather's getting sunnier later and it'll be light until ten. I'll keep an eye on the road while I'm cycling back and maybe I'll spot it.'

'I could give you a lift?'

'You'd never get my bike into your Mini. I'll be fine Cath, honestly.'

'If you're sure.' Cath looked her up and down. 'You're dripping all over the floor. Go and change. Don't worry about making Jay's Americano, I'll do it for you, then I'll open up. Apparently, there are a couple of coaches coming in this morning, Lily hasn't completely abandoned us, she's promised to take a break from helping out at the restaurant today to pop in to help us out with lunch.' Cath peered out of the window. 'It's brightening up. Do me a favour, will you please give Jay a chance? There's a lot more to that man than you see at first glance.'

Chapter Seven

So, I'm-not-swimming girl worked in the café. Jay was surprised, he'd thought she was just another tourist, destined to be here one day and gone the next. Instead she lived and worked here and, from the nurturing glances Cath had been giving her, there was a story there. Not that he was interested.

Jay picked up the Americano Alice had handed him and took a sip. Urgh, the drink tasted awful, how could you work in a café and not be able to make a decent coffee? She was obviously well out of her comfort zone. He'd have to pour it down the sink when she wasn't looking.

Which wouldn't be long.

Alice had been whirling in and out of the small kitchen like a hyperactive yo-yo all morning. She must have been hovering over customers on the other side of the door catering to their every whim. He shook his head as he perused the cupboard. He couldn't imagine what she'd done to it, she didn't look the type to be swinging from shelving.

Alice swept into the room.

'Whose genius idea was it to nail the cupboard shut?' he grumbled, running a finger over the large nail someone had bashed into the bottom, splintering the door.

Alice fired him a look of disgust that did strange things to his stomach. He really needed a new girlfriend.

'Cath and I both thought it would be better to do that than lose any more of the crockery. I assume you have a better idea, perhaps you'd have used your laser vision to hold it shut?'

'At least that wouldn't have damaged the wood.' Jay stroked his finger across the bottom of the cupboard looking for more nails, trying not to watch the strands of blonde hair falling out of her ponytail. Alice narrowed her eyes at him, were they grey? He hadn't noticed the colour on the beach. Not that he cared. 'It's too heavy for one person to get down when it's full, I'll need help.'

'I'll do it.' Alice frowned. 'Unless you don't trust me?'

'I'm not going to answer that without a weapon in my hand.' He took in her small frame; she didn't look strong enough but he'd been impressed with the speed she'd cycled, the power in those legs. 'Okay.'

Alice looked surprised.

'It's not exactly life-threatening,' he explained, easing himself up onto the counter and putting his large hands underneath the edge of the cupboard. 'If I hold it upright, can you use the claw of my hammer to take the nail out, then empty it?'

'No problem.'

Alice went to get a chair and hopped up. Even with the uniform on, Jay could see her arms and legs were lean with a hint of golden brown tan. She had long legs, even though she was small, and a solid strength to her body. He took the weight of the cupboard, grunting.

'It's heavy,' he mumbled, averting his eyes from her small waist as she reached up to work on the bottom of the door. She had the nail out in seconds, impressing him, then pulled it open.

'Damn,' she muttered, her full lips forming an appealing pink pout.

'What?'

'Some of it's broken.'

'I guess that's what happens when a full cupboard almost falls off the wall.'

Alice sighed and began to pull down the crockery, placing the cups, plates and bowls in neat piles beside her. One pile of broken and the other of salvageable items. She worked quickly and efficiently and the cupboard lightened as she progressed.

'Watch your fingers on the broken bits,' Jay said, watching her small hands grab and swing a jagged piece of glass onto the counter. 'They look sharp.'

Not as sharp as the look she gave him.

'Superhero, remember.' He shrugged. 'All part of the job description.'

'Telling people what to do?'

'I'm just trying to save you from a cut finger, it's no big deal.'

'I can save myself. Besides, haven't you fulfilled your quota of rescues today?'

'Always room for one more.'

'Then look for hedgehogs on your drive home. The cupboard's worse than I thought,' Alice said as she emptied the last of it. 'The wood's all split at the back.'

She hopped down from the chair, out of the way, and he slowly let the bottom of the cupboard drop further down the wall, before moving round to view the damage. He smoothed his fingertips over the crack.

He loved the texture of wood, always had. He'd built his first chair at school when he was only sixteen. He'd been surprised to find it in his mum's bedroom when he'd been draining the radiators a few months before. God knows why, it was an ugly thing. But he'd never forgotten how much he loved the feel of it under his hands, the way it felt to create something that would last no matter what. He unscrewed the unit and put it on the floor. He'd have to go into town later and pick up supplies. The job wouldn't take long, he should finish today and could then cost up the extra shelving in the larder.

Alice pulled the bin closer and started throwing the broken crockery into it as the door banged, signalling Cath's return. She was laden down with a tray of dirty plates and mugs.

'The last lot of customers are leaving, where were you?'

'Sorry, I was helping.' Alice bobbed her head in the direction of the crockery.

'You got it off the wall.' Cath put her load down and began to pack the dishwasher. 'What's the damage?'

'More broken stuff and a very sick cupboard.' Alice looked miserable. 'I'm sorry.' She tossed a couple more cups in the bin.

'I can do that.' Jay threw in some plates. 'I'm wearing gloves.'

'It's my mess.'

He continued to chuck the broken bits away, despite Alice's glares.

'Don't look like that,' Cath admonished. 'He's a good carpenter, I don't want you scaring him off. Besides he's right, if you cut yourself you're going to bugger up that training schedule of yours. You load the dishwasher, I'll get the rest of the stuff from out front. Simon's expecting at least four coach loads today and the castle restaurant's fully booked for lunch so we're bound to be busy.'

'Is that the grandson of the previous owner, Simon Wolf?' Jay asked, Cath nodded. 'I didn't realise he'd taken over already.'

'He turned up a few weeks ago, when Jack Wolf retired due to ill health. Apparently Simon was running a place somewhere in Australia, he only came back because Jack begged him. Simon's okay, a bit of a slave driver, so we need to make sure we're ready before the rush. Have a chat with Jay while you're packing stuff away, Alice.' Even he could hear the calculation in Cath's voice. 'Tell him about your training, he might have some tips. You've done the triathlon, haven't you Jay?'

Turning he caught Alice's face. Wow, her permanent expression seemed to be mad, or maybe it was just him?

'You're doing the triathlon?'

'Yes.' She turned her back, clearly wanting to avoid further conversation with him.

'How's the training going?'

'Fine, good, great.' Alice started to stack plates and cups into the dishwasher with military precision.

'You done one before?'

She shook her head without turning.

'Is that why you're cycling to work?'

'Yep.'

'How long have you been training?'

'I moved to Castle Cove four months ago. Started training a month after.' She glanced over her shoulder and something dark flashed across her face.

'You enjoying it?'

Alice paused. 'Yep.'

'Anyone ever tell you, you talk too much?'

Alice straightened, closed the dishwasher door and turned to face him. 'I'm the strong silent type.' Her expression was deadpan but he could see a brightness in her eyes. So, she had a sense of humour. He leaned against the counter and folded his arms. Her eyes flickered across them momentarily before she averted them to the cupboard above his left ear.

'I've done the triathlon a few times, are you training with anyone?'

'I'm fine.'

Was she? Her face said something was going on but he didn't know her well enough to read it and, despite the attraction he felt, did he want to get involved? 'When you swim, you should go with someone.'

She pursed her lips.

'The sea can be deceptive.'

'I can assure you I haven't swum in the sea alone recently.'

'I could swim with you if you'd like?'

Did he really just ask that? He should swallow his chisel, or worse, drink that awful coffee, for pulling a stunt like that.

Alice cleared her throat. 'I appreciate the offer, but I like training alone. I won't do anything stupid, so you can fold up your cape.'

'Sure.' What was he trying to do here, get involved with a complete stranger? 'I'm going into town to get some wood.' And a decent cup of coffee. Jay didn't wait for her answer, instead he turned and headed out of the kitchen and through the café without looking back.

He'd got as far as the pickup when his pager went off.

The sea looked choppy and full of secrets today. Jay checked the controls as he steered the lifeboat along the coast. 'How long did his parents say he'd been gone?'

'Two hours, they said he was going for a walk, but didn't take any food or a coat and he's been gone way longer than expected.' Shaun shook his head ignoring the gusts of wind blowing in his face and lifted the binoculars, scanning the rugged coast.

There weren't any people about, probably because of the earlier rain, which tended to scare off all but the most determined dog walkers. Miles of sand stretched along the coast, framed by waves seeped in seaweed, which meant they didn't get a lot of swimmers round this side either. A blessing on a day like this.

Tall grey cliffs took over where the beach ended; here giant rocks dipped their toes into the waves, then rose upwards for about twenty metres. Shrubbery and grass topped them off, looking like a bad haircut.

During the winter, they had to keep the boat away from the edges of the beach because of crumbling rocks. Today they kept away because they didn't want the sea to smash them into any hidden boulders where the water got shallow.

'Tide came in fast this afternoon, he could be stuck along here somewhere, maybe sheltering on top of one of these rocks. Wouldn't be the first time,' Shaun said.

'Does the boy have a mobile?'

'He's not answering it.' Shaun shook his head. 'It's beautiful here, but when I have kids I'm going to fit them with a tracking device, or tie them up so they can't leave the house.'

'Not sure that's legal. Besides, if you want kids, you'll have to find a woman first.'

'I'm finding plenty,' he grumbled. 'Just none I want to keep.'

'Maybe it's because you're dating the wrong ones?'

Shaun grunted.

'Are you still not talking?'

His expression darkened. 'I told you I don't want to talk about her.'

Jay sighed. 'You said the boy was fourteen? If his girlfriend of two months dumped him on Instagram, he's probably gone off somewhere to lick his wounds or to listen to miserable music on Spotify. I'm sure we'll find him.' He curled his fists. Steve had been fourteen.

'Give him a few more years and he can work it off in the pub like the rest of us, hell, I'll give him a job. I hate this bit.'

Jay jerked his head in agreement. Once you found them it was fine, until then, you just didn't know. 'There's no way he'd have gone for a swim?'

'Never learned.'

Neither of them commented, but something unpleasant lodged in Jay's throat. Images swept through his head as they scanned the rocks but he pushed them away. He wasn't sure he'd be able to deal with finding the body of a teenage boy. All the years he'd been volunteering, he'd never had to encounter it.

Shaun thumped him on the shoulder. 'We'll find him Jay, and he'll be fine. You know you didn't have to do this one, right?'

'We don't get to pick and choose.'

'Is that clothes?' Shaun pointed to the rocks.

'Where?'

'I can see something moving.'

Jay hit the throttle and the lifeboat shot forwards.

Chapter Eight

Alice narrowed her eyes at the tools Jay had left on the kitchen floor as Cath swept in with a tray of dirty cups and plates, barely missing the hammer.

'Don't touch them,' Cath barked. 'It's crazy out front and Lily hasn't turned up to help with lunch, can you pop to the restaurant and ask her to get a move on please? There's another coach-load of tourists due soon.'

'Sure.' Alice trotted out of the front of the café, past the patio and turned right. The weather had brightened and sun shone on the stone pathway leading to the grand staircase at the entrance of the castle.

Cove Castle rose above Alice as she headed towards it. Stepping inside the glorious Cinderella-style grey stone building with turrets and tall slim windows and walking up the staircase always made her feel like a princess. She grinned in anticipation.

The huge oak doors stood open, ready to receive the many visitors who flocked to the castle at the weekend, eager to see the newly restored grand hall, library and chapel. A few years earlier, the castle had been run down and there had been few visitors, until a mystery injection of cash sent to Simon Wolf's grandfather Jack had funded the much-needed restoration work. Since then, visitor numbers had soared.

The entrance buzzed with people and Alice took a moment to look up at the intricate arches and pillars that made the hall so imposing. There were paintings of various kings, ladies and earls on the walls and a large, carved stone fireplace that Cath had said they decorated at Christmas with holly and candles. Today it was filled with pottery and sculptures.

Alice hurried through the hall into the grand dining room, which had the same vaulted ceilings and stone walls. The floor was buffed oak and there were almost twenty tables, already laid for lunch with starched white cloths, candelabras, sparkling glasses and shiny silver cutlery. She spotted a napkin that was a little too far to the right and moved it as she passed. As she did, Anya Jenkins, one of the waitresses, came flying out of the kitchen at the end of the room. Anya was five foot nothing and her white blonde hair had been styled in a pixie cut, making her look like a forest nymph.

'Alice,' she grinned. 'It's all kicking off in the kitchen. You might want to come back later.'

'Why?'

'Marta West, who runs Picture Perfect, the gallery in town, is having a ding dong with Simon Wolf. Apparently, he's trying to charge her for displaying art from the gallery in the castle.' Anya hooted as something smashed.

'I need Lily though.' Alice gritted her teeth and continued forwards.

The kitchen was an interesting mixture of medieval and modern. A huge stone fireplace dominated the end of the room and multiple copper pots hung above it as well as inside. Around three of the walls, shiny metal cupboards housed more equipment; below them an industrial oven hummed next to a hob busy with bubbling pots. Alice smelled lamb and her stomach grumbled.

In the middle of the room sat a large counter covered in chopping boards, pots and pans. Someone had been preparing lunch but everything sat abandoned. Instead, the kitchen staff gaped as a show unfolded.

At the edge of the counter, Simon Wolf, the man responsible for running Cove Castle, stood with his arms folded. His square jaw was set firm and his dark grey eyes narrowed as he watched a woman rant.

You could tell from her sharp grey business suit that Marta West was usually an elegant woman. But today, her hazel eyes flashed and the large auburn bun on her head was shedding hair at an alarming rate.

'I've had an arrangement with the management for the last three years,' she said, her small hands curled into fists. 'Cove Castle displays work from my gallery free of charge and in return, I promote the castle to my customers.'

Simon shrugged. 'It's a small fee. You've got work displayed in the restaurant, café, hallway and in most of our busiest rooms. I assume you've got an advertising budget and I'm happy if you pay monthly.'

'That's not the point,' she snapped.

Someone tapped Alice on the shoulder and she turned. Lily King was five seven, with perfectly styled dark brown hair and an open, sweet face that could be described as beautiful when she didn't look so worried.

'I'm sorry,' she whispered. 'Are you here for me? I've just realised the time. I got distracted.' Lily nodded her head towards the arguing couple.

'We need to get back, Cath's on her own,' Alice whispered.

'No problem.' Lily glanced towards Simon and Marta, who were still arguing. 'Simon knows I'm helping you today, I won't interrupt.'

'What's with those two?' Alice asked as they headed through the restaurant into the hall.

'I'm not sure. Every time Marta comes to the castle they end up fighting. I'd never seen her get worked up about anything until Simon moved here.'

As they approached the café they saw a line of people disembark from a coach in the car park.

'Looks like we're in for a busy day.' Lily said as they broke into a run.

☆

Cath locked the door of the café and flipped the sign to closed as Alice flopped onto a chair and wriggled her toes. Lily came out of the kitchen looking calm, collected and not even a little tired.

'I'm glad that's over.' Lily sank into a chair.

'I know.' Alice slipped off her shoes. 'All that training, you'd think my feet would be able to handle walking around the café for a few hours.' She rubbed the pads of her feet with her fingers, digging deep and winced. The cycle home would be a long one, but at least Mr Superhero wasn't around to moan about her lack of lights, and the weather had brightened.

'Did you hear from Jay?' Alice asked.

'Not yet.' Cath checked her watch as she finished polishing the last table then shut the orange blinds over the deep windows at the front of the café, blocking out the sunshine. 'Not sure he'll make it back tonight.'

'Is he always unreliable?'

'Jay's the most reliable man I've ever met.' Lily muttered as Cath snorted.

'Unreliable's not a word I'd use to describe him.' Cath said. 'I expect he got called out. It's not like the cupboard is urgent, he knows we won't mind waiting.' She raised an eyebrow. 'Will we?'

'No.' Lily agreed.

Alice frowned. 'His tools were all over the floor, I had to step over saws, screws and hammers every time I went into the kitchen.' She'd almost tripped a couple of times.

'Until you moved them.' Cath smiled. 'He'll crack up when he sees what you've done.'

'If he's so concerned with safety, he'll thank me.'

Cath pulled out a chair and flopped beside her, closed her eyes and leaned her head back. 'That's it, I'm done. I feel like I've walked to the arctic and back while being hunted by a pack of hungry polar bears.'

'Not all the customers were bad.'

'A couple got close. I almost asked you to bring out some ice cream.'

'I've given up assaulting customers.' Alice wriggled her toes. 'I need to get up but I'm not sure I have the energy.'

'I've got to.' Lily hopped up suddenly and headed for the door checking her watch. 'I promised Simon I'd do a shift in the restaurant tonight.'

'Now?' Cath looked shocked.

Lily shrugged. 'I don't mind, I'm enjoying being in the kitchen with the chef.' She flushed. 'See you both tomorrow, I'll be working until lunch, I can pop in after?'

'Perfect.' Cath nodded, locking the door as Lily disappeared, watching her head for the restaurant. 'That girl needs to learn to say no.' She shook her head before turning to take in the room. 'It's so tidy in here.'

The ten cream tables were neatly aligned along the three walls, with a couple in the centre of the room. Each was already laid for breakfast, with a new perky flower in a vase at the centre. 'I've got to admit, the way you reorganised this room was genius, I still don't understand how you knew how to do it?'

Alice smiled. 'Simple, I calculated the distance from the counter, along with the number of chairs at each table to work out maximum efficiency.' She laughed. 'You and Lily thought I was a nutcase.'

Cath's curls bobbed as she agreed. 'A couple of the customers commented too. But I'm sold now, it does take less time to serve. Still don't know why, but I won't worry my pretty little head over it, I've got you, at least for a few more months.'

'We're a good team.'

'We are. You know you don't have to spend so much time in the kitchen? I don't have to do all the serving, I'm happy to share, Lily and I always do.'

'You're both better with people. I've always been good at the background stuff, ordering stock, organising tables, doing bookings, stock taking.' She cleared her throat. 'Tidying, that kind of thing.'

The ease with which they'd slipped into their respective roles reminded Alice of the six years working at Taste of Rome. She'd quickly been absorbed into the routine there, and after her parents had split, it had been a great place to lick her wounds.

'It works for me. I've never been able to say goodbye to the last customer without having to spend an hour tidying after they left. I can't believe how lucky I was that you came looking for a job just as Lily got asked to cover maternity leave at the castle restaurant. Never leave.' Cath put a hand over hers. 'Seriously.'

'You know I'm going to Thailand in September to visit my dad.' Alice smiled to soften the blow. 'Maybe you'll visit? Dad's got a decent-sized house with his girlfriend, Beth. It's on the beach and they'll be plenty of room.'

Cath pushed her long fringe behind her ears revealing a flash of disappointment in her green eyes. 'Not sure I'll have the money. Dan wants to expand his plumbing business and get a new van, it's going to take at least another year until we've saved enough. How long will you stay with your dad?'

Alice shrugged. 'I'm keeping things open. I've never met Beth, I'm sure she's great but it'll be odd seeing him without Mum.' Her voice cracked.

'How long were they divorced?'

'Six years. I haven't seen Dad since he got on a plane a year later.'

'Wow.' Cath straightened her legs, she was a little taller than Alice, but sometimes seemed to tower over her. 'Why haven't you seen him?'

Alice shrugged. 'I was angry about the divorce, I thought it was all his idea.' She grimaced. 'But when my great aunt died, Mum moved from London to Castle Cove so she could live in her house, and every time I saw her Mum seemed happier, lighter somehow. But now she's dead too.' She shook her head. 'I didn't visit enough.'

Cath patted her hand. 'I don't think we ever feel like we see our family as often as we should.'

Tears pricked Alice's eyes. 'It never seemed like the right time. Now it's too late.'

'You're here now, making changes. I think you should be proud of yourself.' Cath's smile was fast and welcome. 'I'll miss you when you go though, maybe you'll come back?'

Alice looked around the café. 'I love it here, but I need to travel, have adventures, really live.' Her throat tightened.

Cath sighed. 'Talking of adventures, do you fancy going for a drink tonight?'

Alice closed her eyes again. Her feet hurt and she didn't feel like going out, but Cath had asked four times now.

'Go on. You're only young once, and the amount of time you spend training or working, it's a wonder you haven't collapsed with exhaustion. Besides you might get to meet my man Dan, he'll be there tonight, assuming he hasn't run out of money again. Mind you, he'll probably just borrow it off of me.' She laughed.

'Where do you want to go?'

'The Anglers, on the promenade.'

'I run past it on my way to the beach.' It was less than two miles from her mother's house – her house now. Alice hadn't got used to it being hers. Even though she'd cleared out most of her mother's things ready to rent it out when she headed for Thailand, at night, when she was alone, she still felt her presence.

'Meet you at eight?'

'Okay, but I need to get going, and I'll do something about the kitchen before we leave.' Alice slipped her feet back into her shoes. 'It's a mess.'

Cath pursed her lips. 'Lily just wiped the tops down, the dishwasher's unpacked, even the food in the fridge has been organised by use-by date.' Cath caught the look on Alice's face. 'Not that I'm complaining, I don't know how we managed before you came along. If only you could tidy up my life as easily. The kitchen's fine, you should get going.'

'There are tools all over the place.'

Her friend smiled. 'You've already arranged them in size order and put them on the side, you planning on filing them in the larder? Not sure what Jay would make of that.'

Someone knocked on the door making them both jump.

'Speak of the devil.' Cath unlocked the door. Jay had changed since this morning and his hair was wet. He looked round at the empty café. 'You okay?' Cath asked.

'You shut?'

Alice tapped her watch. 'Half an hour ago.'

'We got a shout, I left my phone in the pickup so I didn't get around to calling. Sorry.' The apology sounded like an afterthought.

'I thought we'd frightened you off.' Cath said. 'Everything okay?'

His expression blanked. 'A boy went missing, we found him half way up a cliff on some rocks and got him home in time for tea.'

'Bet there was a bit more to it than that? Do you want to talk about it?'

'It's fine. He'd lost his phone, didn't hear the last of that.' His blue eyes clouded.

'I'll bet his parents were pleased?'

Jay lifted a shoulder. 'I thought I'd get the tools out of your way before you closed. I can't come tomorrow because there's a training thing I need to do, and I'm booked up early next week. I'll be back on Thursday if that's okay?'

Cath followed him into the kitchen. 'The tools weren't bothering us, were they Alice?' she smirked.

Jay stopped dead. 'You organised them?'

Alice shrugged.

'If I stopped still for long enough, she'd tidy me up. You should get her to take a look at your books.'

He rolled his eyes. 'They're fine.'

'Shaun once told me your accountant threatened to sack you.'

Jay glowered. 'Shaun has a big mouth.' He picked up his tool bag and began to chuck all the tools inside it.

Alice winced. 'Don't you have a system, won't they get chipped?'

'It's either in the bag or I'm using it, that's my system. And I'm pretty sure they can handle getting tossed about.' He slung the bag over his shoulder. 'I'll get out of your way.'

He left without looking back.

'Grumpy.' Alice returned to the kitchen so she could wipe the tops where the tools had been.

Cath grabbed the cloth from her hand. 'He's not grumpy, he's tired and probably dealing with things he doesn't want to face. One day, you might get to know him better, then you'll understand.'

Alice watched Cath disappear into the café, wondering what her friend meant.

Chapter Nine

The boy had been fine, but seeing him hurt and near the water had brought back memories Jay wasn't ready to deal with. Didn't *want* to deal with. He shrugged off the feelings and threw his tools in the back of the pickup. His dog, Zeus, simultaneously whined and wagged his tail as he hopped into the driver's seat. He'd parked next to Alice's bike, which sat exactly where she'd left it this morning. She'd be leaving soon and although it wasn't late – only just past seven and it would be light for hours – rain was on the way and how safe would she be without lights, even with that reflective jacket?

Damn. His fingers gripped the steering wheel. He knew he wouldn't be able to leave without making sure she was all right. Maybe he could fix the lights before she got here? He'd have to be quick, he could only imagine her reaction if she caught him.

Shaking his head, he hopped out of the truck feeling irritated, then knelt so he could spin the front wheel of her bike. Dammit, the tyre looked flat.

'What are you doing?' Alice's voice came from behind his left ear and he sighed. Why wasn't she more like Mel? She'd have been in the bathroom getting changed for at least another half hour.

'You've got a puncture,' he grumbled as she came to look. He caught a whiff of something appealing, like chocolate, probably from the cakes she'd been serving in the café. 'Do you have a repair kit?'

'I do – did,' she corrected frowning. 'It was in my backpack this morning but when I got changed at the café I couldn't find it. It might have fallen out somehow when I cycled here, I remember going over a bump, and my bag was unzipped when I arrived.' She looked thoughtful. 'Or maybe it got caught up in my clothes and I missed it.'

Alice put the backpack on the floor, and unpacked it quickly. 'It's definitely gone.'

She looked so devastated by the admission he didn't have the heart to call her on it, but who cycled on dark, lonely roads without checking they were carrying a way to fix a tyre? Had she really lost it or had it never been there in the first place?

Alice glowered at the bike.

'It'll fit in the back of my pickup if you want a lift?'

'I can walk. It's not far if I head along the promenade.'

'It's going to rain.' Jay could feel the weight of it in the air.

'I… ' Alice bit her bottom lip.

'You can even lift the bike in yourself.' Jay walked to the truck and opened the back, standing beside it with his arms folded. She frowned but dipped her chin in agreement.

Jay forced himself not to help as Alice slung her backpack and helmet inside, but when she struggled with the bike he grabbed it.

'Thank you,' she said, but he wasn't sure she meant it.

Jay opened the passenger door and whistled. Zeus hopped into the back and barked, then they both waited as Alice flipped the remains of lunch – an empty coffee container and Mars bar wrapper – from the seat on to the floor with a noisy exhale.

'That was too easy, I thought you were going to complain about me lifting the bike.' Jay started the engine.

Alice leaned against the headrest. 'Maybe I'm mellowing.'

His snort made her open one eye and fix him with it. 'I didn't mention the litter, I ought to get points for that.'

'I'll bet it cost you.'

Alice cocked her head. 'You think you have me all figured out?'

'I think order and independence are imprinted in your DNA. I think you hate it when you need help, and your repair kit isn't filed in your backpack under E for emergency.'

'E's for chocolate, I usually put it under R for repair.' She closed her eyes. 'And I'll have one back in there this time tomorrow.'

Huge drops of rain hit the windscreen as Jay drove past the spot he'd started to follow her this morning. 'We'll take the long route home and look out for your repair kit. If we find it, I can help you fix the tyre if you like?' He ought to have his head examined for offering to help her again.

Alice laughed. 'Do you think if they checked *your* DNA under a microscope they'd see flashing blue lights?'

Jay smiled. She was funny when you got to know her, and an excellent antidote to a shitty day. For the first time in a few hours Jay felt himself relax. 'You don't sound as irritated about it as you did earlier, am I growing on you?'

Zeus barked and she turned to stroke his head, earning a zillion brownie points from both of them.

'My feet hurt, I'm tired and you're driving me home. I'd be an idiot to be annoyed about that. I'm sure I'll be back to my normal grouchy self tomorrow so you can ditch the superhero cape.'

'Not sure I can fight my DNA, I respond to bribery though.'

Alice turned to face him, her hand still stretched in the back, stroking Zeus's head until the dog was practically purring.

'What, more coffee?'

He couldn't hide the grimace, you couldn't pay him to drink any more of that. That was the only explanation he had for what came out of his mouth next. 'A date.'

'With you?' Alice sounded so horrified Jay almost laughed.

'I'm afraid Zeus already has a girlfriend. Why not me?'

They drove past the brewery and into Castle Cove, passing his mother's house. Jay saw a light on in her kitchen, even though she didn't need it on an early evening in June. When they hit Cliff Hill he stopped as a couple walking a dog crossed the road. 'Where are we headed?'

Alice pointed forwards. 'Second right, take Henry Street and you'll want the second left after that… I'm not looking to get involved.'

'Damn,' he growled. 'And I've already got the engagement ring from Grandma.'

'Ha, ha.' Alice shook her head. 'I'm here to do the triathlon this summer, and I've got to finish it.'

'Why?"

Alice tensed. 'My mother used to compete every year. I promised to join her and kept putting it off. Then she died.' Her voice wobbled.

Jay fought the urge to comfort her. 'So, you're doing it for her?'

Alice shrugged and he could almost see the weight of guilt on her shoulders. 'It's fitting.'

'What happened?'

'Aneurysm.' She grimaced. 'Five, no, six months ago. Feels like yesterday.'

'I'm sorry.'

Alice brushed the sympathy aside. 'It's left here, then you just carry on up the hill. I'm near the top on the right,' she paused for a beat. 'Completing the triathlon's important to me, dating might interfere with my training. It's not—'

'On your agenda?' Jay guessed, stopping to let a couple with a pram cross the road.

Alice shrugged.

'And do you ever deviate from your plans?'

'I—' She shook her head. 'Right here.' Alice pointed to a space outside a terrace of Victorian houses and he pulled in. 'Thanks.'

She sat for a bit looking out of the window at her house. 'I'm trying to.' Alice opened the door, avoiding his eyes as she turned back to pick up the rubbish she'd pushed on to the floor earlier. 'We're very different.' She waved the empty coffee cup at him.

'Because I'm untidy?' Jay hopped out of the pickup and opened the boot, lifting her bike out which she immediately grabbed, accidently dropping the Mars bar wrapper onto the floor.

He tried to pick it up but she beat him to it, groaning as the bike prodded her stomach.

'Is that supposed to be evidence of our incompatibility, because I can easily make that rubbish disappear?'

Alice shook her head. He picked up her helmet and backpack before closing the boot.

'I thought I'd put it in the bin. Damsels in distress prefer a tidier chariot.' Alice turned to wheel the bike to the front of one of the houses.

'In my experience, damsels in distress don't care what you turn up in as long as you rescue them.' Jay smiled. 'Besides, maybe I like mess.'

Zeus barked, not happy he'd been left in the pickup.

She fished keys from her backpack. 'I like order.'

'I got that.' Jay backed off as she opened the door, unsure as to why he kept pushing her, except that she fascinated him. 'I'm pretty sure being messy isn't catching.'

Alice looked uncomfortable. 'Being messy probably isn't, going out with you on the other hand… ' She shook her head looking surprised at the admission.

'Is that a compliment?'

'Not really.' She choked.

'At least think about training with me? It's a lot more fun if there are two of you.'

'You setting up your next rescue?'

'Will you need it?'

Alice narrowed her eyes and he had to fight the smile.

'Thanks for the lift,' she grumbled, before slamming the door.

Chapter Ten

'Here, come, sit.' Cath nudged Alice onto a corner bench by the window in the Anglers. It was good to get off her feet, it had been a rush getting ready after Jay had dropped her, and since her tyre was flat, she'd had to jog from her house to meet Cath on time.

The pub looked modern. The walls were decorated with pastel blue wallpaper and light wooden floors that made the atmosphere clean and bright. Colourful pictures of boats, cliffs and some of the castle were hung around the walls.

Alice glanced around. A few people were eating burgers and one had a curry. The food looked good. In all, the place was a vibrant mix of comfortable and trendy. Locals must have felt the same because the place was packed – people stood at the bar and in between tables and there were few spaces to sit.

They were about an arm's length from a small stage area with a chair, microphone and selection of guitars. Someone was going to sing. Alice closed her eyes. She could be cleaning out her fridge right now.

Alice peeled the black woollen cardigan from her shoulders.

'Nice top.' Cath pointed to her blue camisole, the light from the lamp above them making the sequins sparkle.

'I'm not sure,' she mumbled. 'I'm worried it's a bit too *hey look at me*. I bought it three years ago but I've never worn it. I thought it would be hot in here.' She played with the straps, feeling stupid. 'I'd have been better with one of my running tops.'

Cath grinned. 'Don't be silly, you look amazing, besides it's attracting attention and you need to have a bit of fun, you haven't been out with anyone since you arrived in Castle Cove, and that's four whole months ago.' Cath waggled her eyebrows at a couple of men at the bar. 'We might not have to buy you any drinks tonight.'

'They're looking at you, not me,' Alice murmured. Cath's green dress was short and showed off her toned legs and arms, her hair looked extra curly tonight and she'd added a sparkly clip that glittered under the lights. That combined with her green eyes and permanent smile made her a knock-out. 'I still can't believe how much chocolate cake you can eat without putting on a pound.'

Cath snorted. 'Lucky genes. My mum was the same, but she said it all went downhill at the age of thirty, so I've got another two years to stuff my face. Once I lose my looks I can focus on my career.' She grinned.

'Running Castle Café?'

Her friend nodded. 'I like it. Lily loves the restaurant, I think she secretly wants to work there full-time, not that she'd tell me. But I really enjoy where I am. The customers are great, well most of them, and there's plenty of variety – I've been working there for almost five years and every day is different. Plus, Simon isn't so bad once you get to know him. That guy over there is definitely checking you out, you should go and talk to him.' Cath changed the subject, pointing a fingernail at a man at the bar who blushed and looked away.

'I didn't come to Castle Cove to get involved with anyone.'

'Who's talking about getting involved?' Cath ran a finger through one of her curls. 'You're young, free and single, seems to me your adventures should include at least one hot kiss.'

Alice's mind flickered to Jay. 'I'm worried getting involved with someone would interfere with my training.'

'You don't strike me as the kind of person to let anything get in their way once they've made their mind up, Alice, have a little faith in yourself.'

A barman arrived holding a tray with a couple of glasses and a bucket piled with ice surrounding a bottle of prosecco.

'See.' Cath furtively pointed to the men at the bar as a tall, handsome redhead approached their table beaming.

'A gift for my beautiful girlfriend and her beautiful friend.'

'Dan.' Cath stood, looking confused.

'I saw you across the room without a drink and couldn't resist.'

'I thought—' She blinked. 'That was really sweet of you, thanks.' Her cheeks flushed as she hugged him, then she turned. 'Alice, this is Dan Bates, my boyfriend. Dan, this is Alice Appleton.'

'I've heard all about you.' Dan took her hand and kissed the top of it. 'Cath never said how pretty you were, no wonder I heard a couple of guys chatting about gorgeous women when I came in.'

'Dan, you're impossible, I thought you said you were working late?'

He grinned. 'I've been putting in a bathroom all day.' He turned to Alice. 'I've got my own plumbing business.' His face beamed with pride. 'I told the client I had an important meeting, and said I'll finish putting in the toilet tomorrow. It's their second bathroom, they'll be fine. A couple of the guys said they were coming down, and I knew you'd be here so I didn't want to miss out. Also, I got a haircut.' He swept a hand over his head downwards over his Calvin Klein polo shirt and Paul Smith jeans.

'New outfit too?' Cath looked surprised.

'Sale.' Dan smoothed the material on his shirt. 'Thought I'd better snap them up while I could.'

'You look great,' Cath took a moment to admire his outfit.

Dan poured them both a glass of prosecco with a flourish. 'Wanted to look good for my best girl.' He waved over her shoulder. 'Paul and Tom are here, you want to join us or are you girls happy chatting?'

'We're good,' Cath beamed, but Alice wasn't sure if the smile was real. 'Maybe pop over later.'

'I'll keep an eye on the bottle, let me know if you need more, lovely to meet you darling girl.' He took Alice's hand again and made a charming performance of kissing it. 'Next time we need to have a long chat, I'd like to know more about this triathlon you're doing, I might have a try myself next year.'

Cath chuckled. 'You'd need to get out of bed before six for the training.'

Dan's eyes widened as he did a comical shudder.

'Good to meet you too.' Alice rose to kiss him on the cheek before he headed back to his friends.

'Nice guy.'

'Always.' Cath watched him getting absorbed into his crowd of friends. 'Life and soul of the party, it's what attracted me to him at first. He was so different from the boy I dated all through sixth form and beyond.' She frowned, still watching him.

'How long have you been together?'

Cath counted on her fingers. 'About nine months, it's been… a whirlwind. Never a dull moment.' She chuckled. 'Dan's a lot of fun.'

'And you aren't?'

Cath straightened her dress. 'We're good for each other. I can be too practical sometimes, too boring.'

'Doesn't sound like you.'

'Not any more.' She picked up her glass.

'What do you mean?'

Cath's eyebrows drew together. 'My parents behaved like they were retired when they were still in their forties. You're only as old as you think you are, and I'm not ready to be old yet, I want to have fun.' She looked over at Dan with a faint smile and repeated. 'He's a lot of fun.'

'I can relate to that.' Alice nodded. 'When I lived in London I never used to go out or do anything except work. I came to Castle Cove to change that.'

'You've hardly been out since moving here, so we've got some serious catching up to do.'

Alice grinned as Cath picked up her prosecco. 'To having fun.' They clinked glasses. 'May tonight be the start of many new adventures.'

'Sounds good.' Alice glanced across the pub. 'Sure you don't want to join Dan and his friends?'

'I'm really happy here,' Cath said. 'We've got a good view of the stage and they'll just talk about football.' She flashed a quick grin.

'They're great, but the conversation can get a bit brash and most of them don't have girlfriends so I end up sitting there feeling like a gooseberry. Besides it's nice to catch up with you properly, it's not easy having a conversation in the café.'

'Especially not when I'm pulling cupboards off walls and throwing desserts over customers?'

Cath snorted. 'Don't forget your penchant for insulting carpenters. I haven't had so much fun since I started working there, never a dull moment with you either.'

'You're making me sound exciting, I knew coming to Castle Cove was a good idea.' Alice looked around the room. 'Will someone be singing later?'

Cath's eyes shot towards the bar. 'Probably, Shaun's got a knack for spotting talent.'

'Shaun?'

Cath flushed. 'He runs this place. Took over five years ago, he's pretty good at it.' Her eyes shot towards the bar again. 'Not sure if he's here today though. He's a good friend of Jay's, we all went to school together, although I was in the year above. My mum tells me we were friends in toddler group way before that. Shaun volunteers on the lifeboat as well… maybe Jay will introduce you.'

'I don't see why.' Alice ran a finger across the top of her glass ignoring the tingling under her skin when she thought about the man who'd driven her home tonight.

'I have a feeling Jay was quite taken with you.'

'I got the feeling he'd flirt with anything with a pulse.'

Cath considered that as she took a sip of prosecco. 'I wouldn't say that. He flirts, but who doesn't? And he's nice with it, not leery and he never makes you feel uncomfortable. When he dates, he's pretty solid and always loyal.' Her eyes skittered towards the bar again. 'There's Shaun.' The man in question was almost six foot, with dark brown hair and a face just the right side of handsome. His nose looked slightly bent which only added to his good looks. His lips formed a grimace as he glanced in their direction before quickly turning his back. 'Looks like he's busy.'

Alice sipped some prosecco, enjoying the feel of it sliding down her throat.

'So, Jay was flirting with you?'

'He gave me a lift home.'

'And?' Cath leaned closer.

'Nothing… I get the feeling he could be quite distracting, that's all.'

Cath feigned disinterest, pursing her lips. 'It's none of my business.'

'But you want to tell me anyway?'

Cath picked up the beer mat from the table and tapped it with her fingernails. She'd be a natural at interrogation. 'Only if *you* want me to.'

'I'll be wondering all night otherwise, go on, give me some of your sage advice.'

Cath looked serious. 'I've known Jay most of my life and I can tell you, he's a safe pair of hands if you're looking to dip your toes in the dating scene.'

'Why do you think I'm looking to do that?'

'You're here for a reason. You're training like a demon, it's like you're running from something, maybe a broken heart?' Cath blurted.

'No, I don't mind talking about it – at least I don't think I do – prosecco has been known to loosen my tongue, and I'm not used to drinking.' Alice tipped her glass in Cath's direction. 'No broken hearts, and more like running *to*. I came here to make changes in my life. At least this is the first step. It took me months to pluck up the courage.'

'Months?' Cath tipped more wine into Alice's glass, her lips curving.

'Okay, years. I was working at Taste of Rome for six years before I finally made a change. But I've wanted to do it.' Her voice became wistful.

'You moved after your mum died?' Cath guessed.

Alice sucked in a breath. 'The world looked different after she'd gone.' She shrugged and sipped more wine. 'Everything I thought was important didn't seem to matter somehow. Mum's house was empty and she'd left it to me, so I thought, what the hell.'

'So, you came.' Cath nodded. 'Left everything. I'm really impressed.' She picked up her glass so they could toast. 'I get the feeling you used to do something better at the restaurant than serving tea, coffee and sandwiches?'

'That life's behind me.' Alice offered. 'I've no plans to go back to it.' She was embarrassed to admit how empty it had become.

'What do you want?' Cath refilled their glasses again.

Alice rolled the question over in her mind as she sipped more wine, feeling her body loosen and relax. What did she want? 'I'm not sure… wild adventures?'

'And is that what you're getting now?' Cath looked confused. 'I don't mean to be funny, but you've not done anything adventurous since you arrived.'

'Everything I do here's an adventure, in comparison to my old life. In London, going to Tesco was the highlight of my week.' Alice confessed. 'The triathlon's a big one, the rest I'm working up to.' Though the thought of heading off to Thailand with no real plan beyond helping her father made her feel nauseous. But she'd have to get over that.

'What about men? In my experience, having a little romance can be the best adventure of all.' Cath leaned across the table so they were almost nose to nose.

'It might complicate everything.'

'Scared?'

Alice pondered the question as she finished her glass. 'I don't know, maybe, it's not something I planned on.' She thought back to her conversation with Jay earlier, to the way he made her body tingle and fizz. 'Maybe that was wrong.'

'I'm just saying it might be fun and it certainly beats spending all hours training.'

Cath's eyes darted to the bar again and back to her drink – had this Shaun made a reappearance? Alice turned her head to the side so she could see and her eyes met Jay's. He flashed a grin she could only describe as cocky and raised an eyebrow, and she turned back to Cath as her heart raced.

'You okay?'

'Sure.' Did her voice sound a little too bright?

'Hello again.' All of a sudden, Jay was squeezing in beside her and putting a pint on the table. He nodded at Cath who sat opposite. The pub was getting busier and warmer and as he leaned his head in so they could hear above the noise, Alice caught a whiff of sea salt. 'I wasn't expecting to see you again so soon.'

The space seemed to get smaller with him in it. As he moved over his leg touched against hers, making her blood race.

Cath sipped more prosecco, looking towards the bar again. 'Alice needed to get out and I thought I'd join her. You here to sing?'

'I'm supporting the main act.'

'I see you brought your fan club,' Alice observed. A group of girls in the corner giggled as they checked him out.

It didn't surprise Alice, a man like Jay attracted attention. He was tall for a start, and had a face too handsome for his own good: eyes that were too blue, jaw a little too chiselled, lips that made women want things they couldn't put a name to, and if they could they wouldn't admit it.

Funny how nature did that sometimes, threw together a combination of genes and chromosomes, and created a face that turned most of womankind into a quivering bunch of hormones. Everyone knew personality trumped looks, until they got a whiff of a pair of cheekbones that triggered a bout of amnesia.

The girls didn't look much over eighteen, and for some reason Alice couldn't fathom, seeing them drooling over him annoyed her.

'Aren't they a little young for you?' Her words tumbled out before she had time to stop them.

The edges of his eyes creased as he smiled, making her insides somersault. 'You worried about me or them?'

'I was making an observation.' She stared into her glass, embarrassed.

'As you'll know from earlier, my tastes run a little older.' He turned to face her and she could smell mint on his breath, his eyes were so blue up close. 'I also prefer blondes.' He lifted a finger and brushed a strand of her hair back from her face. 'Especially ones with bad tempers.'

Alice jerked back, blushing as she looked at Cath, who signalled a thumbs up.

'I don't have a temper.'

'Then perhaps it's just me you don't like?' Jay leaned back, looking amused.

'I never said that.' Alice scowled. 'You just...' *confuse me.* The man was impossible, she couldn't decide whether she wanted to thump him for trying to rescue her all the time, or leap onto his lap for the same reason.

'What?'

Someone shouted something across the bar before Alice could answer and Jay glanced up. 'Looks like I'm on.' He tipped a thumb towards the stage. 'I hope you'll stay long enough to watch, we could continue our discussion later?'

'You sing?'

'He's really good,' Cath mused. 'I've been telling him to go on *Britain's Got Talent*, but he's not interested.'

'I need to get ready.' Jay winked at them before heading to the bar and Alice dragged her eyes back to her drink in case she did something stupid, like watch him.

'I think he gets embarrassed about all the attention,' Cath said. 'Women pretty much throw themselves at him after he's played.'

'Must be hard for him to resist?' Alice felt a prickle of jealously, which was ridiculous.

'Oh, he doesn't take them up on it,' Cath confided. 'At least, not any more. He's been seeing some girl for the last few months but they've just split up, can't remember her name.'

'He doesn't look very heartbroken.' Alice watched him saunter towards the stage saying hello to most of the women on his way, then he turned and threw a smile in her direction, making her stomach flip again.

'Not sure how serious things were, I've never seen Jay get too involved.' Cath cocked her head. 'I'd say he's exactly the type of man you should be looking for if you are after a wild adventure with no strings. Besides, imagine that face serenading you. A man who sings, what could be better than that?'

What indeed? But did she have the guts to find out?

Chapter Eleven

Jay opened the door of his house and switched on the lights. Peter Tennant, the teenage son of his next-door neighbour, dog-sat for him occasionally and had obviously been in because a light was on.

Jay headed for the kitchen to the left of the hall and Zeus greeted him, thumping his paw on the black tiles of the kitchen floor, before chasing his tail. The view of spinning white gloss cupboards must have made Zeus dizzy because he slumped down suddenly with a whine. He'd been alone on and off for about four hours while Jay had been in the pub, and even though he'd had a long walk earlier, he was obviously itching for fresh air.

Jay checked his watch, it was after eleven, but he wouldn't be able to sleep, neither would the dog.

'Walk?' he asked, as if Zeus would actually say no.

The dog shot from the room and was by the front door before Jay had even moved. If he went out for an hour and walked along the seafront, he'd be able to work off this restlessness.

When he'd been in his early twenties, he'd have distracted himself with a girlfriend. There'd been plenty of volunteers in the pub tonight, but he was past that. Shaun would accuse him of getting old, and maybe his friend was right, although when did twenty-seven become old?

He pulled on a light jacket and trotted outside. It was a beautiful night, still warm even though the sun had set over an hour ago, but he could feel the wind from the sea. It would be a great night to be out on the water, to feel the spray on his face as he headed into the horizon with no plan for where he might end up.

As he approached the sea front, Zeus stayed just ahead, stopping now and then to sniff at tufts of grass that had battled with the tarmac and won. Jay took a deep breath and smelled salt, feeling calmer.

The Castle Cove promenade looked empty and Jay stood on the pavement for a while with his hands on his hips, watching the waves crash in and out. Zeus got bored after a few minutes and began to head for the town centre, passing the Anglers, which was closing, spilling customers onto the street where they wandered on the pavement next to the beach, past pots filled with purple and pink infusions of fuchsias, lobelia and petunias.

As Jay followed, he heard bubbles of laughter mingling with the footsteps of couples and friends as they headed home in bunches. Some had brought their drinks out in glasses from the pub – they'd probably return them in the morning, most did. Staying out late at night drinking, then heading home with friends for another pint was something Jay would have done about a zillion years ago. He couldn't remember when things had started to change, maybe two years earlier when he'd hit twenty-five and had begun to wonder if this was all there was to life.

God, he felt old.

Jay continued along the sea front, heading towards the castle. Zeus trotted along, stopping every now and then to glance back to make sure he hadn't lost his master. Making a last-minute decision, Jay changed direction and headed back down Castle Road, towards the High Street. If he followed the road up, he could walk through the middle of town, then cut back past the caravan site, maybe head on to the cliffs after that. The moon was full and the sky looked clear, so visibility would be fine. If he took that route, he could see if there was a light on at Alice's house. She'd left while he'd been singing and he had no idea if anyone had walked her home. Probably not, because Cath lived closer to town.

He wanted to know Alice had got home safely. While he knew the streets were busy enough and she'd probably be fine – Castle Cove was usually a safe place to live – in summer the flood of tourists meant anyone could be walking about. Something was telling him to check on her. Trouble was, he wasn't sure which part of his anatomy was talking.

They hit Alice's street within twenty minutes and Jay paused at the bottom of the road, feeling like an idiot. He shouldn't be here, but Zeus was already running ahead and he couldn't disappoint the dog, could he?

He put his hands in the pockets of his jeans and walked up the hill, checking each house as he passed. Most of the lights were off, no surprise at half eleven. Would he even remember which one was hers? Zeus stopped, sniffed at a gate and whined but didn't enter.

Jay recognised the house, even though he hadn't taken time to look properly when he'd dropped Alice off earlier. The building was pretty and old, probably pre-nineteen-hundreds. From outside he could see it was a two-up two-down arrangement, with tall bay windows filled with original glass that would make the house a bugger to heat in the winter. Colourful tiles lay a tempting pathway to the front door, which was one of those old-fashioned stained-glass affairs with a huge silver knocker set in the centre. White shutters closed the world out, but he could see a hint of light above in the hall and front room, which told him Alice might still be up. He itched to knock, but it was late and what would he say? So far, she hadn't seemed very impressed by him. They'd chatted on the drive home and at the pub, but she'd still turned him down when he'd asked her out, and had left while he was singing, without even nodding goodbye.

He took another couple of steps and was just past the house when he heard a front door closing. He turned as Alice walked through the gate onto the pavement wearing black joggers, her blonde ponytail providing a brief flash of colour.

He flexed his fingers. If she went on the road like that, no-one would see her. 'No reflector gear?'

Alice stopped at the end of her pathway. 'Jay?'

'Yes.'

She glared. 'Why are you here?'

'Walking Zeus.'

Even in the dark he could see she wasn't pleased. Zeus returned and circled her trainers, checking for food.

'On my road?' Alice glowered, bending to stroke the dog's head. 'At this time of night?'

Women didn't usually look so horrified at the idea of him turning up on their doorstep. He tried not to be offended as he pointed up

Princes Hill. 'Zeus is a night owl. We're heading for a walk on the cliffs and this is the best route.'

'It's dark.'

'I'd noticed.' Jay considered his next words carefully, he didn't want to offend her. 'Where are you headed dressed all in black?'

'I don't feel tired, thought I'd walk it off.' Alice admitted. 'I haven't done enough training today.'

'We could head in the same direction? I'm walking Zeus and I'd appreciate the company. You can protect me if we run into ruffians.'

Alice half smiled, at least he thought it was a smile. 'You get a lot of those around here?'

Jay nodded. 'Hundreds. Also, there's a good hill.' He gestured towards the top of the road. 'It's not a triathlon but its exercise.'

And she'd be far safer with him than alone. Not that he'd mention it.

Alice chewed her bottom lip.

'No offers of dates or help, I promise.' Jay held up his hands in mock surrender.

'What if I decide I want to jump off a cliff using just my t-shirt as a parachute?'

Jay grinned trying not to visualise that. 'I think I'd at least have to mention how cold you'd get, what with the headwind and everything.'

Alice tipped her head and smiled. 'I guess I can walk with you. Aside from ruffians, someone needs to make sure you don't get accosted by those groupies from earlier.'

'God forbid.' Jay coughed. Before he'd left the pub he'd had at least one phone number shoved in his pocket, which he'd found when he got home, but he didn't think any had followed him. He glanced down the street to make sure. A kitten trotted up the road and meowed and Alice bent to pick it up.

'Cute.' Jay rubbed its head and was rewarded with a purr. 'Yours?'

'Nope.' She admitted, stroking the cat's head too. 'A stray trying to adopt me, keeps darting in the house every time I get home.'

'Don't let Zeus see it, he's got a particular love of cats.'

Alice checked the dog wasn't looking before disappearing into her front yard to drop off the kitten. She returned a few seconds later.

'Do you want to set the pace?' Jay started to walk and she followed. They didn't talk, but he could hear her settling her breathing. 'How's the training going?'

Alice shrugged without looking at him. 'Three months ago, a small incline and I'd have been on my knees, but since I've been training every day it's gotten a lot easier.'

Alice sped up into a slow jog and he matched her pace, enjoying the warmth hitting his joints and the sight of her Lycra-clad legs pumping the ground.

'It's up there.' Jay pointed to a small entrance off the pavement, and matched her step for step as she headed for it. They stayed level, watching Zeus as he bounded in front, ridiculously pleased with his bonus walk. It was a good ten minutes before either of them spoke and that was when they reached the top of the hill and hit the small steep climb to the cliffs. They turned to look down over Castle Cove. There were still a few lights on and they could see the multicoloured mishmash of roofs and street lights dotted in between like fairy lights. Behind them the path to the cliffs looked dark in comparison, and Alice reached into her pocket and pulled out a torch.

'You were prepared,' Jay murmured and she grinned. It was the first time he'd seen her really smile and he felt like he'd been punched in the stomach.

When they hit the top of the hill, they stopped for a few moments. The full moon sat high in the sky creating a pathway of sparkles on the sea that ended at the horizon.

This was his favourite kind of night, even the soft breeze coming off the sea felt warm, the weather having turned sunny again after the short spell of rain.

'It's pretty.' Alice breathed in deeply.

'It is, isn't it?' Not everyone felt like that. Mel had hated coming out at night, she hadn't been that keen in the day either if he was honest. She had always preferred being indoors which is probably why she'd gone into hotel management. They used to joke she was more mole than human.

'I love it here.' Alice took another deep breath and moved into a calf stretch. His eyes hovered on her curves before he dragged them off to look at the view.

'You said your mum used to compete in the triathlon here. So you know Castle Cove?' Jay forced himself to look straight ahead.

'We used to holiday here with my aunt when I was a child,' she added. 'I'm living in Mum's house now, when she died it passed to me.' Alice stopped talking abruptly and took a deep breath closing her eyes. 'I've never gotten over that smell. I used to buy candles called sea spray, but it's not the same, is it?'

'I don't know much about candles,' he said, deliberately making his voice a little deeper in response to the question.

'I'm sorry.' Alice stifled a giggle. 'Have I insulted your manhood?'

'Absolutely. You need to ask me about beer, I think my testosterone levels have dipped dangerously low.'

'I think you've got some to spare.'

Okay, he hadn't been expecting that. Their eyes caught – and he saw heat – before she flushed and looked away.

'There are a lot of stars.' Alice waved a hand at the sky, talking quickly. 'My dad once tried to teach me about them, but I'm rubbish at remembering where they are.'

Jay looked at her but she was facing the sea again. Had he imagined that look? Was his attraction reciprocated?

'We learned about them when I was doing my lifeboat training,' he confessed, still studying her. 'Actually, I knew them already, it's part of the boy code.'

'The same one that says you shouldn't have a clue about candles?'

'I think the rules appear on the same page.'

'Figures it wouldn't be alphabetical,' she sniggered.

Jay liked that sound, he didn't know Alice well, but he got the feeling she didn't laugh much and suddenly he wanted to hear that noise again.

'That one over there,' Jay pointed towards the sky. 'That's the Plough.' He moved closer and stood behind her so she could follow the direction of his finger. 'It's easy to remember because it looks like a saucepan, see the handle there.'

Jay didn't touch her but standing behind with his arm pointing towards the horizon meant he could smell chocolate cake again. He resisted the urge to lean into her hair.

'I remember, my dad used to say seeing it made him hungry.' Alice chuckled and he wanted to punch the air.

'Look upwards from the edge of the pan, up there, that's the North Star, it's guided sailors home for generations.'

'Does it guide you, when you're out on the water?'

'We're a bit more technical now, but I always look for it. I like knowing it's there, so whatever happens I'll be able to find my way home.'

And didn't that sound stupid and sentimental, maybe the candle question *had* affected his testosterone?

'That only works if you know where home is,' she said, almost too softly for him to hear.

'You don't?' Jay asked, but felt the distance as she walked away, heading for the pathway that ran alongside the cliffs. He followed and she didn't speak for a while.

'Not right now.'

'Not Castle Cove then?'

'The house is here, whenever I want it. But no, I don't think Castle Cove is the right place for me at the moment.'

Jay wanted to ask why but instead he focused on walking and letting her talk. In the end she answered anyway.

'I've got a lot of living to catch up on. I'm heading for Thailand after the triathlon, to help my dad run his diving business, after that who knows, I want to travel.'

'Ah a free spirit, that'll explain the candles.' Although it didn't explain the need for systems and order.

'Yep, you summed it up, free-spirit-in-training, that's me.' Alice twirled under the stars, her arms stretched skywards then continued walking. 'What about you?'

'Me?' Jay waited until they'd both stepped over a stile. Alice's torch shone on the ground in front to light the pathway, but he was glad the moon had reached so high.

'I grew up here, lived in Birmingham for a few years.' He didn't mention that he'd hated it. 'Missed the sea, so I came back.'

'Do you have family here?'

Jay shoved down the sharp pain in his chest triggered by the question. 'My mum lives in Castle Cove.'

'What about your dad?'

Jay frowned. 'He left when I was seventeen and I haven't seen him since, there's no-one else.'

'I'm sorry.' Alice's brow puckered.

'Don't be. I don't miss him. I love it here. There's nowhere I'd rather live and I love what do.' He'd had plenty of opportunities to live elsewhere, but he loved his life. Aside from the recent restlessness, he wouldn't change a thing, except for Steve.

'Ah.' Alice smiled suddenly, lifting the mood. 'Your double life as a superhero-stroke-carpenter, I can see the appeal.'

'Don't forget I volunteer on the local lifeboat.'

'Part of any decent superhero's job description, right alongside leaping tall buildings with a single bound.'

'I try to avoid that,' he said smiling. 'It's not good for the knees.'

'And you're alone?' Alice stumbled over the words and walked further ahead as she said them.

'Alone how?'

'Cath said your girlfriend had moved to Dubai?'

They'd been talking about him? It was stupid how pleased he was to hear that. 'Oh, that, alone, yes, aside from Zeus, why?'

Alice sighed. He almost didn't hear it but the wind chose that exact moment to blow the sound in his direction. He waited to see what came next, he could almost hear the whir and click of her brain as she thought of what to say. In comparison to the impulsive, wear-your-heart-on-your-sleeve Mel, Alice was fascinating to watch.

'I was rethinking.'

'What?'

'That date, is it still on the table?'

'You're changing your mind?'

Alice stopped suddenly to take in the view again. She didn't look at him. 'Maybe. Okay, yes, I've had some time to think.'

Jay smiled. 'What, you've decided an opportunity to go on a date with me is too good to pass up?'

Alice frowned, making a hefty dent in his ego. 'I'm here for adventure.'

'And I'm adventure?'

Alice pondered the question. 'You're a man I don't know very well.' She broke off. 'I haven't dated in a while, I'm doing lots of things I haven't done before. If you want to call that adventure, yes.'

'So, I'm a tick in a box?'

Alice bobbed her head, a hint of a smile on her lips. 'Yes, if you like.'

'Any stranger would do?'

She looked surprised, mulling the question over before grinning. 'I considered Ted Abbott but he's a little old for me.'

'I guess I should be honoured I pass muster. And you haven't met anyone else in Castle Cove you'd like to date since you arrived?'

Alice lifted her shoulders. 'You said Zeus was already taken. Besides, I've been training most evenings since I got here, the rest of the time I've been working or clearing out my mother's things.' She swallowed. 'I haven't been looking. You're probably only the second man outside of work I've spoken more than three sentences to since I arrived four months ago.'

'Gee, you sure know how to make a man feel special,' he teased.

'I think your ego can take it.'

Jay put a hand on his chest. 'I may never be the same. Not sure I can pass up the opportunity of an adventure with you though. I'd be delighted to take you on a date.'

'Nothing serious, I'm only looking for fun.' Alice looked at him, her eyes solemn, and a ridge embedded in her forehead that told him what she was saying was important.

Jay nodded. Why not? It wasn't like he was looking for anything serious either, especially not with someone planning on leaving town. 'Fun's okay, I can do that. You'll have to stop yourself from falling for me though.'

Alice snorted, denting his ego even more. He'd need a panel-beater to straighten it out after this conversation. 'I think I can handle it.'

'So, adventure.' Jay scratched his chin, making a big deal out of it. 'Is that what you want from our date?'

'Of course.' Alice looked so sober he wanted to reach across and rub the troubled lines from her forehead. 'To clarify, I don't consider a ride on the teacups at the fairground adventure.'

'Ah, depends if you're eating candy floss at the same time – and *damn*, I always do that on a first date.'

'I used to dream about paragliding. I've never tried, have you?'

'Overrated. I might take you for a meal at the pub,' he quipped. 'If you're feeling really brave you could try the chicken curry, it'll bring tears to your eyes.'

'Or abseiling?'

'You're scaring me.' Jay pretended to shudder. Zeus brought him a stick and he threw it back in the direction they'd walked.

Alice shivered suddenly and he wanted to offer her his jacket, but when he started to take it off she shook her head, then pulled a fleece from her backpack and put it on.

'It's getting cold.' *And dark, not to mention late.* 'We should head back. There are clouds gathering, if the moon gets covered, we won't be able to see, which is—'

'—dangerous.' She finished for him, sounding amused.

'I'll walk you back and we can swap numbers. Are you free next Saturday?'

He'd be racking his brains all week to figure out a way to impress her. Why it mattered, he didn't know.

'I can be.' Alice looked towards the sea again, her expression unreadable. 'I'm working and then I need to run, but I'll be free by five, is that okay?'

'If I get called out, I might have to postpone.' Jay let it hang there. Some women – a few he'd dated – had been irritated that he'd put a rescue first, so now he made a point of saying something up front, in the hope that it would save complications and irritations in the long run.

Alice didn't look surprised, or upset. 'I wouldn't expect any less and I certainly wouldn't give you a hard time about it.'

'Okay.' Something settled in his chest. 'Good, great.'

'So, now we've cleared that up, how about I race you home? Last one back gets to pick the litter up in your car.'

Alice took off suddenly at a sprint – with the torch – with Zeus following closely behind, leaving him in the dark, feeling more than a little surprised.

Chapter Twelve

Towel, check. Wetsuit, check. Sun, check. Sea, check. Nerves, check.

Alice put down her towel and wriggled out of her trainers, scanning the beach, which was getting more crowded by the minute. Her day off from the café had coincided with a heatwave, even though it was only mid-June, and the sand was filled with people determined to enjoy the tropical Friday afternoon.

Red, blue, yellow and pink towels and a showroom of umbrellas littered the sand. Families played ball games, kids dug sandcastles with their multicoloured buckets and spades while parents looked on, thumbing through paperbacks or licking ice creams.

A couple next to her ate sandwiches from a large green ice box filled with lager cans.

A child shrieked suddenly and Alice stood, checking the sea for signs of a problem.

Her heart had thumped most of Beethoven's Fifth Symphony before she saw a group of kids batting a ball over a net. One of the boys had tumbled onto the floor with a bikini-clad girl and they simultaneously laughed and screamed, hugging as they hit the sand.

Alice closed her eyes as her heartbeat slowed, then pulled off her shorts, revealing a wetsuit, and folded them into a neat pile along with her t-shirt and hat. Her small backpack lay hidden underneath and she spent a few more moments arranging and rearranging them, glancing every now and then at the lifeguards. Were they paying attention to the water or checking their phones?

Alice pulled off her sunglasses and stood as a cloud covered the sun giving them all an unexpected dose of shade.

Would the sea be cold today?

People ran and splashed in and out of the waves, some surfing, some playing. The sound of laughter mixed with the hush of foam and sea spray. She checked the lifeguards again – they were one hundred per cent focused on the sea, even Jay wouldn't find fault.

Years ago, Alice wouldn't have cared about lifeguards or cold, she'd have swum anywhere, pounded the waves until she was out of breath. She'd been known to lay flat in the water, out of her depth, with her head looking skywards, floating and thinking, without a care in the world.

She let her feet squeeze the hot sand and took a couple of steps, feeling strangely lightheaded. The beach was long and the walk felt long too. As she got closer to the sea, her head filled with dread, drowning out everything.

People continued to run and walk around her as if she were invisible. She balled her hands, letting her fingernails pinch flesh and bring her back to reality.

Alice tried a couple more steps, almost spinning round and tripping when a man jogged past, knocking her sideways.

'Sorry.' He stopped and helped her stabilise.

'My fault.' Why did her head feel so fuzzy? 'I wasn't watching where I was going.'

He looked into her face, perhaps checking for signs of alcohol. 'You okay?' She knew him from somewhere, but couldn't place him.

'Great,' she chirped, glancing towards her towel. 'Just going for a swim.'

'The sea's that way?' The man pointed to the waves.

'Ah, yes, I'm okay, really.'

He cocked his head. 'I knew I'd seen you before. You know Jay? You were sitting with him in the pub the other night.' He looked up the beach before turning back to her.

'I know him a little, you are?'

'Shaun, from the Anglers.'

'Of course… and you're a friend of Cath's?'

Shaun grunted, then put his hand out so she could shake it. His fingers felt hot.

'You're freezing,' he said.

'It's colder than it looks, I'm not used to the fresh air. You should finish your run, it's a beautiful day for it.'

Shaun's forehead creased, not so easily distracted.

'I'm good, honestly, I might change my mind about the swim… '

'You'll feel better once you're in, it's always the first few steps that are the worst,' he reassured her.

'That's what my mum used to say.' Her voice came out wistful. 'Thanks, perhaps I'll see you again.' Alice took a few more steps, not waiting for his answer and didn't turn back, even as she approached the water.

'Knees.' Alice shivered as her feet hit the cold waves. A giggling toddler with yellow armbands ran past, followed by his dad. Their splashes had her sucking in a breath.

Alice stopped, looking down, focusing on the warmth from the sun hitting her back. Someone shouted but she didn't look up, instead she moved in further. The breath caught in her throat again and she stopped, closing her eyes.

'You okay?' Alice recognised the voice immediately and looked up. A pair of sharp blue eyes studied her face.

A large wave hit her thigh and the next breath came on a whoosh. Alice stumbled towards the shore, not waiting for Jay. She knew she looked odd, but to hell with it. When she hit the beach, she turned to watch him stride after her, his wetsuit clinging to his body, exposing perfectly muscled forearms and legs.

'I'm great.' She tried to smile to prove it, dragging her eyes upwards to his concerned face. The sand felt warm here and Alice's legs began to heat up, bringing her heartbeat down. Her hands gripped into fists, frustrated she was totally off schedule.

'Have you been in?' Alice asked.

'Yep. Thought I'd get some fresh air, keep an eye on things while I'm here, this is the busiest it's been so far this year.'

'Where's Zeus?'

'My mum likes to have him sometimes, he's on a visit.' Jay scanned the beach. 'Still on for our date?'

'You packed the parachutes already?'

His laughter warmed her belly. 'No, but the teacups are ready to go.' His eyes drifted to her feet and skimmed upwards. 'You didn't get very far out?'

'I left my stuff over there.' Alice pointed up the beach, towards her pile of belongings. 'I was thinking it might not be a good idea to go in and leave it, the beach is busier than I expected.'

'I'll watch it if you like? Maybe don't swim for too long, it's still only the middle of June, even in a wetsuit it gets cold and you're at risk of hypothermia.'

Alice tutted. 'The sea is busy, I might run first.'

'Is it worth changing again? In the triathlon you'll be swimming first, and it'll be busier than this so it'll be a good idea to get used to it, maybe do a quick ten minutes and when you've finished I'll run with you?' While Jay talked, his eyes watched the sea, but somehow, he managed to make her feel like she had all his attention.

'You'd run in that?'

'No way, trainers in the car. It's only fair you give me the chance of a redo after my humiliating defeat on Saturday night.'

Alice fought the smile. 'Zeus did look embarrassed. Okay.' She glanced at the sea again searching for excuses. The thought of coming clean made her knees go weak. 'I'll show you where I left my stuff. We didn't see you at the café yesterday?' she said making conversation.

'Another emergency. Cath said it would be okay if I came next week.'

They trudged up the beach and Alice focused on the sand. Maybe she could have a sudden bout of stomach flu? Or remember she'd left the oven on? If she was lucky someone would have stolen her mobile and they'd spend the next hour talking to the police.

They approached her towel, and she could see nothing had been disturbed.

'Here.' It had taken them only seconds to get there, but the walk back would feel longer. She'd have to tell him, she'd never be able to go in. 'Um.'

'Jay!' The shout from across the beach caught everyone's attention. Shaun ran towards the shore following the two lifeguards and immediately Jay sprinted after him. Alice watched him eat up the sand, admiring the speed and athleticism of his body. Even after her months of training she wouldn't be able to keep up.

The couple who'd splashed them earlier were shouting; she could see a man further out paddling and waving, holding up a tiny shape wearing yellow armbands. The sea seemed to roar louder, and people began to yell from the edge of the waves. Alice headed towards them, wanting to see more, but not wanting to see anything at the same time.

The lifeguards were in the sea and got to the scene first, grabbing the child. Within seconds everyone was back on the beach but the small crowd had multiplied. People were shouting as the lifeguards put the child in armbands on the sand and gathered round in a flurry. One opened a medical bag and pulled out pieces of equipment. Alice could see tubes, a blanket and some kind of mask. The crowd hushed as they worked and a baby started to cry. A lifeguard sprinted to a truck further down the beach and pulled out a walky-talky, speaking urgently into it. The small figure on the ground didn't move and Alice's stomach churned. Then suddenly, the child screamed and began to wriggle. His father pushed the lifeguards aside so he could grab and cuddle him close, his face ashen.

Alice watched Jay standing on the sidelines watching the action unfold. Goosebumps rose on his arms and legs and he looked so worried that she had an unexpected urge to hug him, but stopped herself.

Even when the toddler was declared fine, his expression didn't change.

☆

'Running on sand's a lot more difficult than on tarmac,' Jay explained as he pounded the hot beach, waving at a couple of life-guards as they passed. His mood had lifted since he'd put on trainers.

Beside him, Alice wiped sweat from her forehead, trying to ignore the ache in her ankles and the sand that had somehow made its way into her socks Houdini-style. 'Maybe I need better shoes?' she gasped, watching as he began to overtake.

'It's worth going to a specialist shop. I can recommend one. They'll check what type you need, you might need trainers to compensate for the way you run.'

'What does that mean?'

Jay dismissed the comment by waving a hand. 'I'm not insulting you. We all run in different ways, have different gaits, use different parts of our feet. You can get tailored shoes for it, helps stop injuries. When did you start training?'

'Almost fifteen weeks ago.' Alice was getting cramp in her left calf muscle, but didn't want to break their stride so carried on. She did feel her cheeks flush when he obviously slowed so she could catch up.

'And you're up to how many kilometres?'

'Five or six I think.' She slowed her breathing to short pants so she didn't sound so out of breath. A dribble of sweat ran down her cheek.

'In how long?'

'Forty minutes.'

He rubbed a hand across his forehead. 'You might need to work on your speed.'

They ran past a couple of sandcastles which Alice dodged, almost tripping but recovering just in time. 'I am, it's just taking a while. I wasn't very fit when I started. I'm only planning to finish the triathlon, not win it.'

'Why wouldn't you want to win? Do you fancy a quick jog across the cliffs?' Jay pointed upwards. 'There are some pretty views and the ground is less uneven, easier to negotiate.'

She nodded because it was easier than talking.

Jay went ahead. They passed through a small gate and he trotted up the path, which steepened quickly. The track was tarmacked most of the way up and lined with rough bushes and piles of white sand. Alice looked at her feet; sprays of sand shot out of her trainers each time she hit the floor. Jay didn't look back as he launched himself upwards; he didn't sound out of breath or look tired and he'd already swum that morning. She slowed to a crawl as she headed up the pathway.

Alice was half way up when Jay trotted back to join her. He looked fresh and pink-cheeked and not even a little out of breath.

'How are you doing?'

'Not... quite... as... well... as... Saturday.'

'Off day?'

'No,' she panted. 'Uphill... harder... and... you... had... no... torch.'

'You still made good time.'

Alice blew out a breath. 'Not... great... at... hills.'

Jay slowed down a bit more. 'It'll get easier, this is the worst bit.'

She didn't bother to answer, but three minutes later the path began to even out.

'You can go ahead if you like.' As her breathing slowed, Alice managed to get the words out.

'I'm not in a hurry. What are your training plans for this week?'

She huffed. 'Cycling to work or running each day, I do the plank, lunges, swim a bit,' she fudged. 'My mum used to say it's more about endurance than speed.' She ignored the dull ache of grief in her gut.

They reached the top and Jay stopped, jogging from one foot to the other as he looked at the view. Sun glittered on the sea and the sky was blue and cloudless. A couple of sail boats bobbed in the distance and a lone paddle-boarder headed into shore.

'It's just as pretty in the daylight,' Alice said.

'Mmmm.' Jay didn't look away. 'It's deceptive.'

'You like volunteering on the lifeboat?' She joined him, jogging gently on the spot as her heartbeat calmed.

'I don't like seeing people in danger, but doing something to help makes me feel good.'

'You've saved a lot of lives?' Alice watched as he considered.

'My team has.' He chose his words carefully. 'It makes it worthwhile when you save someone, but sometimes we're too late.'

'What happens then?'

He frowned. 'Shall we run?'

Jay took off suddenly without waiting for her, although he didn't go fast, so Alice knew he was aware of where she was. She followed him slowly, watching him run. Complicated man. Something was definitely going on underneath the surface.

Alice let her eyes follow the path of his body from his feet upwards. She hadn't met many men who looked like him. Even some of the younger waiters at Taste of Rome, with all of their gym time, preening and hair products couldn't quite match up.

Dammit she was perving again. She increased her speed to catch up, then her foot caught on something suddenly and she launched forwards, grasping with her hands to try and stay upright. Her feet went out from under her and she shouted as she flew downwards.

Her hands slammed onto the ground, her knees grazed chaffing grass and sand, and she felt an agonising pain in her ankle.

'Bugger,' Alice groaned, lying flat on the floor as tears pricked her eyes. 'That really hurt.'

'You okay?' Jay was kneeling beside her in seconds, his hands on her shoulders. 'Don't move yet, does anything else hurt?'

Gentle fingers moved down her back as she tried to turn. 'I'm fine... ow!' Her ankle protested as she sat up.

'You've scraped your knees.' Jay said, helping her to sit upright.

She moved her leg and stopped when a sharp pain shot from her ankle again. 'I might have pulled a muscle somewhere.' She ran a hand over her foot. 'Bloody idiot.' She'd been too busy watching Jay's form rather than the floor. 'Serves me right, I wasn't paying attention.'

He tipped her chin up and looked into her eyes. 'I don't think you're concussed, did you hit your head?'

'I think my ego's more bruised than my body,' she admitted. 'My ankle is painful.'

He ran gentle fingers over it. 'Can we take your trainer off?'

'Only one way to find out.' She undid her laces but Jay took over and slowly removed the shoe, before tipping out the sand. The movement made her wince.

'Were you trying to take the whole beach home?' Jay joked as he angled her ankle gently to the side. 'I don't think you've broken anything, feel okay?'

'Yes, ow.'

'Sorry. Ready to head back?'

'There's a bus in forty minutes.'

He looked annoyed. 'Don't be silly, I'll drive you, we should probably pop into the hospital on the way, we can get your ankle checked.'

'I can get there.'

Jay ran a hand through his hair making it stand on end. 'Your stuff is in my truck anyway.'

'To keep it safe while we were running, I don't want you to go out of your way.'

Jay stood, holding a hand out to help her up. Alice joined him and tried to put her weight on her left foot, but the pain stopped her.

'Looks sore?'

'I'll be fine if I take it slow,' she lied, limping a couple of steps, but he walked in front of her.

'I'll carry you down the hill.'

'Not necessary.' She blushed. 'I can walk, I'll just take it easy.'

'If I carry you, we'll get there faster.'

'And I'll feel like a total idiot.' She hobbled further forwards, ignoring the shoots of pain. 'I'm not totally inept.'

'Putting your weight on it now might make it worse,' Jay explained. 'It's up to you, but if you let me at least help you down the hill, I can move my pickup closer and you won't have to try to use it. If you walk on it now you might end up having to rest for the next few weeks.'

'How will I train?'

'Exactly.' His lips tightened as he watched her process the information.

'Fine, but I'm going to feel ridiculous.'

Before Alice could change her mind, Jay swept her up into his arms. Her ankle felt uncomfortable but she shifted until the pain stopped. She wound her arms around his neck and inhaled the scent of the sea.

'I feel like Scarlett O'Hara.'

Jay snorted. 'You've certainly got the temperament for it.'

'Are you saying I'm difficult?'

She was close enough to see his lips twitch at the corners. 'Let's go with feisty.'

'Semantics, and a brave word considering I'm close enough to pull your hair.' Alice tugged a stray strand curling at the back of his neck to prove it.

'Ouch, don't forget I could drop you.'

She mock gasped. 'And risk your superhero licence? Never gonna happen.'

'One day I might surprise you.' They hit the pathway and he began to walk down. Even though Jay was carrying her he wasn't a bit out of breath. The sun beat on their heads but he didn't even look hot.

'You're very fit.'

He grinned. 'Thank you.'

'Ah, there's that ego again. I meant in shape.'

'Thanks again.'

She poked out her tongue.

'My job's physical, I run most days, walk Zeus, swim every other. I love being outside.'

'I can relate to that, not usually as much adventure indoors. I never realised how important it was to be outside. How many times did you win the triathlon?'

Jay paused so he could count. 'Eight I think, haven't done it for a few years now.'

'Right.' She tracked their progress, they were almost at the beach. 'So you know what you're talking about?'

'Better than some.'

'Do you think I can do it?' She regretted the question as soon as it had left her lips.

'Of course.' They reached the beach and Jay put her down carefully next to the half-gate. Alice rested one arm on it so it could take some of her weight. 'Why would you ask me that?'

'No reason.' Alice gazed at the sea. 'Sure you don't mind getting the car? It'll hurt to walk on the beach and I really don't want to be carried.'

'I don't mind.' Jay jogged onto the sand and Alice watched him go, trying not to put weight on her ankle. She moved her gaze to where the late afternoon sunlight sparkled on the sea, and children ran in and out of the waves as if they were harmless.

Would she ever be able to join them? Alice winced, determined not to feel sorry for herself, but the question haunted her. Was her dream of completing the triathlon destined to ever become a reality?

Chapter Thirteen

'I really don't think this is necessary,' Alice grumbled as Jay approached the hospital. 'There aren't any spaces to park and I don't want to wait. If you drop me home, I'll put some ice on the ankle, take a paracetamol and it'll be fine.' Her voice had taken on a pleading quality.

'There's an urgent care unit, it shouldn't take long.' Jay swung the pickup into an empty space and turned to face her.

'In some countries they'd call this kidnapping,' she grumbled.

Jay laughed, a quick rich rumble that made her pulse perk up and take notice. 'Happily, in ours they call it being sensible. Let's just get the ankle looked at and I'll drop you home after, it'll be quicker than getting the bus.'

'You said it wasn't broken, and I'm sure it's fine.' She thought about waving her ankle in his face and rotating it but knew it would hurt too much.

'Better to check, don't you think?' His voice was gentle. 'Being stubborn is one thing, but if you damage yourself trying to run or cycle with an injury, you might have to pull out of the triathlon.'

'But what if they say I can't do it?' Her voice sounded small and she looked out of the window at the other cars, forcing the tears back. 'I'm not sure I'll be able to stand it.'

'I don't think they will.' Jay put a gentle hand on her shoulder. 'But it's better to know now. If the worst happens, there's always next year?'

'No there isn't.' Alice tried the door handle, feeling angry. 'By next year I'll be in Thailand.'

She opened the door and got out of the pickup slowly, taking care not to jerk her ankle. 'I made a promise.' That sounded so inadequate, she hobbled towards the sign saying 'Urgent Care'.

As they approached Alice could see the waiting room was small and lined with orange and chrome chairs, all of them occupied. A couple of vending machines loomed in the corner, one with a piece of laminated A4 stating it was 'Out of Order' and the other filled with a variety of crisps and chocolate treats. The walls were decorated with colourful posters warning of the dangers of everything from smoking and drugs to unexplained lumps.

A snotty toddler screamed through his dummy while his dad nursed what looked like a cut finger. In the corner, near the window, a woman in a red summer dress held a bowl under her friend's chin. Next to her a teenager dressed in cricket whites pressed an icepack against his jaw, not quite covering the dried blood that had trickled down his neck. His mother talked into her mobile, darting anxious looks in his direction. Alice averted her eyes as she shuffled inside.

'Take a seat, I'll check you in.' Jay pointed to the empty chair in front of the main desk.

'I can do it.' Alice hobbled in front of him, earning herself a loud sigh. 'I don't want you telling them I've broken it, it's just a bruise.'

Jay stood silently beside her until the woman at the front desk looked up. Her white blonde hair was decorated with pink highlights and she wore more make-up than Alice would apply in a whole year. Her eyes caught on Jay immediately and her face lit up.

'What are *you* doing here? Rescuing another damsel in distress?' Her eyes skimmed over Alice, barely taking her in.

'Hi Tina.' Jay shot her a smile that should come with a health warning for the weak-hearted. 'The patient has a sprained ankle, or a bruise.' He touched Alice's back easing her forwards. 'Probably not serious but best to check it out.'

'Off duty?'

'Jay's never off duty,' Alice muttered.

The woman's eyes narrowed as she checked out Alice's Lycra outfit and found it wanting. 'There's a fair wait.'

'We'll probably leave it then.' Alice started to turn around, but Jay put a hand on her shoulder.

'That's fine, we understand. How about you check the patient in while I find somewhere to sit?'

Alice narrowed her eyes.

Jay raised an eyebrow. 'We're not going anywhere until someone checks your ankle. It's partly my fault you're here at all.'

'Don't see how that works; my ankle, my stupid fault I wasn't paying attention to where I was going and tripped.'

'My idea we go running on the cliffs,' Jay added, sounding irritated.

'For goodness sake.' Alice turned back towards Tina, pushing her temper down. 'I'm not registered with a local doctor.'

'Doesn't matter.' Tina tapped something into her screen. 'Can you tell me your name and date of birth please?'

By the time she'd finished, Jay had found them seats and bought a couple of steaming cappuccinos and slices of chocolate cake. He hovered as Alice slowly sat but didn't try to help.

Alice looked at her cake. 'I hate these places.'

'What's not to like; the sick people, boring wait or bad coffee?' He stared into his cup as if he was waiting for it to morph into something more interesting.

'They usually mean someone you know is sick, or dying, or you are.'

'The upside is many get well or fixed.' He leaned back and crossed his legs at the ankles.

'Of course they do,' she admitted. 'I know that. It's just sometimes they don't.'

'You talking about your mother?'

'It was quick.' Alice rotated her ankle and felt the bite.

'Sometimes quick is better, for the person.'

Embarrassment made her flush. 'I'm sorry, I'm being insensitive. I guess your job brings you here all the time, you must hate it?'

'We only come if we want to. The paramedics usually meet us somewhere, and take over.'

'But you come? That girl, Tina, knew you.'

Jay waved the question away. 'I went to school with her, I think we dated for a while when we were teenagers.'

'Cath said you were… popular.'

'Is that a nice way of saying I got around?'

'You dated her, we're going on a date, I rest my case.'

Jay laughed. 'I never dated Cath, she and Shaun fell head over heels with each other in sixth form.'

'Cath dated Shaun?' Alice asked, surprised.

Jay nodded.

'I guess it should have been obvious, there was something going on the other night in the pub, but I couldn't put my finger on it.' Alice paused, feeling strangely hurt that her new friend hadn't confided in her. 'So he's the man she dated for ten years?'

'Yep.'

'Any idea why they broke up?'

'Shaun's not one for sharing and that conversation has been off limits since it happened.'

'Okay.' Alice sipped some coffee, feeling her mood darken.

'In answer to your original question, I haven't dated the woman I just bought coffee and cake from, and Olive who works in our local vet's doesn't fancy me... ' He smiled, his eyes sparkling.

'I got the feeling Tina knows you from somewhere more recently?' Alice blushed, knowing she was being nosy.

'Ah, sometimes I come to check on people. It helps close the circle, I like to see things work out.'

She nodded, feeling a little overwhelmed. 'I'm sorry for being such a cow before, you're not exactly what I thought.'

'What, a bossy, cold-hearted superhero, hell-bent on rescuing women, even if they haven't asked?'

'Well.' Alice flushed. 'Yes.'

'Yet you still agreed to date me?' Jay mimicked shock.

'My standards are low.'

Jay chuckled and took a bite of his cake. 'So, what did you mean on the beach when you asked if you could do the triathlon?' His blue eyes drank in her face.

'Nothing.' She felt her cheeks heat. 'I'm just nervous, that's all.'

'Any particular reason why?'

'Ms Appleton.' A nurse walked into the waiting room with a clipboard and Alice sprang up, forgetting her ankle until the sharp pain reminded her.

'Yes.' Jay took her arm as she let herself lean on him.

'I'm a triage nurse.' The woman started talking as she led them both into a small cubicle with a desk, chair and a hospital bed. Smiling, she pulled the curtain closed. 'Mr O'Donnell, haven't seen you for at least a week.'

'It's been quiet.'

'I know he's pretty to look at, but are you okay with him staying?' The nurse asked Alice.

'It's fine.'

The nurse sat in a chair. 'Why don't you sit, and tell me what's wrong.'

'She twisted her ankle.' Jay murmured.

'Doesn't look like there's anything wrong with her mouth though.' The nurse frowned.

'Sorry.' He zipped a finger across his lips.

The nurse knelt down and lifted Alice's ankle, running gentle fingers over it.

'I tripped when we were running. I'm sure it's only a bruise but he insisted I come to get it looked at.'

'We'll soon know.' The nurse continued her examination. 'Does it hurt?'

'No, yes— ow.'

'I assess cases before you see the doctor so I can prioritise urgent cases. There might be a bit of a wait until you see someone. Have you taken any painkillers?'

'No.'

'I'll get you some paracetamol, tide you over until you see the doctor.'

'Do you think it's broken?'

The nurse put her foot gently on the floor and stood up. 'It's not an obvious break, more likely you've strained it, but we can't always tell from looking. There's a little swelling, nothing major, you've still got movement.'

'So, I'm a non-urgent case?'

'Yes.'

'Roughly how long is the wait?'

The nurse winced, looking embarrassed. 'Depends on who else comes in, and how urgent the cases are. A couple of hours, three tops.'

'How about I go home, ice it, and see how I feel tomorrow?'

'It's up to you. If it still hurts and you want it checked out further, you'll be able to get an X-ray here tomorrow if you need one. Depends what your plans are tonight.'

'What about running?' Alice asked.

The woman chuckled. 'Even if it isn't broken, it obviously hurts, no running for a few days, at least until you can stand and walk comfortably.'

'Cycling?' Alice asked, feeling desperate. 'Swimming?'

The nurse gave her a gentle smile. 'Why don't you see what the doctor says?'

Alice stood. 'I really think I'll feel better after a rest and some sleep. If it's not better tomorrow I'll come back.'

'Let me give you something for the pain first.' The nurse said. 'Is he going to drive you home?'

'Yes.' Jay jumped in.

'Lucky girl,' the nurse winked. 'Give me a minute and I'll get your painkillers.'

Jay stared at Alice after the nurse had disappeared through the curtain. 'You know it would be more sensible to wait?'

'I know, but I'll come back tomorrow if I need to.'

'Are you working?'

Alice nodded. 'Saturday's one of our busiest days.'

'I can take you to the café in the morning if you're feeling okay. I'd planned to pick you up anyway, for our date.' He added.

She frowned at her foot. 'I guess parachuting's out?'

'I'll come up with a plan B.'

'Promise you're not going to wrap me in cotton wool,' Alice pleaded. 'My ankle will probably be fine by tomorrow and I don't want to be treated like an invalid just because I was silly enough to trip.'

'Accidents happen,' Jay said mildly. 'And I promise we'll have an evening of adventures, even if I have to carry you for the whole date.'

Chapter Fourteen

'You should have called,' Cath fussed as Alice circled the kitchen trying not to put too much weight on her ankle.

'I didn't want to bother you and Jay had it covered. Besides they just sent me home with some painkillers, wasn't much anyone could do.'

Cath frowned at her foot. 'How long do you have to take it easy for?'

'Not sure yet.'

Cath picked up a chair from the corner of the kitchen and placed it in the centre of the room near the dishwasher. 'You should sit, I'll bet that nurse told you to keep the weight off?'

Alice rolled her eyes. 'Don't you start. I've been pampered and nagged to within an inch of my life. You've no idea how many times Jay told me to put my feet up when he drove me home last night.'

'I always did like that man.' Cath's expression was wistful.

Alice hobbled past the chair and took a handful of clean plates out of the dishwasher.

'You will not.' Cath said. 'Jay called me before he dropped you here, said you had to rest that foot or else.'

'God.' Alice rolled her eyes. 'It's like having my own personal minder.'

Cath put her hands on her hips. 'You should be so lucky. He said I needed to remind you that if you don't keep the weight off it, it might not heal in time for your training. Are you sure you don't need to go back to the hospital for an X-ray?' Cath eyed her foot suspiciously.

Alice shook her head. 'I don't need one. Despite appearances, it feels a little better today. I think if I do as I'm told and take painkillers I'll be okay.' She glanced around the kitchen with a frown. 'Are you sure I can't help at all?'

'Nope,' Cath said. 'Lily's coming in a bit so you can relax. Just chat when I come into the kitchen. Dan's been away for a few days and I've been missing having company.'

'I'm sorry Cath.' Alice got up and shuffled to her friend, placing a hand on her arm. 'I didn't realise.'

'It's okay.' Cath smiled but Alice could see through it. 'He'll be back soon, and to be honest I'm just happy he's taking such an interest in his plumbing business, he's so much more enthusiastic about work recently.'

The bell over the door went. 'That's probably Lily. Sit.' Cath pointed to the chair with a grin before bouncing into the front of the café.

Alice perused the kitchen; the counters were covered with cups and plates, some of them clean and some of them still in piles as a result of the broken cupboard. As Jay had mentioned on the beach, he still hadn't been back to mend it because he'd had a couple of client emergencies, and Cath had told him not to worry. He needed to sort it soon though, the mess was driving her mad.

Alice edged to the counter and pulled some mugs out of the dishwasher and placed them on the side. She wouldn't be able to put them away, but at least she could make some space. She'd almost finished when Cath whizzed back into the kitchen and screeched.

'If you don't sit down Alice Appleton, I swear I'll superglue those feet of yours to the floor.'

'Fine. I'll sit.' Alice raised her hands in mock surrender and plopped onto the chair.

'How about I get the café books for you to look at? You can tell me where I'm going wrong? Simon complained yesterday that he couldn't understand any of my figures.'

'Fine, sure,' Alice agreed, feeling her spirits lift.

☆

'Is this okay?' Later that afternoon, Jay laid out a soft rug on the sand and lowered the picnic basket next to it. He watched Alice grimacing as she lowered herself down.

'I feel like giving you a sticker for not offering to help.' Alice adjusted her sunglasses, squinting through the dazzling sunshine and pulled off her sandal. The painkillers meant her ankle didn't hurt so much today. Hopefully she'd be able to get back to her training soon.

She dipped her fingers into the warm yellow sand and let it fall through like an hourglass.

'Enjoying yourself?'

Alice picked up another handful. 'Yes. This is ridiculously relaxing.'

Jay grinned. 'You need to get out more...'

'I don't know, I've been shouted at on the beach, stalked on my bike and injured while jogging, I'd say my life in Castle Cove has been action-packed.'

'Is that your way of saying thank you?'

'Maybe.' Alice scanned the beach. She'd never been to the secluded cove before, even the car park looked empty. Sun beat on her shoulders, even though it was past five o'clock. Soft waves lapped at the shore making her long to dip her toes without having a panic attack.

'You need some lotion on those shoulders?' Jay asked suddenly.

'Ah, okay.' Alice reached into her bag and pulled out her factor 30. 'I can do it.'

'Don't doubt it.' Jay knelt beside her and hearing him squeeze lotion on his fingers, she smelled coconuts and almost flinched when he touched her. Had it been that long? Her body relaxed as he smoothed cream into her back.

'Your skin's hot.'

Alice cleared her throat.

'Feel okay?'

'Yep.' Her voice sounded high. 'Is this all part of an elaborate seduction technique?'

Jay's fingers dipped to the top of her t-shirt and then ran along the edge until he hit her bra strap and followed it to her shoulders. Alice fought a shiver, feeling ridiculous.

'Maybe. I've been practising this particular technique since I was sixteen, is it working?'

Alice swallowed the affirmative. 'Do you want me to give you a score out of ten?'

Jay laughed. 'I'm guessing you're not impressed?' His fingertips traced the tops of her shoulders along the tip of her collarbone then glided up her neck.

'I... ' She suppressed a shudder. 'Well—'

'I think you might have burnt here a little.' Jay put a finger at the top of her spine where her neck started. His fingers reached the top and slid sun cream across the back of her ear making her lips tingle. 'Does it sting?'

Alice couldn't find any more words, her body was on fire.

'Well?' Jay's voice sounded close to her ear, or maybe that was her imagination?

'I, er, no.'

Jay eased his fingers back down to her shoulders and then pulled away. Alice heard the lid snap back on the sun cream before she could form any more of an answer.

Jay plopped down next to her, his t-shirt and cargo shorts setting off his long, lean limbs. She dragged her eyes to the sea as he popped open the top of the picnic basket. 'It's hot, do you fancy a drink?'

'You've got water?' she asked, feeling jittery.

'Fizzy, I promised adventure.'

Jay's jokey tone put her at ease, even though she wouldn't forget how it felt to have him touching her.

'Is this plan B?' Part of her felt disappointed.

'Not quite.'

Alice cocked her head, watching him. 'What are we doing, abseiling down those cliffs?'

Jay smiled. 'Nope, but we could start with a swim?'

'Not sure my foot's up to that.' She sipped her fizzy water to hide the flush of her cheeks and watched him drink some too. 'Besides, I forgot my wetsuit. Sorry, I know you said to bring one.'

'That's fine, probably best to leave it another day, I don't think Nurse Ratchet would appreciate it if you strained it again.' Jay poured her more water. 'Let's eat, then we can hop in the car, there's a small dock a few miles down the coast, Shaun's got a boat there we're going to borrow.'

'A boat.' Her heartbeat thundered in her throat.

'It's a beautiful sunny afternoon, we can head towards the Castle Cove rocks, there are some stunning views and coves if you know where to find them. If you don't fancy eating now, we can take the picnic. It's not parachuting, but you won't sprain your ankle.'

'What about Zeus?'

'He loves being out on the water, you don't mind him playing gooseberry?'

'Not if he doesn't.'

Jay considered her for a moment. 'Don't you like boats?'

'I do.' Alice let hair slide over her face. Jay had an uncanny knack for reading her emotions, one she could do without. 'Just not been in one for years, are you sure it's safe?'

Jay looked amused. 'Aside from the holes in the bottom, but I've got buckets so we won't sink.'

'Sorry, forgot who I was talking to for a nanosecond.'

Jay pulled out a tray of chicken and a couple of plates from the basket.

'You know, I'm not that hungry any more, maybe we should eat later?'

Jay put the chicken back, grabbing a leg first.

'How big is this boat?' Alice swallowed more water to clear the dryness in her throat. Maybe it would rival the QE2.

'Big enough for the two of us and Zeus. I think we could squeeze a couple more in if we wanted to.' He stood and threw the picnic hamper over his shoulder. 'We can find somewhere to go ashore if we want to picnic, or eat on our knees.'

'Knees work.' No way was she getting out near the shore, what if she fell in?

Jay looked pleased. 'In that case, we can stay out late, follow the North Star home.'

'Ah, well, won't it be more dangerous in the dark?'

'Don't you mean adventurous?' Jay laughed. 'Fully equipped. Even has night lights, no chance of running into trouble with me. Don't worry, I'll get you home before you turn into a pumpkin. Shall we head for the boat now? It's a short drive and we can change and leave our stuff in the truck?'

'Sure.' Alice agreed reluctantly. At least she had the ride there to come up with an excuse. She limped towards the car, glancing back at the beach.

A boat trip? She'd have preferred the teacups. It would take a miracle to stop Jay from finding out her secret once they hit the water.

Chapter Fifteen

'You ready?' Jay asked.

Alice tried to smile as she looked around the jetty. Blazing sunshine made the sky a vibrant blue and the water was like glass, nothing to worry about. Zeus zipped past her launching himself at the small boat, landing perfectly on deck even though there wasn't much room between the seats.

'Impressive.'

Jay looked like a proud dad. 'He's always had good sea legs. Don't be shy, hop in and join him, I'll fish out some life jackets.'

'It's small.'

'Big enough for us, plenty of places to sit.' Jay's eyes were fixed on Alice's face.

'What's it called?'

'*Titanic*, Shaun has a twisted sense of humour.'

'Funny.' Alice grimaced, fighting the rising bile in her throat. 'Is there a bathroom somewhere?'

'Over there.' Jay pointed to a white building they'd driven past on the way into the boat yard and dangled a set of keys from his fingers. 'You can let yourself in, or I can do it for you?'

'I'll be fine, won't be a sec.' Alice wanted to run, but her ankle wouldn't allow it, so she hobbled over to the building, opened up and let herself inside. She closed her eyes and leaned back against the door fighting the rising panic.

'It's a boat,' she murmured. 'A perfectly safe boat with a terrible name, driven by a lifeboat volunteer stroke superhero. What's the worst that could happen?'

It could sink. You could drown.

'I will not.' Alice splashed water onto her face, then glared in the mirror at her pale cheeks. 'I can't think of a good enough excuse not to do this, besides, Jay won't let anything happen to me.'

It's not him you've got to worry about.

'He won't let me fall in, and the boat won't sink. I'll be fine, I'm being ridiculous.' Alice went to the toilet and took her time washing her hands. She even applied more lippy. By the time she limped back to the boat she felt calmer. Ignoring her shaking legs as she made the half leap, half stumble onto the deck of the boat. It bobbed a couple of times, but felt safer than she'd expected. It wasn't cold, and there was plenty of shelter from the tall windscreen at the front. There were padded white seats along the back and sides and she quickly went to sit on one, facing the driver's seat where Jay sat.

'Want to come up here and check it out?' Jay noticed her focusing on it. 'I'll put the picnic down there if you're hungry? Or there's wine.'

Jay handed her a lifejacket and she tugged it on. 'Nice boat.' At least it seemed to do all the right things, like float.

'Shaun looks after it.' Jay put a lifejacket on Zeus, then fired up the engine and steered it out of the dock. Alice sat where she was, holding onto her seat, her fingernails gripping the white plastic padding. Jay hummed as he manoeuvred them out into deep water.

Alice adjusted her sunglasses. At least the weather still looked good, the sun was high in the sky and the water only rippled but she could feel a cool breeze.

'You can move if you want?' Jay turned.

'I'm all right here.'

Zeus put his head on her knees and she let go of the bench with one hand so she could stroke his head, holding fast with the other.

'You'll see more next to me.' Jay looked at her oddly, it might have been her imagination but Zeus looked confused too. 'Or you could sit up the front, you'll get a great view?'

'Next to you will work.' Alice let go of the bench after a couple of tries and hobbled to Jay's side. In front of him was a dashboard of buttons and a small screen.

'This is high tech.'

'Shaun had it built especially. We've seen so many things go wrong with boats or the people driving them on our rescues, he wanted to cover all bases. There are even backups of backups on here.'

The windscreen shielded them from spray but didn't obscure the view. They were heading out to sea; all she could see was the horizon and a few bobbing boats to her left.

'Not many people about.'

'We'll see more on the journey.' Jay flicked a couple of buttons. 'See over there?' He pointed left. 'That's the start of Castle Cove's famous rocks.'

'Why are they famous?'

'Depends on which story you believe. Legend says smugglers used to hide things in those rocks and spread rumours about monsters to scare people off.'

'Doesn't look very comfortable.' Alice watched the sea roll in and hit them, sending up sprays of white foam into the blue, cloudless sky.

Jay laughed. 'It wasn't the smartest plan, because the water gets high and things get washed away. I thought we could head past, then get a bit closer and find somewhere to stop?'

'Sure.'

'Enjoying yourself?'

Alice nodded, surprised. This felt like old times when her parents had still been married and they'd go out on adventures together, before the divorce had changed her life. Her stomach had stopped clenching once they started moving. Jay was right, the views were incredible.

'You do this a lot?'

'The only time I've been on a boat recently is on a rescue.' Jay flicked some switches and pushed the throttle without looking at her. He steered them further along the coast and within a few more minutes he'd found a quiet place to stop. The craft bobbed but Alice felt safe enough to hobble back across the deck to where she'd been sitting before. The views were less obstructed from there. Zeus came up to nudge her hand and she stroked his head.

'Fancy a drink?'

'Yes please.' Alice leaned back and closed her eyes relishing the warmth from the sun as Jay opened the hamper.

'Want wine?'

Alice grinned, feeling a flutter of excitement in her belly. 'Small one please, I think wine on a date is obligatory.'

Jay handed her a glass filled to the brim.

'Where's yours?'

'In charge of a boat, not a good idea. I'll have one later.' He watched her take a big sip. 'How's the ankle?'

'Forgotten about it, that's a good sign. Hopefully I'll be up to training tomorrow. Swimming at least.' Alice drank more as something began to beep in the background.

'Radio,' Jay explained. Picking up a mouthpiece, he spoke into it. She couldn't hear but Jay's shoulders tensed; after a few terse sentences he hung up.

'What's up?'

Jay turned. 'Lost swimmer, last spotted somewhere round here. He's experienced but three hours overdue.' He tapped the throttle. 'Shaun says they've just received a call from the coastguard, thought he'd let me know in case I saw anything.'

'You want to look?' Alice sipped more wine.

'They're out now, coastguard too.'

'More eyes?'

Jay looked torn.

'Is it because of me?'

'It's not a good idea to get you involved, and I'm not supposed to.'

What if the man was barely hanging on? 'I'm fine. I'll stay out of your way, I can look from here, I've no intention of moving.' Alice patted the seat, then poured the rest of the wine out of the boat so it didn't spill when they moved and put the glass back into the hamper. 'We can just help to find him, we don't need to get involved.'

'Sure?'

'If it was me, I'd want as many people as possible looking.'

'Okay.' An emotion flashed across Jay's face and he fired up the engine. 'Thank you. I... not all my dates end like this.' He steered the boat forward. 'Hopefully it won't take long and we'll get back to our picnic.'

He'd already turned to face the front and the boat was shooting through the water, picking up speed as it skimmed over the waves.

'What are we looking for?' Alice shouted.

Jay didn't turn around but she could hear him answer. 'White swimming hat, that's all I know, he swims here a lot and could be anywhere along the coast.'

Her eyes scanned the surface. It was so hard to see, harder than she'd expected. Even though her ankle protested a little at the movement, she shifted to the right so she could scan a bigger area and gripping the edge of the boat, she leaned out over the water, squinting as sunshine hit her eyes. The boat was high in the sea, but Alice felt exposed. Cold spray hit her on the face and goosebumps prickled across her body.

'How can you tell what's a hat and what's a wave?' she shouted, trying to distract herself.

'You can't. Just look for anything odd. Sometimes we have to go back and forth a few times. Anything you think looks strange tell me and I'll bring the boat around.'

'I can't imagine being in the sea for that long.' She shivered involuntarily. 'He'll be so cold.'

'He's wearing a wetsuit, otherwise he'd probably be dead or suffering from hypothermia by now, but we need to find him soon.' Jay went quiet as they continued looking. Even Zeus whined, picking up on the tension.

'I don't know how you do this.' Her heart raced, with a strange mixture of excitement, anticipation, and dread.

The radio beeped again.

'They haven't found him.' Jay explained after a brief conversation. 'Shaun says he's heading further along the coast but asked us to stay looking around here. That way we cover more area. Okay?'

'Sure.' The small buzz the wine had given her was gone. Alice held onto the edge of the boat tighter as she turned to look behind them. Trails of white foam left a bubbly stream in the dark water. They were close to the coast, but to the left and behind she could see nothing but sea.

'The poor man must be terrified,' she mumbled, more to herself than Jay.

'There!' Jay shouted suddenly, pointing in front of them.

Alice inched herself forwards until she could see where he was looking.

'I don't see anything.'

'It's gone now.' Jay pushed the throttle again. 'I'm sorry, if that's him we have to get there. I've had people drown when I've been just seconds away.'

Alice searched the water, squinting against the sunlight. 'Hat, I think that was a hat! But it's gone now.' Her heart pounded, deep in her throat. 'Do you think he knows we're close?'

'I hope so.'

'There.' Alice spotted something to the left of them. 'I'm sure I saw something.' Jay didn't question it, he headed in the direction of her finger.

'I see him.' He'd brought the boat round in seconds, radioing Shaun at the same time.

'Oh, my God, is it him?' Alice couldn't see anything but sea any more, had he gone under the boat?

Jay ran to the edge and looked over. 'He's fine, he's hanging onto something. We need to get to him. I shouldn't help but Shaun's too far away to wait. Zeus, get out of the way.' The dog moved instantly. 'The boat's going to bob here while I try and get him but we need to be quick or the tide will move us, I'll need your help.'

Alice jerked her head, her eyes widening.

'Can you get closer to the edge?'

'Sure.' The word caught in her throat, but she hobbled next to him. Her breathing hitched as she looked into the dark water. The man was hanging onto a rock, gripping it with both arms; he looked tired, and his complexion almost matched his hat.

'Can you move?' Jay shouted.

The man barely opened his eyes as he lifted his head and tried to focus. 'Don't… think… I… can… let… go,' he rasped.

'I'll get you, it's okay.' Jay ran to the back and pulled up the white seat she'd been sitting on earlier. Alice got a brief glimpse of a first aid kit, emergency flares, life jackets and a life preserver. Jay quickly grabbed the ring. 'If I throw this to you, can you get it over your head?' Waves lapped at the swimmer, covering his face.

'Not sure.' The words came out slurred and one of his hands started to slide downwards.

'I'm going to have to go in.' Seconds later Jay kicked off his shoes and tied the rope attached to the preserver to the boat.

'What?' Panic clawed at Alice's stomach. 'Won't Shaun be here soon?'

'Can't wait, sorry.' Jay lifted himself up and over the edge, slipping into the water. Alice heard him gasp and then there were splashes as he sliced his way through the waves. Alice watched, transfixed, as Jay caught the man by the shoulders just before he disappeared under. The swimmer looked unconscious, but Jay managed to wrap the ring over his head and pull him through it without letting him slip under the water.

'I'm going to swim back,' he shouted. 'Can you help me pull him, the tide's working against me? When I get there, I'm going to need your help getting him in the boat, okay?'

'Yep,' she squeaked, fighting the growing sense of panic. She'd have to lean over the edge, risk sliding in the water – she could already feel the cold seeping into her bones. Her stomach performed a perfect triple somersault, like her vital organs were auditioning for Cirque du Soleil.

Jay began to swim and Alice pulled herself together, picking up the rope and tugging on it. The rope burned her hands, but between them they got the swimmer to the edge.

'Right.' Jay sounded out of breath. 'If I push from the bottom, can you help pull him in?'

'I'll try.' Her stomach somersaulted again.

'If you can lean down… Not that far,' he snapped as she curved her body downwards. 'Up a bit, now grab here.' Jay took her hands and placed them just above the swimmer's waist. 'Grab a handful of wetsuit if you can, yes, like that, now on three, I push and you pull.'

Alice could smell the water, she shivered but refused to look. The wetsuit was hard to hold onto and it felt freezing, but she grabbed it.

'Three, two, one, pull,' Jay shouted, heaving the man's body up. The swimmer moved. It wasn't easy but she put her whole body into it, ignoring the sharp pain in her ankle – there wasn't time for that.

'One more.'

Alice pulled again, and this time the man plopped over the edge like a seal, unconscious. She dragged him into the small space between the seats on the deck. Zeus looked over the edge of the boat and whined. Alice quickly checked the man's airway, he was breathing – thank God – and she put him into the recovery position, picked up the picnic blanket and laid it over him, then went to find Jay.

'Not sure how I'm going to get up. The sides are too high to climb especially when I'm weighed down with wet clothes.' Jay was hanging onto the side of the boat, bobbing in the water. He looked pale and had started to shiver. Despite the sunshine, the water was freezing.

'I'm not leaving you there, it's too cold and you're not wearing a wetsuit.'

'Shaun will be here soon.'

'Not soon enough.' Alice reached a hand down, not looking at the water. 'If you hold onto to me, maybe I can pull you up?'

'You're not strong enough.'

'Then climb up over me, use my body as a ladder.' She got onto her knees and leaned over the side, then closed her eyes. 'Go on, I'm not sure what to do with this guy, he's out cold and might be badly injured. I need your help.'

'Hold on.' Jay answered after a long pause, then he grabbed onto her shoulders, using them to lever himself up. He was heavy and she felt her body slide downwards as her knees left the floor. Dammit, why hadn't she thought she needed to hook her feet into something?

'Oh, oh, no.' The words came out in a sharp breath as she felt herself lurch downwards. Jay wasn't holding her now; his hands must be firmly hooked into the boat but gravity had its own momentum. Alice grabbed onto the sides, feeling her body slide further downwards, but somehow she managed to suction herself vertically to the edge, holding on to the top of the boat with the bottoms of her legs and feet. Cold water licked her face and she began to hyperventilate, pushing her hands on the side, trying to crawl back up away from the sea and the cold.

Don't panic, don't panic, don't panic. The words filled her head like a mantra. *You can't go in.* She'd drown if she did.

Alice slipped down further and started to scream but her descent was stopped suddenly by a large pair of hands yanking her back in the boat. Jay placed her onto the white padded seat and turned quickly, dripping all over the floor as he checked the swimmer.

'Still out cold,' he said. 'But he's alive. You've done all the right things, he's started to shiver which is a good sign.'

Shaking from head to toe, Alice blew into her hands but couldn't find enough breath. *In, out, in, out,* she said the words in her head, trying to calm her breathing.

'Are you okay?' Jay was in front of her, his face pushed into hers. 'You're breathing too fast.' Jay pulled her to her feet and she winced as her ankle twinged. 'You're cold,' Jay said gently, opening the lid of the white seat and pulling out packs of emergency blankets. He unwrapped one quickly and pulled it round her. 'Sit.' Jay pushed her to the floor and knelt in front of her, taking her hands in his.

Behind him the man groaned and Jay closed his eyes for a second. 'He needs to get warm. I know it's not a cold evening but his body temperature will have dropped.' He turned quickly to rip off the picnic rug and wrap the man on the floor in one of the blankets.

'Stay here, help's coming, do you need oxygen, do you feel okay?'

The swimmer shook his head. 'I'm fine, just tired.'

'We'll get you to shore in a minute, and the lifeboat team has called an ambulance.' Jay leapt back to Alice. 'You okay?' he asked.

'Can't… breathe.' Alice put a hand to her chest.

'You're hyperventilating.' Jay reached behind her quickly and pulled a small paper bag from the box. 'Shaun thinks of everything, here.' He opened the bag and blew into it, then bunched it at the top. 'Breathe into it, slowly.' He stroked her shoulder while she did, and the ridge in his forehead deepened.

'I need to use the radio to check how close Shaun is. Breathe,' Jay ordered, shooting to the front of the boat. He was back in seconds. He sat beside her and pulled her to his chest, hugging her shoulders as she breathed. His touch helped her system calm.

In, out, in, out, the bag worked to control the panic and by the time Alice heard Shaun's boat her breathing had slowed, in sync with her heartbeat, and she'd stopped shivering.

'You okay now?' Jay asked. 'I need to speak to the guys for a few moments, is that all right?'

'Yes.' Her voice shook.

Jay disappeared for what was probably only a minute or two but felt like longer, and Alice heard movement as the swimmer got transferred to the other boat.

Zeus came to lay his head on her lap and she stroked it, dropping the bag so she could take in sea air.

Jay sat beside her again. 'You calmer now?'

Alice almost leapt up. His clothes were soaking, and his arms and legs were covered in goosebumps. 'Why haven't you used one of these?' She ripped the emergency blanket from around her shoulders and covered him with it.

'I'm fine.' Jay tried to give it back.

'Me too and I'm not cold, I didn't go in, thanks to you.' Angry now, she pulled the blanket round him again. 'You're dripping all over the floor.'

'You were hyperventilating.' Jay caught her hands and held them.

'A little.' Alice frowned at their linked fingers.

'Because you were scared of falling in?'

'Ah…' She didn't want to lie. 'It's embarrassing. We were rescuing that guy, then you had to rescue me.'

'That's not how I see it. You helped save him, helped me. If you hadn't, I'd have been in there for another five minutes, might not have made it at all.' His voice deepened, making her shiver even more. 'You were terrified?'

'You had to rescue me,' she grumbled.

'And you didn't complain once.' Jay tipped her chin so she could see his face. 'I call that progress.'

'I can't believe you're dripping all over the floor trying to console me.'

'Want to tell me what happened?' he asked gently.

Alice turned away and faced the back of the boat so she didn't have to look at him. 'It's too embarrassing.'

'How about I take you back to mine and show you my most embarrassing secret?' Jay moved in front of her. His eyes flashed with humour and she laughed.

'That's very tempting but I'll have to pass.'

'I'm serious, maybe you can help me with it?'

'That line usually work?'

Jay considered the question. 'First time I've tried it so I'll tell you later. Come back.'

'Why?'

Jay flashed his teeth. 'It's still early, not long enough for a first date. Besides, I need to shower.'

'I'm not going to sleep with you.'

'Well, okay.' Jay looked thrown. 'That's… that wasn't what I was thinking, although, I can't lie, the idea is appealing. But I don't usually let women have their wicked way with me until at least the third date.' His eyes crinkled. 'At the moment, I'm offering you some food, a drink, the chance to talk.'

Alice closed her eyes and nodded. That was exactly what she needed.

Chapter Sixteen

Jay's house sat on a street of small white houses close to the beach. He pulled into the pebbled driveway and they hopped out of his truck without speaking. Even though the day was still warm, Alice had put the heater on full blast so Jay wouldn't get cold and had picked up an empty water bottle and crisp packet from the floor, both of which she carried as they approached his front door.

Jay unlocked it and guided her into the hallway, walking ahead, switching on a couple of lamps until they hit a huge open-plan living area with a big corner sofa, chair, coffee table and dining table with an assortment of bookcases.

The living room ended with a huge set of bi-folding doors that led to a deck. Jay took the rubbish from Alice and headed to the kitchen and she wandered to the windows, taking care not to put pressure on her ankle. The painkillers had worn off hours ago, and it ached.

Alice looked out of the window. The deck had been cleaned recently; there were two chairs and a table, so maybe Jay didn't have a lot of guests? A couple of tennis balls sat on the floor under the table, probably Zeus's. Beyond the deck stretched a short green lawn, and at the end an open fence and gate with the beach beyond it.

Alice leaned her head against the glass and watched foam dance on the water, as the waves rolled in and out. If she wasn't such a coward they might be bobbing up and down in there now. She shivered.

Jay appeared from the kitchen and handed her a glass of wine. 'You'll be okay for a few minutes?' He looked down. 'It won't take me long to change.'

'Sure, don't rush.'

'When I come back, we'll talk, okay?'

Alice didn't answer. He disappeared and she walked to the oak bookshelf positioned to the right of the large windows. There were a couple of photos on it: one of a couple of boys on bikes next to the beach, the other of the lifeboat crew. Jay stood in the centre looking tanned and handsome. He seemed different in his kit, more serious. The rest of the shelves were packed with an eclectic mix of paperbacks and hardbacks, fiction and non-fiction, in no particular order. Alice scanned them twice, trying to work out his system. They weren't arranged alphabetically, by author, colour or size. She tapped a finger on *Moby-Dick* and moved it after *Les Misérables*, as both were Penguin Classics and the same size.

Alice heard the shower, and continued to sort through the books, arranging them in title order, separating the paperbacks and hardbacks onto their own shelves because they looked better. When Jay reappeared ten minutes later she'd finished.

'I hope you don't mind,' Alice said, embarrassed. 'I thought this would make them easier to find, and they look better.'

'I don't mind, and they do look better.' Jay paused and she could feel his presence, like a low buzz across her shoulders. 'Most people organise by author.'

'I thought about that, but the books lined up better this way, also, you don't seem to have much by the same author.'

Jay ran a finger along some of the spines. 'I'm a promiscuous reader, there are a couple of authors I keep coming back to but otherwise I prefer reading what I fancy at the time.' He scratched his chin, he hadn't shaved and had the beginnings of a five o'clock shadow which only succeeded in making him even more attractive. 'Didn't take you long to do that.'

'I—' Alice shrugged. 'Organising is something I'm good at, it relaxes me. Maybe that's my superpower.'

'That's what I wanted to talk to you about.' Jay moved closer and she could feel his breath on the back of her ear, which did funny things to her insides, so she sidestepped him and moved back to the centre of the room. A large orange box sat on the coffee table that hadn't been there before he'd showered.

'Your etchings?'

Jay snickered. 'I usually save those for the second date. This is what I wanted to talk to you about, my embarrassing secret.' He moved away from the bookshelf and took off the lid. 'My accounts.'

Alice laughed. 'I can see what you mean. It's almost equally embarrassing how much I want to get my hands on them.'

The box literally overflowed with receipts and slips of paper. She pulled a few out but, much like his bookshelf, there didn't seem to be a system.

'You're drooling.'

'Where are your invoices?' Alice burrowed deeper into the pile of papers.

Jay pointed to the box. 'There are some papers at the bottom, and I've got most of them on computer, I just haven't printed them out.'

'And you need me to do what?' Alice pulled out a receipt from a local hardware shop she recognised, along with a couple from the Castle Café. 'Murder your bookkeeper?'

Jay ran a hand through his wet hair. 'Put them in order, log them into a spreadsheet. No bookkeeper, I have an accountant, but last year he told me if I gave him a box again, he'd sack me. I had someone lined up to help, but she… moved away.'

'I'll take a look.' Alice bent to pick more papers out of the box. 'I can sort and log them. You'll need to email me the invoices. It won't take long, if I have questions I'll call.'

'I'll pay you.'

'I don't want your money,' she said, insulted. 'I think I owe you something after the number of times you've rescued me.'

'Superheroes do it for love, not money.' Jay narrowed his eyes as she pulled out more receipts and began to make piles. 'I didn't mean for you to do it now.'

'It's no problem.' Stupid how much she was looking forward to getting stuck into such a familiar process, to commit to a challenge she already knew she could beat.

Jay looked uncomfortable. 'I've got until September, and you haven't finished your drink.' He pointed to her glass. 'I still want to know what happened on the boat.'

'Oh.' Alice put the receipts back in the box.

'You have no idea how miserable you look right now.' Jay said half smiling. 'I'm not going to force you to tell me, I just thought I could—'

'Help?' Alice flopped back into the chair, fighting the smile curling her lips. The man was incorrigible.

'I shared.' Jay pointed to the box. 'I risked ridicule and disgust.'

'I think you know me enough to understand I'm more excited about that box than disgusted. We all have our gifts.' Alice paused. 'This obviously isn't yours. Besides, you might not be so kind.'

Jay just looked at her.

'Fine.' Alice considered the box again.

'Do you want to tell me before you try to elope with my invoices?' Jay waited.

'I'm afraid of the sea.'

His expression switched from teasing to serious. 'You can't swim?'

Alice looked at her fingernails. 'I can.' She ground her teeth. 'It's… difficult to explain.'

'Try.'

'This is more embarrassing than a box of receipts.'

'It's a bit more serious if you're doing a triathlon. I saw you at the beach in a wetsuit, and I took you out on the boat, it didn't even occur to me you'd have a problem with water.'

'I… I thought I could work myself up to going in.'

'I shouted at you.' Jay looked pained.

'You didn't know.'

Jay leaned forwards. 'Did you make it into the sea?'

Alice shook her head. 'I was telling the truth.'

'I don't understand, what happens when you try?'

'I panic, feel sick, shake. I… I fall apart.'

'You've always been afraid?'

'It's… recent.'

'Do you know why?'

Alice picked up her wine and swallowed a large glug. 'It's going to sound ridiculous.'

'I'm not going to judge you, people can develop fears at any stage of their lives.'

Alice got up and walked to the window, looking out. 'What do you feel when you see the sea?'

Jay must have moved because suddenly he was standing beside her. 'I feel excitement. I love the way it feels to be on the water, the way I feel. Powerful, useful, excited. I think of the water as a living, breathing thing, sometimes it's my friend and sometimes it's my enemy, but I always respect it.'

'I feel cold.' Alice shivered. 'I can't get past it. Cold and scared. I put my foot in and my body goes into meltdown. Today, when I thought I was going in—'

'What triggered it?'

'It's ridiculous, but it started with a dream.' Alice's forehead creased. 'Soon after Mum died, I dreamt about her drowning, and I've had the same nightmare a couple of times since.' The memory made her wince. 'In the dream Mum's swimming and I'm watching from the beach – she doesn't know I'm there. A wave comes out of nowhere – a big one – and she's pushed under the water.'

'What do you do?' Jay asked softly.

'Nothing. I'm there but it's like I'm frozen so I can't help.' Bile rose in Alice's throat as she relived it. 'I'm screaming but there's no-one to help and I feel so guilty because I can't. I watch to see if she reappears – she doesn't, she's gone and then I wake up.' Tears pricked her eyes. 'I thought it was all part of my grief. That I'd get over it. But then I signed up for the triathlon soon after coming to Castle Cove and the first time I tried to go into the water I started to panic.' Alice stopped, remembering the pain in her chest, how she couldn't breathe. 'Since then, every time I've tried to get into the sea it's got worse.' Even now, talking about it, she could see her hands quake.

'You've tried, how many times?'

'Feels like hundreds, maybe twenty. I've been running and cycling. Recently I gave myself goals: stand in the water for five minutes, get up to my knees. It isn't getting any easier and now I'm scared I won't be able to compete in the triathlon.' Admitting it brought tears to her eyes.

'It's only two months away.'

'I know… ' Alice faltered.

'Let me help.'

'Sorry?'

Jay went to get more wine and filled her glass. 'I can help you with the swimming.'

'I don't see how.'

Jay pointed to the table. 'I look at that box and it gives me palpitations. I'm not comparing receipts to genuine fear, I'm just saying we have different skills, different ways of looking at things. I love the sea, letting me help isn't going to hurt. Besides, I'm more than qualified to rescue you. What have you got to lose?'

'I'm scared.'

'But are you more scared of doing it, or not doing it?

Chapter Seventeen

'You'll love it in here.' Cath took Alice into Little Treasures, Castle Cove's antique shop, making the bell above the front door ding. She tugged her through the clutter as a man with salt-and-pepper hair, aged in his mid-fifties, appeared from the office. 'Alice this is Ben Campbell, he owns the place.'

Ben gave Cath a quick hug.

'Ben's local now, but he used to commute to London every day so he could work with the Met Police. Until a few months ago, Alice lived in Highgate,' Cath explained.

The edges of Ben's eyes crinkled. 'I retired so I could move back to Castle Cove a couple of years ago and haven't looked back. Do you miss the big smoke?'

'Nope.' Alice admitted, letting her eyes stray to a pile of vinyl LPs on the floor. 'This is a great place.'

'Thanks.' Ben nodded. 'My wife Mary opened it. She had a talent for finding gold in amongst clutter. I took it over full-time when she died.'

'I'm sorry,' Alice said, feeling awkward.

'How's Emily?' Cath changed the subject.

'Loving Nepal.' Ben grinned. 'I'm not sure she's ever going to want to come home.'

'Emily was a few school years behind me, she's a nurse,' Cath said, as her eyes wandered around the room, catching on a set of brooches on a 1940s sideboard. She bent over to take a closer a look.

'I'll let you browse.' Ben waved towards the back of the shop. 'Just shout if you need anything.'

'Nice to meet you.' Alice said, as her eyes caught on a lamp in the corner next to an array of mirrors. 'This is gorgeous, I love gold.' Alice went to finger the tassels on the lamp and looked at the price. Fifty-two pounds – she couldn't justify spending the money, especially when her savings were disappearing at an alarming rate.

Cath hopped from one foot to the other, looking excited. 'Just buy it. The mermaids at the bottom remind me of you, especially now you're not shuffling everywhere.'

Alice wriggled her ankle. It had only been a week of hobbling, but had felt like longer.

'Buy it.'

'I—' Could she? Silly to make a fuss over such a relatively small decision but she wasn't used to frivolous spending. 'I don't need it,' she murmured, more to herself than Cath. 'And I'm going to Thailand in September, what would I do with a gold lamp with mermaids on it? It won't fit in my backpack.'

'Leave it in your house. Think about it, where would you put it?' Cath tapped a finger on her bottom lip, considering the shade again, making Alice's heart swell. She could tell by Cath's expression that her friend hated it, but was taking the decision seriously because she knew it was difficult for Alice. 'I always think it's important to have a good plan.'

'Remember who you're talking to.' Alice laughed. 'I have a plan. It would go in the front room, next to the fireplace.' She could already imagine how it would look. She could pick up cushions with mermaids stitched on to match, and in winter it would add a soft glow to the room.

But she wouldn't be in the house by winter.

'I don't need it.' Alice headed for the door just as it opened and Marta West walked in. Alice hadn't seen her since her run-in with Simon at the castle restaurant. Today, Marta's long auburn hair was piled in a perfect bun and there were no wisps escaping. She wore an elegant black dress that ended just above her knees and she looked business-like and out of place in the rambling shop.

'Marta.' Cath passed a cabinet proudly displaying a silver and white tea service and gave the woman a swift hug. 'How are you?'

'Great.' Marta grinned. 'Haven't seen you since our cocktail night at the Anglers last time Dan was away.' She shuddered theatrically.

'Yep.' Cath laughed. 'Not sure I'll be able to face another margarita for a while. This is Alice, she works with me at the café.' They turned to greet her properly. 'Marta owns Picture Perfect, the gallery in town.'

'Lovely to meet you.' Marta flashed a smile as they shook hands.

'I haven't seen you at the café for a while.' Cath said.

Marta's expression clouded. 'Your boss Simon – Wolf by name, wolf by nature – he's refusing to let me display my art unless I pay a fee.'

Cath grimaced. 'He mentioned I might have to remove the photographs of the castle but didn't say why.'

'Simon wants to charge me advertising rates. I told him exactly where he could shove his invoice.' Marta stopped suddenly and shook her head. 'Apologies, I know he's your boss, but the man has no understanding of a mutually beneficial relationship. On a more pleasant note, is Ben around?'

Cath nodded. 'In the office.'

'Great.' Marta smiled. 'I've got a set of paintings he's going to love. See you later Cath, good to meet you Alice.'

'You too,' Alice muttered, heading for the front door. When she reached it she turned, 'You coming?'

'Yup.' Cath followed slowly, glancing back at the lamp a few times. 'We could probably knock the price down,' she mused as they headed along the high street. 'Ben's often willing to do a deal if stock isn't selling.'

'Is that your way of saying it's awful?' Alice teased.

'Uh uh.' Cath shook her head smiling. 'I just never figured you for the kind of woman who'd have such… romantic tastes.'

'I'm not, I'm more practical, which is why I didn't buy it.'

Cath's mobile rang and she dug around in her bag while Alice admired a set of sparkly earrings in a nearby shop. She couldn't remember the last time she'd been window shopping just for the fun of it.

'I can't do it Dan, I've got to work in the morning.' Cath's voice changed. 'How long will you be gone?' Cath stepped aside to avoid a couple of shoppers. 'So, the party will be that good?' *It's Dan*, she mouthed, pointing to the mobile. 'I'm in town with Alice… yes I can meet you, we'll walk to the cafe if you like?'

Cath looked in her handbag for a lipstick. 'Dan's been invited to a party in Birmingham.'

'Long way?'

Cath bobbed her head. 'He loves a party. Doesn't seem to matter how far away it is. I can't make it, I'm working tomorrow, so he wants a kiss goodbye – he's such a sweetheart.' She applied some red to her lips as they headed down the high street, past the wine shop, Marta's gallery, the wedding shop and bakery. The sun was hot again today, so they ducked down a side street onto the promenade so they could walk next to the beach and cliffs. When they arrived at the café Dan wasn't around.

'I'm sure he won't be long, we could have a drink and wait?' Cath pointed to the tables on a small patio just outside the café where they'd have a pretty view of the cliffs and sea.

'Sure,' Alice agreed. There were plenty of free seats, the sun was still out, but a gentle breeze had put a chill in the air so almost everyone sat inside. They pulled out seats just as Lily came out of the front holding a pad.

'How's the shopping going?' she asked.

'Successful. We found a lamp that Alice refuses to buy but I'm going to talk her into eventually.' Cath teased. 'How's it been?'

'Fine. Busy. Simon sent Anya to help me. She's inside grappling with the cappuccino machine, I swear it hates her.'

Cath laughed just as an older rotund lady ambled towards them.

'Olive.' Cath got up.

'Cath Lacey, haven't seen you for ages,' the older woman rasped as she approached. She was carrying a large flowery shopping bag piled high with strawberries and green beans. 'How are your parents?'

'Oh, you know,' Cath looked uncomfortable. 'Nothing changes.'

Olive nodded. 'I've just seen Ted. He'll be along in a bit. He got some fruit and veg from the farm when he dropped off their post.'

She plonked the bag onto the floor with a deep sigh and nodded at Lily. 'You're looking tired, burning the candle at both ends?'

Lily flushed.

'She's working here and helping Simon at the restaurant.' Cath's tone told Alice what she thought about that.

'I like it,' Lily said brightly. 'I'm learning loads.'

'How's the boyfriend?' Olive asked.

Lily frowned. 'Rogan's still away on business. What can I get you?' She changed the subject, tapping a pencil onto her pad.

They all ordered coffees and Lily disappeared as Olive pulled up a chair. 'You're the new girl?' She screwed up her face so she could peer closely at Alice; her face powder was dark orange and stopped abruptly at her jawline. 'Ted said you were pretty. You look like your mum.'

Alice's stomach dived. 'You knew her?'

The woman nodded and held out a hand. 'I'm Olive Simms, I work at the Castle Cove vet, I know everybody. Genevieve came in to ask about getting a cat a few months before—' Her round face fell. 'I was so sorry to hear the news.'

'Mum wanted a cat?'

Olive shrugged, her green overcoat was a good two sizes too big and hung off her shoulders. 'She hadn't decided between a cat or a dog if I remember correctly, and wasn't rushing into it. She talked about you.'

'She did?' A wave of emotion made Alice whisper.

'Said you managed a restaurant?'

Alice nodded, unable to form any words.

'She mentioned you worked too hard.' Olive must have noticed Alice's face drop because she quickly added, 'But she was proud of you, couldn't wait for you to come to watch her compete in the triathlon. Your mum mentioned it was a tradition.' Olive stopped suddenly, probably realising she'd put her foot in it again.

'Ah.' Cath interjected. 'Alice is doing it this year instead.'

Olive nodded and patted her hand, just as Lily turned up with their coffees. 'She'd have loved that. She was planning to run around the Isle of Wight, did she tell you?'

'Yes.' Alice murmured. She'd been really excited on their last call. 'She was quite an adventurer.' She trailed off as Ted approached their table and Olive started to get up. They weren't related but Ted had the same spherical shape as Olive and the same wily smile. He wore shorts and a red fleece and had a postbag filled with strawberries slung over his shoulder.

'Ladies, how lovely to see you all. I've got a letter for you.' Ted pointed to Alice. 'Brought it up in case you were working today.' He reached into his postbag and dug between the strawberries before pulling out a brown A4 envelope.

'Oh.' Alice rose to take it. The postmark read Castle Cove.

'It's all the documentation for the triathlon.' Ted explained.

Alice checked the seal, but it looked intact.

'There's been a batch of them going out today.' Ted continued, his red cheeks wobbling. 'I've seen you running a couple of times while I've been doing my round, you look like you're ready.' He shivered suddenly. 'It's a bit parky out here, fancy moving inside?'

Olive nodded but Cath shook her head. 'We're waiting for Dan. Sorry Alice, he shouldn't be much longer, sometimes he gets distracted.'

'I don't mind.' Alice nodded at Olive and Ted as they said their goodbyes and disappeared into the warmth of the café.

They sat for a few moments in silence watching the sea until Cath hopped up suddenly. 'There he is,' she said, giving Dan a quick hug, dodging the multiple bags dangling from his fingers. A couple of good-looking men dressed in designer jeans and shirts, whom Alice didn't recognise, stood watching them.

'Sorry I'm late love. Georgie, Adam, this is my gorgeous girlfriend Cath. In fact, Adam, I think you two have met?' Adam looked at Cath blankly as Dan picked her up and swung her round, kissing her noisily on the top of the head.

Georgie and Adam headed into the café promising not to be long.

'You work together?' Cath asked.

'Sometimes. They're helping me with the kitchen job,' Dan explained. 'We might go straight to work from the party tomorrow, it seems crazy driving back home first, even if it does mean I miss out on making my favourite woman her breakfast and giving her a good morning kiss.' He grabbed Cath's coffee and took a quick swig before pecking her noisily on the lips. 'Sure you don't want to come, it's going to be wild?'

'Sorry.' Cath looked embarrassed. 'I know, but I've got to work tomorrow, I really wish I could.'

'I understand, it's why I love you babe, you're so conscientious.'

'Not boring though?' Cath flushed.

'Never. Next time?'

'Definitely.' Dan leaned over and kissed her on the head.

'I took a few notes from the savings jar, I'm still waiting to be paid for my last job and I owe these guys a few beers. Is that okay?'

'Sure.' Cath's smiled dimmed and reappeared almost immediately. 'Whose party is it?'

Dan flashed a hundred-watt grin. 'Potential client, you've never met her but she's got lots of friends. Georgie knows her really well and says she's angling for a new kitchen so I'll get in there while I can. Might bring more work. You know things have been quiet recently. I didn't have any work for over two months.' Dan explained to Alice. 'Everything changed with this last plumbing job, but I've got to network if I want to expand the business.'

'I admire how you throw your heart and soul into your job.' Cath flashed a smile.

'Always, babe.' Dan let go of her hand and kissed her on the cheek as his friends returned from the café and handed him a takeaway cup. 'We're going to head off home in a sec so I can pack, it's a long drive and I want to get there early so we've got time to change.' He waved a bag. 'New jeans.'

'More?' Cath laughed.

'I didn't like the ones I bought last week.'

'There are snacks in the fridge if you want to take them for the journey,' Cath said. 'Where are you staying tonight?'

Dan pulled out his mobile as it began to play a Justin Timberlake track. 'No idea, probably kip on a floor somewhere, I wasn't planning on going to bed. Life's too short for sleep! It's Johnny!' He answered and turned his back, jabbering into the phone about cars and the best route to Birmingham. The three of them wandered off towards town and Dan gave Cath a final backward wave.

Cath watched him go with an indulgent expression. 'He always has so much energy, and a constant stream of new friends, I never seem to meet the same person twice. Never a boring moment with Dan.'

'Where did you meet?'

'Down there.' Cath pointed back towards the promenade. 'I'd split up with my long-term boyfriend a month before and was feeling really blue.' She sighed.

'Jay mentioned you dated Shaun?' Alice confided.

Cath blushed and looked away. 'Yes. Sorry, I don't know why I didn't want to tell you. I think in some ways I'm still quite raw about it and he can be funny with me.' Cath shrugged her small shoulders. 'We'd been together for years.' Her face clouded.

'You were telling me about when you met Dan?'

Cath nodded, her face brightening again. 'I went for a walk on the beach, and there was this man with bright orange hair, running in the sand and laughing, wearing nothing but a pair of red boxers. It was September and he said he was testing his costume for Halloween.' She grinned. 'It was the funniest thing I'd ever seen.'

'What, and you started talking?'

'He ran up and asked my name.' Cath smiled. 'I'll never forget it. I couldn't tell if he was crazy or a dreamboat, but he asked me out for a drink, then made me pay because he'd spent all his money on caffeine drinks, but I had such a good time. I'd been so unhappy about my break-up with Shaun and he took my mind off it. It was a while before I agreed to date him, or, you know, but he helped.'

'He's good for you?'

Cath's eyes shone. 'Dan's so different from anyone I've met before, he doesn't care what he does, or who he talks to. Sometimes, I'll admit, he can be reckless and irresponsible. He says life's too short to worry about following rules, and doing the right thing; that we should focus on just having fun, there are plenty of years to grow up. I have such a good time when I'm with him.' She stared into her coffee. 'And that makes up for everything else.'

'Like what?'

'Ah.' Cath screwed up her face. 'He's forgotten we were meant to be going to the cinema tonight, just him and me. It's not a big deal.'

'You want to come around to mine?'

'Thanks, but I'm a little tired. It'll do me good to have an early night. Means I'll be on top form when he gets back, we really do have so much fun.'

'Fun's important.'

'It's easy to get bogged down in the day to day.' Cath agreed. 'To spend too much time being serious and fixating on what your next step in life should be, getting married, settling down.' She sounded irritated. 'Thinking about stuff like that instead of living and enjoying it.'

'That's exactly why I'm here.' Alice admitted.

'And it's what I've been focusing on since things ended with Shaun,' Cath said.

'But it must have been hard… splitting up with him?'

'It was.' Cath's expression changed. 'But we wanted the same things for years, then everything changed and we started wanting different things. He couldn't be bothered to see my point of view.'

'You didn't sort it out?'

'Shaun didn't want to. He was furious when I started dating Dan, but what did he expect?'

They left the café and headed towards the beach and promenade. Kids were playing in the sand, building sandcastles and a couple of people were braving the water. Cath led them towards the sheltered benches facing the beach, where they sat and finished their coffees. A couple of boats whizzed in between the waves in the distance.

'Do you ever regret it, moving here I mean?' Cath asked suddenly.

'No, definitely not.' And if she ever had uncertain moments, thoughts of her mother soon reminded her she'd made the right decision. 'Change isn't easy.'

'No, it's not.' Cath's expression darkened. 'Sometimes change is the hardest thing of all.'

'I wasn't expecting any visitors tonight?' Alice ignored the skip in her stomach and looked up at Jay, who was standing on her doorstep holding a small bag. Zeus sat at his feet wagging his tail.

'No.' Jay held on tight to the lead as the dog started to step through the doorway. 'We're heading for a walk on the cliffs, and I noticed your light was on so I thought I'd say hi.' Something clattered in the front room making them both jump and Jay scowled. 'I'm sorry, I didn't realise you had company.'

'I don't, it's probably the stray. I was having supper.' Alice backed up inviting them both in and headed for the front room. The kitten was up on the large oak coffee table lapping her plate, her fork sat on the multicoloured woollen rug and bits of food were scattered next to it. Embarrassed, Alice picked up the fork and stood next to the large squashy grey sofa she'd been sitting on only minutes earlier.

'Dammit.' Alice was about to shoo the kitten away when it spotted the dog and bolted. Sighing, she collected the plate. Zeus was already hoovering up the mess.

'I'm sorry, we ruined your meal.'

'I was finished anyway. Do you want to stay for a drink?'

'I'd love a beer, thanks.'

'Sorry I've only got wine. You're my first visitor.'

'Wine is fine.' Jay smiled. 'And I'm honoured.'

Alice headed for her favourite room; the kitchen was large and airy and reminded her of her mother. Genevieve Appleton had redecorated after her aunt had died, installing a light blue shaker-style kitchen, with wooden worktops and a huge cream fridge. Alice opened the back door to let Zeus out and pulled a bottle of white from inside the door of the fridge and poured them both a glass, then she put her plate in the dishwasher. Jay leaned back against the oak counter with his arms crossed; the way he was standing made the blue t-shirt stretch across his chest, and she forced her eyes skywards as Jay offered her the bag he was carrying.

'I bought you something.'

'More invoices?' Alice joked as she peered inside, feeling her stomach free fall. 'Lights.'

'For your bike. I wasn't sure you'd have gotten around to getting any.'

'Um, not yet, I fixed the tyre and got a new puncture repair kit but they were out of stock of the lights, thought I'd wait.' Too much information. 'This is… so thoughtful of you, I don't know what to say.'

Jay looked embarrassed. 'It's nothing. I went to Bournemouth, saw the bike shop had a sale so picked a few things up.'

'I'll pay for them, obviously.'

Jay cleared his throat. 'Not necessary, at least let me get them to say thanks for doing my books.'

'I'm enjoying myself.' Alice reddened. 'But thank you, it'll be good to be able to get back on the bike at night.'

'I guess it beats you having me follow you in my truck?'

'That might get a little tiresome for you.'

Jay didn't comment. 'Shall I fix them on?'

'It's not necessary, I'll find a how-to on YouTube and figure it out later.'

'I'm here anyway, and I need to finish my drink.' He gestured towards the hall with his wine glass where she'd parked her bike and headed for it.

Jay knelt and flicked a finger across her old lights. 'Do you have tools?'

Alice dug out a box from the kitchen cupboard and stood in the hall watching as Jay flipped the bike over and undid her old lights then screwed the new ones on. It only took a few minutes and she admired him as he worked.

'They'll flash when you cycle. I'd recommend switching them on whenever you're going to the castle. That road can get busy and people fly down it.'

Alice smiled because instead of feeling irritated, she was warming to having someone worry about her. The kitten reappeared, wrapping itself around her legs so she picked it up.

'Looks like you've been adopted.' Jay threw the tools back in the box. Alice winced but didn't say anything. Maybe he was growing on her?

She took the box from him and returned it to the cupboard. 'I like having the kitten around but I can't take her on, not when I'm leaving.'

'It's hard not to put down roots.' Jay picked up his wine, and leaned against the wall glancing towards the kitchen. 'Zeus must be having a ball in your garden, he's not even paying attention to this little lady.' He stroked the kitten's head, earning himself a purr. 'I was thinking about our conversation.'

'Which one?'

Jay studied her, looking serious. 'I understand why the triathlon is important to you but why are you so determined to leave Castle Cove? I know you're visiting your dad, but what about after? This house is yours, isn't it?'

Alice shrugged. 'It's a boring story.'

'Not to me.' Jay said.

'Shall we sit in the front room?'

Jay followed her and took a seat on the grey sofa next to the fireplace. Alice sat opposite on a wooden rocking chair that used to belong to her great aunt.

'I don't know why you want to know this.' Jay waited and Alice sipped some of her wine, mulling it over. Maybe telling him would help her understand? She exhaled heavily. 'I had a happy childhood so it's nothing to do with that. I'm an only child and we were a close family.' She stopped.

'Were?'

'Six years ago, my parents decided to divorce.'

Jay nodded.

'I don't know the ins and outs. It probably sounds stupid, I know parents get divorced every day, but it was a shock and I couldn't adjust. It was only ever the three of us and my great aunt – and suddenly everything changed. I worked in a restaurant near home, got the chance to live above it so, on a whim, I moved. I used to work long hours.' Alice frowned. 'Once the divorce went through I spent more and more time there.'

'Because?' Jay studied her face.

'I don't know.' Alice waved her hands in the air. 'Maybe because I could control everything there. Paperwork rarely surprises you, it's easy to contain.' When Jay raised an eyebrow, Alice smiled. 'It is for us mere mortals. And it doesn't let you down. I'm not explaining this well,' she grumbled, probably because she didn't understand it herself.

'Go on,' Jay prodded.

'I'm not sure why I'm telling you this.'

'Talking helps?'

Alice rolled her shoulders, of course he was right but it rankled. 'I lost touch with everything. Dad moved to Thailand, Mum was only down the road but I hardly saw her. There were so many shifts, so much work. Perhaps I didn't want to make the time... ' She jumped up. 'Look at the photos on the wall, they'll explain it better than me.' Alice swept her arms around the room. There were pictures everywhere, some of her, some of her mother.

Jay got up. 'This your mum?' Jay pointed to one of her mum standing next to a bike, beaming.

'She'd just finished the London to Brighton cycle ride. That one next to it, there,' Alice pointed. 'That's her after the three peaks.'

Jay moved on to the next picture of her mum in walking gear covered in mud, her cheeks were ruddy and her eyes bright.

'I'm guessing this was her at the triathlon, with you and your dad?' he asked, pointing to the photo above it. The picture had been taken at least ten years before. Her dad had his arm slung over both of their shoulders. Genevieve was wearing her wetsuit. She'd just finished competing. It had been a beautiful warm day and Alice could remember them laughing and playing in the sand, then eating fish and chips afterwards.

'Yep.' Her throat closed. 'I was supposed to do the triathlon with Mum last year, the year before, too. Somehow... ' She trailed off.

Jay nodded. 'Life got in the way?'

Something lodged in her throat. 'Then she died.' Alice stopped, gathering her emotions. 'And I tried to carry on. Only it wasn't the same at work. It's like all the order became chaos, nothing felt right and I realised if I didn't move then, make a change, I never would.'

'So you moved here?'

Alice was rambling, weaving a tale that wasn't going anywhere, but Jay sat there, listening, with an intense expression on his face. She stroked the cat, feeling calmer.

'Mum left the house to me so I had to come anyway, to clear it out. I'd planned to rent it but when I got here, saw all her stuff...' Alice faltered. 'The photo albums, pictures, all the things she'd done with her life, I knew I had to stay. Knew if I didn't sign up to compete in the triathlon, I never would. It's the reason I know I have to visit Dad straight after, and travel. If I don't, I'm just going to get stuck again. Haven't you ever reached a place in your life where you knew things had to change or you'd just go on day in, day out doing the same thing over and over?'

Jay looked thoughtful, then his face cleared. 'Not really, I'm mostly happy with my life.'

'Then you're lucky. I wanted to change mine. This is the place I chose to start, the last place my mother lived, the place I remember being with her. This is where I need to be for now. And I have to do the triathlon. I just… ' Alice blinked. 'I don't know how I'll live with myself if I can't compete. It's like I'll be letting Mum down.'

'So, compete.'

'How? You saw me on the boat, I didn't even have to touch the water and I could hardly breathe.' The kitten snuggled into her, purring.

'I think I can help you.'

'You're busy.' Alice dismissed the offer.

'Not that busy. Unless you don't think I can?'

'It's not that.' Alice closed her eyes. 'Maybe I'm just too scared.'

'Ah.' Jay draped an arm over the back of the sofa. 'You know what they say about fear, don't you?'

'What?'

'You have to face it.'

Chapter Eighteen

At six o'clock the sun still shone in the cloudless sky. It should have been a perfect evening to relax and enjoy the weather, instead Alice sat in Jay's pickup and tried not to think about what she'd be doing in the next hour. Whatever he said about her being safe with him, she wasn't ready to get into the water.

'You okay?' Jay asked for the five hundredth time and she nodded, even though they both knew she wasn't. Alice switched on the radio and 'The Drowning Man' by The Cure blasted out. *Great.*

'I thought we'd start back on the beach where we had our picnic because it's more familiar,' Jay said.

'That day didn't work out so well last time.'

'Now *I* know what we're dealing with and I've been researching techniques.'

Alice grunted.

'Have a little faith. We'll only dip our toes in today, take it slow.'

Alice shook her head, catching sight of the side pocket of Jay's passenger door as she did. 'What?' she pulled out a couple of parking tickets, still wrapped inside the packaging and quickly ripped off the plastic, moaning as she scanned them.

'If you read that it might make you an accessory after the fact,' Jay murmured, reaching across to try and pull them out of her hands. She snatched them back.

'Jay, this one's overdue, you'll have to pay over sixty pounds. If you'd paid in ten days it would have been less than half that.' She turned the other one over; he'd got it the day he'd come to fix the cupboard, when he'd been called out. 'Why did you get this one?'

'Ah.' Jay sounded embarrassed. 'Sometimes when I get a call and the car's parked somewhere, I leave it. It's often quicker to run to the lifeboat station. We aim to be on the water in less than five minutes.'

'If this happened while you were working, we can see if you can claim for them. Don't you have a sign or something you can put in the window when you're out on a call?'

'Zeus ate it.'

Alice checked the fine again and winced. 'We could challenge it.'

Jay shrugged as he pulled into a car park and sat in the pickup watching the sea. 'I must have put them in that side pocket and forgotten, if you leave them on your seat I'll get around to it.' Alice shook her head as she stuffed the bundle into her bag. 'I don't understand how you can leave that kind of stuff. It would drive me nuts.'

Jay's lips curved but his eyes didn't brighten and he rested his arms on the steering wheel. 'I've learned some things aren't impor- tant. They'll get sorted anytime – a cup on the floor, an overdue parking ticket.' He frowned. 'When all's said and done, they don't really matter.'

Alice's stomach twisted. 'But if you sort them out, that's one less thing that's out of your control.'

He smiled. 'Perhaps, but I'm not sure I can work up enough adrenaline to save myself from a bunch of parking tickets.'

Jay hopped out of the pickup and Alice reluctantly followed. He put his towel on the beach and removed his t-shirt, revealing a skin-tight waterproof top that stretched across his chest and ended below his shoulders, defining muscles she could only imagine underneath. Why did some people's DNA create masterpieces, while others more of a wobbly dot-to-dot?

Alice dragged her eyes to the towel on the floor as Jay pulled off his shorts and dropped them next to his t-shirt, leaving everything in an untidy heap that she itched to fold.

'You going in like that?'

Alice blushed and pulled off her top and shorts, placing them in a neat pile, flushing more as he watched. She'd dressed in a short wetsuit that covered everything vital but didn't leave much to the imagination. Jay must have realised he was watching because he turned his back and faced the sea.

'I'm not sure I'm up to this. If you think the panic attack I had the other day was bad, you haven't seen me in full swing, I can out-perform a carnival.'

Jay smiled, turning to face her. 'Shall we try to think positive? Fear is a lot to do with what you fill your head with. If you think you can, you can, if you think you can't, you can't.'

'I've heard it and I definitely can't.'

'We'll see.' Jay grabbed her hand and they walked together towards the sea. Her stomach flip-flopped but she wasn't sure if it was because Jay had taken her hand, or because she was heading for her worst nightmare. She squeezed his fingers.

'I'm not going to let you drown, you're barely going to touch the water today. How about we sit, watch it for a while?'

Alice could feel her body shaking, had a sudden urge to spread herself flat against the sand like a shag pile rug.

'Just here, I'll hold on to you. Take a few deep breaths, in a minute I might ask you to dip a toe in – just a toe.' Jay said, on her sharp intake of breath. 'Has the dream affected how you feel about showers, baths?' Jay continued.

Alice snorted. 'Are you asking me if I wash?'

Jay laughed. 'I'm wondering if there's anything else in the mix.'

'I can get in a pool no problem. The dream was about my mother in the sea, I haven't had any others. There's just something about the cold, dark and waves that triggers the panic.' Alice glared at the water.

'You've got as far as putting your feet in? I saw you.'

Alice nodded and Jay stroked a hand down her back, perhaps trying to calm her but it had the opposite effect. Alice let her eyes slide from the foam up his feet and tanned legs. He picked up a stone and threw it. As it skimmed the waves, her eyes caught on his forearm. Dark blue numbers were stamped beside the crease of his elbow. She leaned forwards to look more closely. 'Eleventh July, is the date important?'

'A turning point in my life.' Jay put his arms by his sides, hiding the tattoo. 'I didn't want to forget it.'

Alice waited for him to explain but he stared at the water until she felt uncomfortable. 'I like that idea, marking the date of something.' She stared at the waves. 'Maybe I should get one so I never forget. I don't want to go back to who I was before, the day I moved to Castle Cove was my turning point. I'm never going back.'

'Remember they don't wash off and you don't strike me as impulsive.'

'I can be.' Alice pouted.

Jay turned so he could tip her chin and look into her eyes. 'Is this the same Alice Appleton who packs her backpack with military precision, and writes meticulous lists?'

'I can make a decision without a list.' Alice pushed her feet more deeply into the sand to help herself stand up, the waves were close, but she ignored them.

'Can you?' His lips curved as he stood too. 'I'm guessing you've even written notes about what you're eating this week?'

'So?' Indignant, she put her hands on her hips. 'What's wrong with that? There's only one of me eating, and it's better than wasting food.'

'You're right.' A slight smile tipped the edges of his mouth. 'But it's the opposite of impulsive.'

'I'll prove it. I'm getting a tattoo and I'll do it tomorrow.' She'd have time before work, especially if she got up earlier. 'I've seen somewhere in the high street, I'll go in the morning.'

'Where will you put it?'

'Oh.' Alice considered. 'I'll make a list.' She grimaced. 'And whether I have a tattoo or not is nothing to do with you, I don't want you to try to talk me out of it.'

'I'm not. Look down.'

Water washed over her feet, hitting her ankles.

'You've been standing in it while we've been talking.' Jay's voice lowered. 'I didn't want to mention it in case you freaked out.'

'I… no, it's okay, I feel okay.' Alice wriggled her toes, swishing her foot through a wave, feeling a gurgle of pleasure deep in her chest. 'I can't believe I'm in the water and I'm not freaking out. Did you distract me? Just then, all that stuff about me being organised, were you trying to irritate me so I wouldn't notice the water?'

Jay gave her a wicked look. 'Did you ever think I might just get a kick out of annoying you?

'It had occurred to me.' She fought a smile. 'And I can't believe I'm saying this, but thank you.'

Chapter Nineteen

Alice marched up to the café's front counter and thumped a book of tattoo designs onto it.

Cath switched off the cappuccino machine, her smile flashing super bright. 'Someone got out of the wrong side of bed today. I'm guessing alone again or you'd be smiling?'

Alice frowned. 'I went to get a tattoo this morning. To prove I could do something impulsive, that I can be impulsive.'

Cath scratched her head. 'Of course, I remember the time you used the blue cloth to clean the sink instead of the sponge.'

'Ha, ha.' Alice slumped onto one of the café chairs as the bell over the front door tinkled and Jay sauntered in with a tool bag slung over one shoulder. He stopped dead when he saw Alice.

'They finished your tattoo already? What did you go for, the two-headed snake or the deranged rabbit?'

'Neither. If you have a tattoo you can't get it wet for at least two weeks, which doesn't work if you're training for a triathlon,' she grumbled.

Jay winced.

'You knew?'

'I remembered last night. I was going to call, but I knew you'd think I was trying to talk you out of it.'

Alice sighed. He was right of course, but it still rankled. 'So you came to gloat?"

Jay shook his head, his expression darkening. 'I came to finish the cupboard and to measure up those shelves you want.'

Alice began to apologise but the bell rang at the front of the café and she shot up out of her seat, but she hadn't even changed into her uniform, she'd been so distracted. Cath pointed a thumb towards the kitchen, gesturing that they should get ready. Jay headed for it. Alice quickly followed. Once the door was closed Jay stepped closer and put a hand against her cheek.

'I'm sorry you couldn't get your tattoo.'

Alice let out a long sigh, feeling her heart kick up a notch. 'I'm sorry for being miserable, you didn't deserve it. I've been thinking about getting the tattoo done all night.' She'd hardly slept. 'I wanted to prove something.'

Jay's mouth jerked up at the edge. 'That you're impulsive?'

'I know you don't think I can be spontaneous,' she protested. 'But this feels right. I love the idea of having something to focus on if I go off track, it's a way of remembering, you know?'

'Yes.' Jay looked surprised. 'That's why I got mine.'

'I hadn't even decided where to put it, not that it matters now.'

Jay smiled gently. 'Does it matter if you can see it all the time?'

'No.'

'How about above your hip bone?' He put a finger to the spot, sending tingles firing downwards.

Alice cleared her throat. 'Possibly, but it doesn't matter, does it? I'm not getting one.'

'Do it when you've finished the triathlon.' Jay looked deep into her eyes. 'Before you leave Castle Cove. Maybe I'll get one done too.'

'Matching tattoos?' Alice giggled, her mood rising. 'What would we go for, the Superman logo?'

'I prefer Batman.' Jay stepped closer. 'Way cooler and we both know you have a thing for rubber.'

Alice hooted and took his hand. 'Thank you for making me laugh. I was feeling sorry for myself and now I'm thinking about you in a Batman suit and that's an image I'm not likely to forget in a hurry.' She wanted to fan herself. 'I haven't let anyone look out for me for a long time and… I've decided I like it.'

Jay looked at their linked fingers and squeezed, then he closed the distance between them and stroked the tips of his fingers down her face. 'I do too. Does this count as our third date?'

'Why not?' Alice asked. 'Beats swimming.'

Jay gave her a slow, devastating smile which lit her insides. 'I can think of plenty more things that'll do that. I've got an idea for somewhere to take you this weekend, but in the meantime…' He continued to brush his fingertips against her jaw tipping her chin up. He was about to sweep his mouth against hers when Alice interrupted.

'I've never been kissed at work before,' she mumbled, wanting to pinch herself because Jay moved back, his eyes crinkling.

'If it's good enough, will you get a tattoo of my name?'

'No.' She choked on the laughter. 'But I might consider Zeus's, his *is* cooler.'

'Let's see if I can change your mind.'

This time Jay didn't wait, this time his mouth was on hers, sudden, fast and hot. He tasted of coffee and dark chocolate, the kind that stayed on your tongue late into the night. The kiss deepened and Alice leaned into it, smelling the sea again, feeling the power of it, the ebb and flow as Jay's arms wrapped around her. Alice gripped Jay's t-shirt, pulled him closer and let herself go. She felt like she was falling; off-balance, out of her depth and out of control but she wasn't afraid. Instead she embraced it. Their mouths fused, in agreement for the first time in weeks.

Alice's heart was pounding and she could feel the tension in Jay's body as she pushed her hands underneath his t-shirt, letting them slide over his back. His skin felt smooth and hot and she heard him moan. He began to pull at the material tucked into her cycling shorts when the bell rang in the café again and Jay shifted away, kissing the edge of her mouth, cheeks and eyelids. Alice's body was shaking and she had to straighten her spine or she might have dissolved into a puddle.

Jay cleared his throat. 'So… '

'Yep.' She muttered, feeling herself sway. 'Maybe Jay is cooler than Zeus after all.'

Jay laughed as Cath hurtled into the kitchen. 'It's getting busy,' she said, taking in Alice's untucked top and smiling.

Alice smoothed down her hair. 'I'm sorry, we were… chatting.' She finished, feeling her cheeks flush.

Cath raised an eyebrow. 'A coach has just pulled into the car park and Olive's here asking after you. See you in a sec.' She rolled her eyes and disappeared into the front.

'Bugger.' Alice picked up her backpack and went to change before heading into the café.

'Alice.' Olive beamed. She sat at a table near the windows. 'I've got something to show you.' She pulled a newspaper out of her flowery bag and placed it on the table with a flourish.

'Oh.' Alice was torn between wanting to see what Olive had brought and helping Cath. 'Can you let me serve a few customers and I'll come back. What would you like to drink?' Alice flashed a smile.

'A hot chocolate and a slice of that Death by Chocolate cake. Don't worry dear.' Olive patted her hand. 'I've got all the time in the world. I'm not working today.'

'Thank you.' Alice gasped, heading for the counter where Cath was making cappuccinos. 'What can I do?'

'Can you cut three slices of carrot cake please?' Cath looked tired. 'You okay?'

Cath nodded. 'I didn't sleep. Dan's decided to stay another night in Birmingham, he's already started work on the kitchen he mentioned, and there might be a party.'

'You mind?' Alice grabbed some plates and began to cut the cake.

'I miss him, but I'm not going to moan about it. I know Dan can't resist a party and it's great he's working.' Alice placed large slices onto the plates and put them on a tray. 'Can you give these to table two?'

'Sure. I'll get the order from nine and when you have a sec, Olive wants a hot chocolate. I'll sort out her cake.'

It took ten minutes before they caught up with the backlog of orders, at which point Alice placed Olive's drink and cake onto her table. Her eyes were drawn to the open newspaper.

'It's your mum,' Olive said, uncurling the paper and placing it face up. It was the *Castle Cove Gazette* and there was a picture of a crowd of people dressed in wetsuits. 'This is her last year, just before she started the triathlon. You were there?' Olive pointed a fingernail at a face in the crowd.

Alice shook her head. 'I was meant to go but there was an emergency at the restaurant,' she said. And didn't that sound ridiculous? What could be so important that she'd missed her mother competing?

'Genevieve would have understood, look how happy she is.' Olive patted her hand. 'You can take the paper home if you like.'

'Thank you.' Alice grabbed the newspaper just as Marta walked in with Simon. Simon Wolf was a man you noticed the instant he entered a room. He had dark grey eyes that seemed to take in everything around him and a square jaw with a dimple in the centre. His full mouth thinned as he stared at the clipboard and pad he held.

'It's only a painting and some pottery,' Marta complained, as Simon wrote something.

'And some photos of the beach.' He pointed at a corner wall near the toilets.

'Josh Havellin-Scott is a talented photographer and a good friend of mine. We're lucky he's agreed to share his art at all. I had to twist his arm.'

Simon frowned and wrote something else on his clipboard. Marta narrowed her eyes and stomped to the counter to order coffee.

'I'm sure we're very lucky.' Simon's tone suggested otherwise. 'But we need to agree something or they'll have to go. I was thinking a commission if you can't pay a monthly fee?'

Heading to the kitchen, Alice thought she could almost see the steam coming from Marta's ears.

'You okay?' Jay asked as soon as she walked in. The cupboard was fixed back on the wall and he'd just finished screwing the door on.

'I'm fine.' Alice snapped, putting the newspaper into her bag. Jay caught her arm.

'What was in that paper?'

'A picture of my mother before the last triathlon. I wasn't there...' Her voice trailed off.

'You feel guilty?' Jay rubbed a hand on her back.

She didn't answer.

'She did it anyway.' His voice deepened. 'I like the sound of your mother.'

Alice nodded. 'She didn't let anything stop her.'

'Then you're a lot alike.' Jay kissed the top of her head.

'I hope you're right.' Alice muttered. But she wasn't so sure.

☆

The Anglers looked busy, and the air seemed heavy. Alice paused at the doorway, and Jay bumped into her back, almost tumbling her forwards.

'Sorry.' Jay guided her inside with a hand at the small of her back, setting off a cacophony of tingles as she moved into the crowd. No-one was playing live but the tables were still packed, with every available space filled. The buzz of conversation hummed under music from the jukebox. 'Still feeling impulsive, because in the absence of a tattoo I wondered if you fancied a cocktail?'

'Will it be blue?' Alice glanced at the bar but couldn't see the shiny oak, or familiar sight of Shaun pulling pints, just a sea of people.

'Can I have one please, I'm feeling the need to be impulsive too. A few days without Dan and I'm starting to feel boring.' Cath nudged between them from behind. 'Where have you been?'

'I had to go for a quick run, sorry.' Alice admitted.

'How's the training going?' Cath asked.

'Well, I can run for forty minutes now without getting out of breath so I'm definitely improving.'

'I don't know how you have the energy after a full day at work, the café was so busy earlier,' Cath sighed.

'What's going on?' Jay asked as they eased their way closer to the heaving mass of people.

'Two of the barmaids haven't turned up, that's what someone said in the loos.'

'So Shaun's alone behind there, how's he coping?'

'I haven't made it to the queue yet.' Cath said as her eyes skirted the rows of people at the bar. 'If it's just him behind there, he's having a crap night.'

'I should help.' Jay said. 'There's going to be a mutiny.'

'Maybe we could all help?' Alice offered. 'We had a bar at the restaurant, I can pour beer, take money?'

'It'll be better for everyone if I stay out here and clear tables.' Cath scanned the room. 'There are lots of empty glasses that need collecting.'

'I'm sure Shaun would appreciate it.'

Cath snorted.

'In his own way.' Jay guided Alice through the pub and to the right, then through a doorway.

'Ignore the mess, I'm always telling Shaun to tidy up.'

Alice almost tripped on a pile of books in the centre of the hallway. 'Were you separated at birth?'

Jay opened a door into the back of the bar. Shaun looked shattered and it was only half past eight. He was almost running between the taps, pulling multiple pints and trying to ignore the sea of irritated expressions.

'Dammit.' Beer spilt over the top of one of the glasses onto his hand.

'Need help?' Jay asked.

Shaun looked at the crowd of impatient people at the bar. 'I think I might be desperate enough.'

'Alice came too.' Jay pushed her forwards.

'Cath's friend.' Shaun's tone wasn't welcoming.

'I've worked behind a bar. I thought you could use some help, but if it's a problem?' Alice began to turn away.

'Yes,' Shaun said. 'Sorry, please. I've had two people call in sick and my back-up is on a ferry to the Isle of Wight, I could use some help.' Shaun looked at Jay. 'You can start by changing some of the barrels. Then you can sort the kitchen, it's a total mess.'

Jay nodded and disappeared through the door at the end of the bar that lead into the back room.

'You really know how to do this?' Shaun looked a little panicked as he handed Alice a bottle of merlot.

'Piece of cake.' Alice smiled, popping the cork before serving her first customer.

It took almost twenty minutes to clear the crowd and Alice felt like her feet were flying. Jay popped a head in briefly to say he'd changed the barrels before disappearing into the kitchen and Cath piled empty glasses in the small spaces she could find at the end of the bar. If Shaun noticed her, he didn't say anything.

She'd missed this, Alice realised. The café was fun and she loved the variety and colour of the locals and even some of the tourists, but she'd missed the vibe of working at night, missed the loud music and adrenaline-pumping atmosphere. She even found herself dancing to One Direction as she used the till.

'You're enjoying this?' Shaun asked after she'd served her first few customers, pinning her with an expression she couldn't read.

'I like being busy.' Alice grabbed two bottles of cola and popped the lids. 'If you moved your glasses from over there up front, you'd be able to deal with some of the non-alcoholic orders more quickly.'

Shaun frowned.

After fifteen minutes, gaps appeared at the bar and with them, Jay. 'Having fun?'

'Beats swimming, but a cup of arsenic would do that.'

'You'll eat those words in a couple of weeks.'

'Mmmmm, you want a drink?'

'It's on the house,' Shaun said from behind her. 'You saved my life tonight and I guess since Jay did a passable job on the kitchen, I owe him a half.'

Jay gave his friend a dark look. 'He means a pint and I'll make you that cocktail if you're still feeling impulsive?' He headed for the bar and began mixing.

'You got a job?' Shaun asked. Scanning the remaining crowd in the bar, his eyes strayed to Cath who was now seated, chatting to Ted and Marta. Alice waved hello.

'I work at the Castle Café, with Cath.'

'Full-time?' Shaun shot back.

'Five shifts a week.'

'You want to work here?'

Alice shook her head. 'I love working at the café, I don't want to give it up.'

'But you're tempted?' Shaun read her face.

'I could do with earning more money.' She still had a lot to save if she wanted to travel after Thailand.

Shaun scratched his chin; like Jay he'd built up a five-o'clock shadow which only made him more attractive. 'The café's daytime, isn't it? How about three evenings a week? You choose which. You're efficient, good with customers, your idea about moving the glasses' – he looked at the spot she'd suggested – 'was inspired. I've had people working with me for months who can't serve a customer as fast as you.'

Alice pursed her lips.

'I'll pay you thirty percent more than you're earning at the café.'

'Stop Shaun, this is embarrassing.' Jay handed her a huge blue drink with ice and sticks with flamingos on the top of them. 'Can't you see she's thinking about it?'

'No,' Shaun searched her face, confused.

'I only think I'll have time to do two shifts.'

'That's okay.'

'And I'm only here until September, is that a problem?'

'I'll take whatever you can give. Who knows, maybe we'll grow on you and you'll stay?'

'No.' Alice fired back immediately, and then registered his startled expression. 'I mean, I'm sure you'll grow on me, but I have plans and I can't change them.'

'Then until September.' Shaun picked up his drink and tipped it in her direction. 'We'll work out the rest later. Why don't you take a break for a few minutes, I can handle this?'

'I'm fine, I've got my drink. Why don't you take a break, you've been at it longer than me?'

Shaun rocked back on his heels. 'I've died and gone to heaven.'

'So long as you don't take advantage of her,' Jay said, which should have irritated her, but didn't.

Jay's blue eyes sparkled under the bar lights. 'You okay? You've been on your feet a lot today?'

'You planning an intervention?'

'I might have a pair of fluffy slippers in the pickup if that would help?'

'My feet are fine, besides it's good training, and I'm enjoying it. I like—'

'Keeping busy.' Jay sipped his pint. 'I know.'

A man came up to the bar and she served him, aware all the time of Jay's eyes on her. Was it odd that her stomach felt all bunched up? That there were tingles on her skin? Did it always feel like this when you were attracted to someone?

'You want another drink?' Alice asked.

Jay shook his head as Cath appeared, holding three empty glasses. 'You look good up there, but if he tries to poach you, let me know so I can punish him. I've got plenty of ideas.' She scanned Alice's expression. 'I'll kill him.'

'He offered me a job, it's in the evenings so I can do both.'

Her friend slammed the glasses on the counter and Alice quickly slipped them under the bar. 'You won't have time if you're training.'

'I'll have days off, and there will be time after I finish at the café, you know how much I hate sitting around?'

Cath's eyes had narrowed to slits and Alice glanced over her shoulder, worried for Shaun if he decided to reappear. 'You want another drink?' she asked.

'I was coming to say goodbye, Ted's leaving and he said he'd walk me home, it's on his way. I'm assuming you've got a ride?' Cath looked at Jay.

'I'll walk her,' Jay replied.

'It's really not necess—' Alice registered both their expressions. 'Jay can walk me. I'm sorry I didn't spend time with you this evening.'

Cath's face brightened. 'I caught up with loads of people while I was clearing tables, just glad His Nibs didn't spot me.' She rolled her eyes and then blew a kiss before leaving.

Alice checked the glasses for cracks before placing them in the dishwasher tray.

'Shaun kept watching Cath while she was clearing the tables. Do you think he still has feelings for her?' Alice asked Jay.

'He wouldn't tell me if did. Whatever happened between them, he won't share.'

'You think there was someone else?'

Jay shook his head vehemently. 'No chance. It's odd because in the weeks before they split, I've never seen Shaun happier.'

A door shut behind them and the man in question sauntered in. 'You can go if you like? I'll finish up. Go finish what's left of your date. Here's a copy of our shifts for next week, you've got first refusal on whichever nights you want. Text me by tomorrow lunchtime so I can divvy up the rest.' He pushed an envelope into her hand. 'That's for tonight, a bonus for the help, we'll be doing normal pay from now on. You—' he glanced at Jay. 'I owe you another half.'

'Pint.' Jay insisted.

'Half, and' – Shaun turned back to Alice – 'tell Cath I said thanks.'

'You were great tonight,' Jay said as they started the walk home.

Alice took a deep breath and smelled the familiar scent of sea salt but she couldn't tell if it was coming from the promenade or him. 'Shaun's been struggling to find someone to rely on behind that bar,' he continued.

'He's doing me a favour.'

A gust of wind blew across the street making her shiver. Jay must have seen because suddenly his jacket was hanging around her shoulders.

'You don't have to do that.' Alice pushed her arms into the holes and pulled it closed around her front. She could smell him on the leather – salt and sea and maybe coffee?

Jay reached across to interlace their fingers, his hand felt large and made hers warm so she held it tighter. Her heart thumped hard as they walked and she couldn't think of anything to say. Grasping for something to talk about, she shot her eyes to the sky and found the North Star. 'I look for it now.'

'What?'

Alice pointed into the sky with her other hand. 'I like knowing it's there, I'll be able to look for it in Thailand, like an anchor.'

Jay squeezed her hand. 'Thanks for helping Shaun tonight, you didn't have to, Mel would have run a mile. Not many people who'd jump in like that.'

'You did.'

'He's my friend.'

'You'd have done it anyway, and it's hardly rescuing someone from a sinking ship.'

Jay sighed, looking grim.

'You okay?'

'Sure,' he muttered and then stopped walking suddenly, jerking her to a stop. 'No, I—' He stood in front and pulled her round to face him. 'You're leaving in September.'

'I am.'

'I know I kissed you in the café, but I don't want to get involved with someone who's about to leave town, I've been there and it doesn't end well.'

Stupid to feel disappointed, he was right. 'Then don't.'

Jay reached a hand up and stroked the side of her face and she leaned into his palm, her hand gripped his and she found herself easing closer, until their toes were almost touching. Then she was looking into his eyes and neither of them were talking. Her heart thumped hard again and even though she could feel a cool breeze against her skin, her body felt hot. Jay tipped her head upwards and brought his lips to meet hers, slowly at first, like a tentative meeting of strangers, their mouths moved against each other, soft, skin on skin. Alice leaned into him even more, found her hands moving upwards until they slid around his neck. The kiss deepened and she tipped her head up further, easing herself closer so she could feel the muscles of his chest, feel the denim of his jeans against her legs. Then suddenly Jay was moving backwards, looking into her face. 'Sorry.'

'Sorry?'

'I'm complicating things again.' He scanned her face, trying to read her expression. 'But damn, you look just like you did when I gave you that box of receipts.' He grinned.

'I—' The bones in her legs felt like they'd evaporated and she stumbled backwards, almost tripping over something invisible on the pavement. She would have ended up flat on her back if he hadn't caught her hand.

'So maybe I'm not sorry after all.' Jay pulled her closer.

'You're not meant to kiss a girl like that and then tell her it's a mistake,' Alice said, feeling grumpy.

'Didn't say it was a mistake, I said I'm sorry, it's not the same thing.' Jay started to walk again and tugged her hand so she followed. 'Maybe I was apologising to myself.'

'Because?' Alice kept her eyes on the pavement.

'For starting something when you're leaving.'

'Oh.' Alice felt uncomfortable. 'So we kissed, twice. A couple of weeks ago you were saying we could date and not be serious, in fact, I remember you teasing me about your grandmother's ring.'

'I'm trying to keep my life simple but in spite of my good intentions I'm not sure I can any more.'

'I'm not creating strings, I'm leaving soon.'

Jay nodded. 'I know. And I'll probably live to regret this, but despite that, I'm wondering if we should just make the most this while you're here?'

'Oh.' Alice stopped walking. 'Yes.' The comment made her ridiculously happy.

Jay stepped in front of her, his eyes darkening. He tipped up her chin. 'So, I vote we ignore good sense and start now?'

Chapter Twenty

'A treetop adventure?' Alice craned her neck searching for the ropes, squinting through the sunshine. 'When you said sensible shoes, I was expecting a long walk, not this.' Something bubbled in her stomach; it could have been excitement.

'Now your ankle's healed, I thought it was time for a proper adventure.' Jay tugged her harness, then stood behind her and adjusted the strap on her waist and she felt his breath in her hair. 'You scared of heights?'

'I think I've used up my quota of phobias, but I haven't had much of a chance to test it.' She looked upwards; at least the sun was shining and there wasn't a beach in sight. 'Remind me again why I'm doing this?'

'You're having fun.' Jay spun her round, the edges of his eyes crinkling. 'You remember that?'

'After a weekend of working on your books I'm not sure I do.'

'I'm sorry I couldn't see you. It's been crazy at work and with call outs.'

'That's okay.' Alice said.

'Besides, I thought paperwork was your idea of a good time?' Jay played with the harness on her shoulders, tightening something she couldn't see. The concentration on his face made her body go hot.

'You okay?'

'Of course.' Alice reassured him. 'Shall we start? It's almost worse when you have too much time to think about it.'

Alice headed for the steps that would lead to the treetops. Her stomach fluttered as she reached the bottom, but the feeling wasn't unpleasant, more excitement than fear. Jay came up behind her and put a hand on her waist.

'Stay close.' Jay spoke into her hair. 'We'll do this together, anytime you're scared or not enjoying yourself, let me know and I'll get you down.'

'You sound more nervous than I do.' Alice looked up, startled when he smiled and leaned down to brush a kiss lightly across her lips. The briefest touch had her body firing.

'I thought about you yesterday.' His voice deepened.

'Oh?' Alice flushed.

'Yes, Shaun got a parking ticket.' Jay grinned, making her laugh. 'You go first, I'll be right behind you.'

'It looks high.' Alice turned and began to climb, aware of him at her back getting another eyeful of Lycra-covered bum.

'The views are amazing at the top. There are two wires attached to your harness remember, as long as you always keep one clipped on, you'll be fine.'

'Clip on, got it, I remember the training.' Alice wanted to salute but wasn't going to take her hands off the ladder. Forget falling, Jay would probably murder her.

They both reached the top and shuffled onto a narrow ledge leading to the first set of ropes they'd need to walk across. Jay watched as she carefully unclipped and then clipped herself onto the rope strung between the first and second platform like a tightrope. Above them thick ropes dangled, each suspending a big chunk of wood that they'd use to walk across.

'They're like stepping stones,' Jay said.

'That wobble?'

'That's part of the fun, if you're clipped on—'

'I won't fall.' Alice giggled. 'I've got no plans to hurl myself off this thing, my weekend wasn't that boring.'

Alice watched the treetops blow back and forth in the wind as she collected herself. 'I've never been anywhere like this.' The ground looked a long way off, she watched a rabbit hop in the undergrowth and disappear. 'My mum would have loved it.'

'Then maybe you're doing it for her?' Jay's mouth moved close to her ear, stroking it with warm air and Alice fought a shiver. 'Like the triathlon. I've been thinking, I'll do it with you if you like?'

'The triathlon?' Alice wanted to turn and look at him, but couldn't because there wasn't enough space. 'I thought you'd won it already, seven times?'

'Not with you.'

'Are you worried I won't finish?' Wind blew across them, ruffling her hair.

'I was thinking it was more like moral support. You'll finish it Alice, I've seen how determined you are, you're just like your mum.'

'Oh.' Tears pricked her eyes.

Jay put a hand on her shoulder and she leaned back against him feeling the light kiss in her hair.

'Are you ready to do this?'

'I guess it beats staying up here, although I could live a little longer with this view.'

'We're lucky, it's a quiet day but there'll be someone along soon.' He put his hands on her hips and gently squeezed, leaving a promise on her skin. 'Be careful.'

Alice took a tentative step.

'Take it slow, I'm right behind you.'

The wood wobbled and she let out a squeak but waited to let her stomach settle before she took another step, then another, until both planks were swinging back and forth, suspended in the air. Her stomach rolled as a gust of wind blew in her face and she tried not to look down.

'You okay?'

'Just getting settled,' she shouted.

'Like it?'

'Yes.' The words came out on a whoosh. Adrenaline fired through her body like a wave of warmth, she took another wobbly step and giggled as her stomach rolled. 'Love it.'

'You sure?' Jay sounded worried so she peered over her shoulder.

'I've felt so little for so long, this makes me feel alive, it's amazing.'

'Have I unwittingly unleashed an adrenaline junkie?' Jay's blue eyes sparkled.

'Maybe.' Alice took another tentative step, then another, speeding up until she hit the other side.

'Good grief,' Jay murmured, but she could hear the smile in his voice. She turned and watch him stride over the ropes without stopping, his long legs travelling fast. Then he was beside her on a tiny circle of wood, and they were so cramped she had to press herself against him, feeling the warmth of his skin through their clothes.

'I want to do it again.' Alice turned letting her body brush against Jay's again. A rope ran across to the next platform with wood panels in threes creating stepping stones. 'That looks less wobbly.' Her voice sounded breathy.

'Maybe we can go across together?'

'Is it dangerous?'

Jay grabbed her hand. 'Twenty-foot waves are dangerous, this is fun. Don't worry, I won't let you fall.'

'I know it. How many times have you done the course?'

'Once. Mark from the lifeboat crew did this the morning after his stag do, there were a few who didn't like it, but I think that was more to do with hangovers than heights.'

'Can we start?' Alice started to move off the platform, stopping dead as Jay gently jerked her back.

'You need to attach your carabiner first.' He unclipped one, accidently brushing a knuckle against the side of her breast as he clipped it on the other rope. 'Looks like I'm going to have to watch you carefully.'

'I don't mind,' she whispered and took another step, holding tight onto the rope. Her body wobbled but the stepping stones were firm.

'Take it slow,' Jay directed from the perch. 'I'll wait here and join you when I know you're comfortable.'

A gust of wind blew her to the side and she bobbed in the air, reminded of swimming, without the fear. On the second stepping-stone she stopped. 'You coming?'

Jay trotted across, focusing on her face as he moved. He came up behind her and waited.

'You just going to stay here?' he asked.

'I like the feeling, it's a bit weird, like letting go.' Alice loosened her grip on the guide rope, but kept her fingers hovering over it. 'I feel free, like I've escaped from something.'

'Paperwork?'

Alice giggled. 'Is there a zip wire coming up soon, I think I'm ready for another shot of adrenaline?' She began to move, treading lightly until she hit the other side and turned to watch Jay do the same. He joined her on the platform and watched her re-arrange the clips.

'Yep.'

'Is it high?'

Jay moved closer so he could adjust one of the ropes. 'Yes. You okay with that?'

'I might scream on the way down.'

'Me too.'

Alice laughed. 'Good.'

Jay leaned in to brush his lips against hers. This time Alice was ready for him and put her hands around his neck, pulling him closer so the kiss deepened. She could smell the sea again, even though they were about a mile in the air and knew the scent came from him. She pressed her body into his and closed her eyes, feeling adrenaline and heat. After a few minutes he eased back and rested his forehead against hers.

'Not sure the top of a tree is the place for this.' Jay twisted to see if anyone was waiting to cross to their station but the ropes were still empty. 'It's a bit of a squeeze.'

'I don't mind.' Her arms slipped from his neck but he put his around her waist and pulled her closer, then shifted so his leg slid up against hers, sending tingles firing outwards.

'After the zip wire, I'd prefer to have more room to manoeuvre,' Jay said.

Oh, well then. 'All right.'

The climb to the top of the ropes was hard, but Jay matched her, taking care not to shake everything and make it harder. Alice had to stop a couple of times to catch her breath. Despite her training, it was hard work pulling herself up. By the time they both made it to the final platform her breath came in short bursts.

'Ready?'

Jay didn't wait for her answer and Alice watched him clip her to the wire, his long fingers nimble and focused. It took effort for her to drag her eyes away to digest the long drop and zip wire tilting steeply to the ground.

Jay squeezed her hand. 'You going to be okay?'

'No idea, but we'll soon find out.' She closed her eyes and took a couple of deep breaths.

'I can go first if you're nervous?'

'I'll go, I'm not much of an adventurer if I chicken out now.' Alice inched forwards but couldn't quite make the leap. 'It's not as easy as it looks.'

'Leaps of faith never are.'

Alice snorted, keeping her eyes shut. 'How do people do this? I think I've changed my mind, I'm not impulsive or brave, I want a ladder.' Her hands shook but she didn't move from the edge.

Jay put a warm hand on her shoulder. 'People do it by trusting the guy who put the frame up, or the friend who says it's safe, trusting themselves to do it right.'

'Is it? Safe, I mean?'

'You think I'd let you step off if it wasn't?'

Alice took a deep breath.

'Well?'

'Thinking about it.' Alice slid closer to the edge, fighting the smile when she heard him grunt. 'Okay, yes.'

Alice stepped off, holding onto the rope and opening her eyes as she began to pick up speed.

'Oh my God this is amazing.' She just stopped herself from screaming 'wheeee' as she whizzed down laughing. She giggled even as she reached the floor, landing feet first in soft wood chippings. Unhooking herself she stepped back and waited for Jay to do the same. He didn't scream, but he watched her all the way and as soon as he landed he unclipped himself and strode over before taking her face in his hands and leaning in for a long, hot kiss.

☆

The roads were clear and Alice closed her eyes and leaned her head on her seat.

'You tired?' Jay moved the pickup into the fast lane and hit the accelerator. 'Traffic's good, it shouldn't take long to get back.'

'I'm fine.' Although her body was still fired up from the kiss after the first zip wire, she shuffled in her seat trying to squash the hormones.

'Up for another swim? Might as well harness all that fearlessness while we can?'

'Sure, okay.' Wouldn't hurt to see Jay in a tight wetsuit either. 'If you drop me home, I'll pick up what I need and we can head straight off.' She watched his hands on the steering wheel, remembering how good it had felt to have them on her. 'Sure you've got time?'

'I'm sure. Would you like to come back to mine after?' Jay asked and Alice watched his Adam's apple bob. 'I could cook?'

'Can you?' Alice stalled.

'What?'

'Cook.'

'Zeus never complains.'

'I need to feed the kitten,' she said, feeling uncertain.

'Are you working tonight?'

'No, tomorrow.'

They fell silent. 'You don't have to,' Jay said gently. 'I'm not trying to push you into something you're not ready for.'

'You're not, I'd love to come, sorry, I just needed a minute to think about it. I haven't been to a man's house in a long, long… long time.' Alice blushed. 'Too much information.'

'It's just dinner.' They both knew he was lying.

Jay switched on the radio and 'Let's Get It On' by Marvin Gaye filled the car. Alice was about to make a joke when his mobile rang so he turned off the music and flipped something on the console.

'Jay?'

'Mum.' His voice seemed to flatten.

'I'm so sorry, love.' Even over the speaker Alice could tell the woman was upset.

'Why?'

'Zeus. I left the back door open, thought he'd stay in the garden.'

A man's voice said something in the background making Jay scowl.

'We think he jumped the fence,' his mother continued.

'We?' He tapped his fingers on the steering wheel.

'He hasn't been gone long, I'm sure he's fine.'

'Where have you looked?'

Alice reached across to squeeze Jay's shoulder.

'I went to yours, Zeus isn't in any of the neighbouring streets, or the park, or beach. I've checked where I've been walking him.'

'It's fine Mum, I'm not far. Look on the beach again, he's wandered there a few times, he might even go back to my house, he's got a great memory for walks.'

'How long will you be?'

Jay checked the sat nav. 'Traffic's good, I shouldn't be more than half an hour.'

'Okay.' His mother sounded miserable. 'I'll check the beach and then meet you at home so we can look together. I'm sorry love.'

'I'm sure we'll find him.' Jay hung up but didn't say anything. Alice watched him turn the wheel. His jawline looked hard from this angle, the edges of his mouth turned down.

'You okay?'

'Zeus doesn't run off, he's probably gone looking for me. I usually leave him with Shaun, but he's been on call, I thought it would make it simpler… '

'We'll find him.'

Jay didn't say anything for a minute; when he did the bottom dropped out of her stomach. 'I'll drop you off so you can get your swimming stuff together, I can call you once I find him.'

'I don't mind helping?' The words sounded a little desperate.

'I've no idea how long it will take.'

'I don't mind, I'd like to help.'

'You'll be better off at home.'

'Sure.' Alice swallowed the hurt. What was going on? The relationship kept leaping forwards before going back. Jay wasn't sharing something with her and she wanted to know why.

Chapter Twenty-One

Jay padded around his mother's front room, almost tripping over a black cat before he took a seat, patting Zeus, who was eyeing the ball of fluff suspiciously, on the head.

'I can't believe he made it to your house.' His mum watched him fuss the dog.

'He's got a great sense of direction.' Jay stared at the cup of leaves swimming in green-tinged water. They'd almost had the conversation about milk again but he'd given up.

'Shame I didn't get to meet your new girl,' his mother mentioned casually as she pulled up her long skirt and sat on the sofa, curling her feet underneath her legs.

Jay didn't want to get into a discussion about Alice, he knew not letting her help with the search for Zeus had upset her, but he wasn't ready for her to meet his mother.

'Who was the man you mentioned earlier?'

Her cheeks tinged pink. 'Ben Campbell. His wife died a couple of years ago and he likes me to give him readings, he just happened to be here when Zeus went walkabout. Finish your tea, I'll read your leaves.' She reached for his cup but he pulled it away.

'I wanted to talk about next week,' he said instead, sipping the bitter liquid and pulling a face.

Shutters come down over his mother's face.

'It's ten years, Mum.'

Her hand shook as she lifted her cup to her mouth without taking a sip and he felt like giving up. She breathed in deep. 'You want to do something.'

'I want to go the beach.'

Jay let that hang and watched her. She'd always been beautiful but had looked tired and beaten down after Steve had died: the weight of grief had taken its toll, dragging her features downwards as if her whole face had set into a synchronised frown. But lately she'd looked lighter, younger, was that because so much time had passed?

'I want us to go where he died.'

His mum sighed again but he wasn't going to give in.

'Just for half an hour, then we can go for lunch, I've already booked a table at the Anglers.'

'Will your girl come?' His mother perked up.

'Not for this, and she's not my girl.'

'Why?' She looked him straight in the eye and he felt a jolt. *Guilt.*

'She's leaving Castle Cove.'

'That's not a reason.'

Jay sipped his tea so he didn't have to answer and coughed as he drank a mouthful of leaves. As soon as his cup hit the coffee table his mother picked it up and he leaned his head back on the sofa and closed his eyes, giving in to the inevitable.

'The girl's in here, what's her name?'

'Alice.'

A floorboard creaked as she got up and paced the room. He knew without looking she'd be holding the cup like a newborn.

'She here for a reason?'

Jay coughed. 'She's stubborn.' And reckless but also incredibly brave. He'd upset her today and regretted it. He'd been so busy keeping her away from his mother he hadn't realised he'd shut her out.

His mum laughed. 'Stubborn, sounds familiar.' She paused as she studied his cup, tipping it from left to right so she could examine it from every angle. 'There's an attraction.'

Did she have to say that? Even at the age of twenty-seven, he didn't want to have a conversation about sex with his mother.

Jay felt the seat dip beside him. 'I get a good feeling about her. You're going to be close, but you've got to let her do what she came here for, does that make sense?'

'Sure,' he stumbled. His mother had always had an uncanny ability to hit the nail on the head when it came to his relationships. He didn't read anything into the fact that she was partly right, it had nothing to do with her spiritual practices, she'd always been sensitive.

His mother spun the cup in her hand and smiled. 'I think your Alice would want to come to the beach too.'

'No.' The word came out so fast his mother looked startled. 'She'll be busy training, and I'd rather keep that day to the two of us, I don't want you to feel left out.'

She looked disappointed as she took his cup and disappeared into the kitchen.

Chapter Twenty-Two

Alice stepped over the mound of sheets that she'd pulled from the airing cupboard, and grabbed the phone as soon as she saw someone was calling from overseas. 'Dad,' she answered.

'Alice, my love.'

She sank onto the sofa, barely missing the kitten who'd taken up residence in the centre.

'Sorry it's been so long,' he said.

'Two weeks isn't long for us.'

Her dad paused. 'It is now we're speaking. I lost you for a lot of years, I won't let that happen again. You okay?'

She closed her eyes, feeling tired, and stroked the kitten. 'Good, great.'

'I just wanted you to know we're looking forward to you coming, Beth and I. Your room is ready at the house. You've even got your own door to the beach, and there are tons of places you can visit when you're not busy. The beaches are amazing if you just fancy lying about. We've got the latest *Lonely Planet* so you can plan your whole trip afterwards while you're here. Not that I'm in any hurry for you to head off.'

'Oh wow.' Her stomach clenched. 'I can't believe how organised you are.'

'Ah, it's all Beth really.' Her dad sounded embarrassed. 'I was a mess until I met her. Kept forgetting everything. The diving business would have gone under if she hadn't come along two years ago and swept me off my feet. You remember how much your mother used to organise me?'

'I remember. I'm not sure we'd have even had milk for tea if you'd been in charge.'

'I always forgot after we split—' He stopped abruptly. 'How's the swimming?'

'Better, someone's helping me now.' At the mention of Jay she frowned.

'You'll love diving, there's so much to see, you wouldn't believe the colours.'

'Great.' Alice shut her eyes. Her big adventure, the one she kept talking about, was only six and a half weeks away, but was she ready for it?

'Can't wait.' The words came out a little hollow. The kitten stretched and found its way onto her knee, purring as it repositioned itself and went back to sleep. Her dad continued to chatter, telling her about the colourful schools of fish he'd seen in the last week.

'We saw some small sharks too. Nothing for you to worry about,' he added quickly. 'Beth knows her stuff. And there are some amazing islands here, places to sunbathe and climb, Alice you'll love it! I can't wait to see you, it's been so many years.'

'Five,' Alice said softly, feeling the weight of grief.

'I wish you'd come earlier, you were always so busy with the restaurant and… I know you were angry about the divorce.'

'Times change,' Alice said quietly.

'You still looking forward to it?' Her dad asked suddenly. 'You seem a little quiet. Are things really okay?'

'They're great, I've just started working at the pub in Castle Cove as well as the café so I can save faster. The house is all cleared out, aside from furniture and pictures, and I'm about to list it with an estate agent so I will find tenants in plenty of time. Dad, I'm fine and I'm really looking forward to coming. I am a bit worried though,' Alice added, aiming to distract him. 'I've never dived.'

'I know.' His voice softened. 'Your mother loved being in the sea. She'd probably have taught you herself if she'd got the chance. She was a much better diver than me.'

'She was good at everything.' Alice admitted.

'You sure you don't mind about Beth?' Her dad asked.

'What do you mean?'

'Meeting Beth, her being with me, it'll be strange, you sure you don't mind?'

'I'm happy for you, honestly.' The kitten's ears twitched and she stroked them. 'I'm glad you found someone to be with.' Her mind flashed to Jay but she dismissed it.

Her dad was silent for so long Alice wasn't sure if they'd lost connection. 'I'm sorry for leaving the way I did.'

'It's fine.' Alice reassured him. 'I understood.'

'I left you.'

'Dad, I was twenty. And you asked me to go with you.'

'But didn't insist when you said no.'

'I had the job in the restaurant.'

'It consumed you.' He sounded unhappy.

'It was what I needed at the time, what I needed for a long time.'

'But not what you need now?'

'I'm—' Alice closed her eyes, thinking of Jay's books, of rearranging the tables in the café, the zip wire today. 'I'm not sure what I need. But I'm sure I'll find out once I get to Thailand.'

After they'd said their goodbyes, Alice picked up her guidebook from the coffee table and curled up her feet, flicking through the pages, making notes against the places she wanted to visit. There was so much to do in Thailand, in a few months she'd be living a totally different life filled with even more adventures.

A life her mother would be proud of.

Chapter Twenty-Three

Why did wetsuits feel tighter every time you put them on? Wind whipped at her body as Alice simultaneously wriggled her bottom and shivered as she tried to get comfortable.

Jay pulled off his jumper and chucked it into the back of his truck, yanking the rest of his clothes off to join them. His chest was broad and strong with a trail of dark hair that dipped from his belly button downwards.

'You okay?' Jay asked.

'Sure.' Alice turned quickly and let Zeus nuzzle her hand. 'I'm glad you found Zeus.'

'Sorry we didn't get to swim last night.'

Alice heard the boot slam and Jay came to join her and damn, the man looked good in a wetsuit. All broad shoulders and long limbs which made her wonder what he looked like underneath the rubber, and didn't that sound odd?

'You missed out on dinner.'

'Zeus first, I get it, wouldn't have it any other way.' Alice nibbled her lip, forcing herself to confront the issue that had given her a sleepless night. 'Shame you wouldn't let me help look though, I'd have been happy to.'

'I should have, I'm sorry.' Zeus whined and nudged Jay's knee and Alice focused on the beach, as something in her chest ached. 'It was a mistake.' Jay continued. 'My mother can be… difficult.'

'How?'

'Ah, she's not great with new people, really shy, I didn't want to overwhelm her, I should have said.'

'Okay.' Alice nodded mollified. 'You should have, but I understand, it's nice you look out for her.'

Jay avoided her eyes and headed for the beach, calling Zeus. Alice left the car park, following him onto the sand, feeling the sun beat down on her back. It was a beautiful day. She watched as Jay picked up a stick and threw it to Zeus who bounded after it. The beach was long and sandy and it took a few minutes to get to the sea. She had to trot to catch up, and when she did, Jay was already watching the water.

'I checked the weather and the wind's steady and it's going to stay fine.' Jay looked at her wetsuit and catapulted his eyes to her face. 'Not warm enough for us to swim without one of these on though.'

'Is it ever?' Alice smiled, feeling the familiar bump of her heart as it sped up, the wave of nausea. 'I thought I was over this.'

Zeus ran towards the water and leapt in and then out again, barking at the waves as if they were living things. Alice buried her toes in the sand, aiming to ground herself. As she did, Jay moved in front, blocking her view. Faced with his chest her heart accelerated again, this time not because of fear.

Jay studied her. 'You're thinking again.'

Alice grimaced. 'I'll try to practise my vacant expression.' Funny how fear seemed to merge into anger so easily.

'Remember how much of this is in your mind.' His voice took on an almost hypnotic quality. 'I'm not saying you don't have valid reasons for being afraid: the dream, your mother's death, plus phobias can hit at all ages and I think your need for control and the fact that the sea is uncontrollable doesn't help. But if you fill your head with fear instead of fact, you're not going to get very far. We'll take it slow like last time, I'm not going to force you into the water, and I'm not going to fight with you either. Distraction isn't a long-term solution, even if it does work.' Jay looked unhappy. 'I won't always be around to irritate you.'

'I know.' But a big part of her didn't want to remember it.

'See if you can access that adrenaline junkie from yesterday.'

'She's still in the high ropes.'

Zeus bounded up and shook himself, making them both wet. He looked so pleased with himself, Alice smiled. 'Maybe he should enter the triathlon, pretend he's me?'

'I think the ears would give him away.'

'I wish I could be more like him though.'

'I don't,' Jay said, turning to smile at her. 'He's useless with invoices, just eats them.'

'I didn't realise you two had so much in common. On that subject, I've finished your books.' They'd been a great distraction after he'd left her to search for Zeus. 'Also, I called about the parking tickets: if you send proof that you volunteer on the lifeboat they'll waive them.'

'Seriously?'

Pride made her grin. 'It's my superpower.'

'Then thank you for saving me.' Jay grabbed her hand and tugged her towards the waves until their toes were practically touching the water. Alice stepped forwards. Her pulse jumped, but not so high, her heart hammered, but not so fast and the nausea had given way to an uncomfortable bubble in her throat.

Maybe she could do this?

'Close your eyes and feel the water stroking your ankles. Feels like feathers, doesn't it?' Jay asked.

'Yes.' Alice closed her eyes, holding his hand tightly.

'So, move a little bit further forwards, let the water stroke your legs, focus on the feeling. Waves can be gentle. Like someone's touching you?'

'It's like they're stroking me, I can feel it now.' The movement was slow, almost erotic. Alice let go of his hand.

'Breathe.' The waves glided over her skin, silky and soft like a lover's hand. 'It's almost at your knees.'

'I feel okay.' Alice giggled. 'I can't believe it.'

'Let's go a little further in.' Jay's voice deepened, making her think of candle-lit bedrooms and warm sheets.

'I'd like to try and swim.' Feeling brave Alice stepped forwards until the water reached her waist. A big wave hit, splashing water onto her face. The cold made her gasp. She must have made a sound because Jay grabbed her hand again and squeezed it.

'Want to head back?'

Alice shook her head. 'I'm not cold.' Her teeth chattered. 'Ignore that, it's not cold, and I'm not scared. I'm not, I'm just getting used to the water. I want to swim.' She still felt nervous, but somehow the paralysing fear had gone.

Jay didn't say anything, but he moved a little closer so their legs touched. Alice could feel the warmth of his skin against hers and the hair on his legs against her calves.

Jay turned and put a palm against her cheek, stepping forwards so he could look into her face. 'If I think we need to stop, we stop, no arguing, agreed?'

'Okay, but remember I'm going to be scared.' Alice pleaded. 'And it might take me a few tries, doesn't mean I need to stop. Tell me we won't give up just because you're worried about me?'

'I'll try not to drag you to shore unless you're actually drowning, but if I think you've had enough, we finish, okay?'

'Fine.' Alice folded her arms so he couldn't take her hand again. 'But you're treating me like a two-year-old.'

Jay's jaw clenched. 'If I were, you'd be paddling. You know what I do, I know this sea better than anyone and it's still a stranger to me.'

'Fine.' The word had a kick to it.

Jay jerked his head, acknowledging her bad mood. 'When you're ready, I want you to dip your shoulders into the water.'

Alice shivered, then stopped her teeth chattering by clamping them together.

'It'll help if you move.'

Alice bent her knees slowly, dipping down a couple of centimetres as her stomach bubbled a complaint.

'That's good.' Jay bent too, going lower so the water rolled over his shoulders. 'Move your arms, pretend you're swimming.'

Alice let herself go lower, felt the water trickle over her shoulders and into her wetsuit. The water pooled at the top and slid down between her breasts. The cold wasn't unpleasant, now she had stroking in her head she couldn't get it out. She moved her arms forwards and mimicked breaststroke.

'How do you feel?'

'Good.' The word hummed between her lips. Before he could ask, Alice closed her eyes and dipped her face and popped it back out again. 'It's freezing,' she spluttered, feeling him nudge a little closer.

'Want to stop?'

Alice waited for the panic attack but it didn't come. 'No.'

'Then let's go.' Jay pointed across her chest. 'We'll stay parallel to the beach so you don't get out of your depth and I'll swim beside you. If you want to stop at any point, you can.'

Zeus barked from the beach and Alice glanced back; even though the water hit just higher than her waist, he looked a long way off.

Alice dipped her shoulders before she could think any more and lifted her feet and suddenly she was swimming. They weren't in a good place because the waves were still breaking next to her, so she swam deeper taking care to keep Jay beside her. Her fingers felt cold but as she pumped the water she began to warm up, and while her stomach seemed to be all over the place, she didn't feel scared.

'You're enjoying it?'

'Once you forget about the cold, it's fine.' Alice swept her hands back and forth under the water. 'I still don't understand why this was so hard for me, it doesn't make sense.'

'Fear isn't always rational. I think that's enough for today. Let's go.'

Alice kicked her legs and angled herself back to shore. Zeus sat on the beach staring at them and she headed towards him. After a couple of long strokes she could stand, she let her feet sink into the sand and waded forwards with Jay beside her. When they reached the beach he grabbed her and kissed the top of her head.

'You were amazing.'

'I never thought I'd actually do it.' A tear tracked its way down her face, surprising both of them.

Jay unhooked his arms from around her so he could bend and look into her eyes.

'I'm fine.' Alice swiped the tear as another joined it. 'I think this is relief.'

Jay pulled her into a hug again with one arm and wiped away more tears. 'I think crying is a normal reaction.'

Alice sniffed, smiling as another tear trickled down her cheek. 'I'm going to be able to compete.'

Jay smiled. 'Never doubted it. Otherwise I'd have wasted a fortune on my entry.'

Alice grinned and Jay grinned back, all the while searching her face. Their eyes met and held and suddenly he was pulling her closer and she was reaching up. When his lips met hers Alice could taste salt – whether it was from the sea or her tears she didn't know, but she didn't care because it tasted just right. Jay kissed slowly around her lips as she linked her arms around his neck. He was so much taller she had to stand on her tiptoes. The beach felt cold but she didn't care because kissing Jay was warming her up. Every nerve fizzed and her good parts joined in. Jay tipped his head and deepened the kiss and she felt herself falling backwards so pressed herself harder against his body. The sensation felt odd, because they were both wearing wetsuits but the warmth was there, and the heat. She pushed her hands into his hair as he pulled her closer still, she felt his fingers on the neck of her wetsuit where the string dangled from the zip, felt a small tug before he dropped his hands and pulled back.

'If we're going to continue this, it had better not be here.'

'Okay.' Alice took his hand. 'Should we change first?'

'We could shower at mine.'

'I've got a change of clothes in your car.'

'You won't need them,' Jay promised, tugging her towards the car park.

Chapter Twenty-Four

'Bad idea,' Jay grumbled as he helped Alice into the truck, trying not to look at how the cheeks of her bum filled out the wetsuit as she slid up onto the seat.

A very bad idea.

Jay opened the back door and whistled for Zeus, who appeared from nowhere and jumped in before he shut it. He tried to calm his body as he walked to the driver's side, thumping the boot as he passed to make sure it had closed properly. He shut his eyes, determined to block out the vision of Alice as she'd looked up at him on the beach with those tears in her eyes.

She'd looked so happy and so... beautiful, and this was a terrible idea but his body was still walking to the other side of the truck, sliding into the seat and starting the engine and he couldn't seem to stop it.

Jay let the engine run as he looked forwards, watching the waves hit the beach. Usually a view like this, a situation like this, would have him gunning the engine but something seemed to be holding him back. Inside his head, Shaun laughed and called him an idiot.

'Everything okay?' Alice put a hand on his forearm, making more than goosebumps stand to attention.

'Sure,' he lied, releasing the brake and putting the pickup into reverse.

'Because if you're having second thoughts you can just take me home, forget that ever happened.'

Seriously? He let the pickup come to a stop. *She* was giving *him* a chance to back out? 'I'm sure.'

Alice raised an eyebrow as if to ask, *what the hell are we still doing here?*

'Are *you* sure? Because you're leaving in a few weeks and you don't strike me as the type of girl who'd… ' Jay left the sentence hanging.

Alice gave him a half-smile. 'I'm not sure I know what type of girl I am any more but I'm trying to be different.'

Well that cleared that up, clear as mud. 'Right.' The word came out in a rush. What was he doing? This was exactly what he'd told himself he shouldn't do again after Mel? Jay pushed the accelerator again, reversing before thumping the pickup into gear. 'Yours or mine?'

'Yours, I think Zeus will be happier.'

Jay heard the thump of a tail from the back and tried not to appreciate that she'd thought about his dog.

Alice sank back in her seat and looked out of the window. He'd checked the floor for parking tickets and receipts before he'd picked her up, he didn't want any more surprises – and maybe she was rubbing off on him? He'd even started filing his invoices in date order, which made this bad idea about a hundred times more dangerous.

They followed the road along the beach and had just turned a corner when Alice bolted forwards, almost hitting her head on the pickup window.

'What's wrong?'

'I—' Alice twisted in her seat tracking a car as it passed. 'I swear I saw Dan.'

'Dan?' Jealousy tickled his chest.

'Cath's boyfriend.' She dug around in her handbag and pulled out a mobile.

'Problem?' Jay pulled the pickup to a stop at a set of lights and studied her.

'I don't know.' Alice pouted at the phone. 'I'm sure Cath said he was away for a few more days.' She scrolled through some messages. 'Uh huh, he's in Birmingham, installing a kitchen in between parties.'

The lights changed and he nudged the pickup forwards. 'Maybe it wasn't him?'

Alice made a huffing sound and dropped the mobile back into her bag. 'I'll ask Cath, and you're right, maybe it just looked like him.'

'You still want to come to mine, you could call her?'

Alice thought about calling Cath for a beat and shook her head. Wisps of blonde hair escaped from her ponytail and framed her face making her look so pretty and vulnerable his hands tightened on the steering wheel.

'Are you trying to talk me out of this?' Alice sounded put out.

'No.' *God, no.* He pulled into a parking space outside his house and hopped out before she had a chance to ask again. What was wrong with him? He was making everything far too complicated, he should be thinking like a caveman.

Home. Hot woman. Sex. No strings. Yeah.

Jay opened the back and Zeus jumped down, heading for the door. Alice jumped down too and followed him without looking back. He dropped his eyes to her bum and felt his body tighten. Better. Now there wasn't enough blood left in his brain to think. Alice turned and smiled, still looking unsure, making him feel like an idiot. A woman like that shouldn't have doubts about the man she was with.

'This way.' Jay grabbed her hand, pulling her to the front door, then they followed behind Zeus until they were standing in the hallway staring at each other.

'I need to feed the dog,' he muttered. If he didn't, Zeus would be barking outside the door which wouldn't do much for the mood or concentration, and he wanted to concentrate.

A lot.

Alice looked down. 'Can I shower?'

'Yes.' Jay pointed to the stairs. 'There's a bathroom at the top, or an ensuite off my bedroom, I'll get you some towels.'

And now he sounded like his mother.

Jay fed Zeus in minutes and closed the door to the kitchen so the dog couldn't follow, then headed upwards and saw the bathroom door had been left open. He heard the spray of water so Alice was probably already inside. Making a quick decision he got towels, walked in, stripped off his clothes and joined her.

Alice squeaked as he entered, surprise turning to pleasure as her eyes flicked up and then down taking him in. Her hair had turned golden in the water and she had bubbles around her face, which he brushed off so they wouldn't go into her eyes. The minute his hand touched her he felt the jolt of attraction and almost had to step back to control himself.

'I borrowed your shampoo, hope you don't mind?' Alice blushed.

'I like the idea of you smelling like me, did you leave any?'

Alice picked the bottle up from the shelf and shook it before handing it over, bumping an elbow on his chest.

'Sorry.'

Jay edged closer brushing a knee across her leg, making her shudder. 'These showers are a little small for two.'

'I guess.' Alice tipped her chin and watched as he poured shampoo into his hand and rubbed it onto his head. The concentration in her eyes, the way she watched him, was erotic and he edged a little closer, enjoying the feel of her skin as it stroked his chest.

'Do you want to switch sides so you can rinse your hair?' she asked.

Jay didn't answer, but he did put the shampoo down before grasping her elbows and spinning them both round until he was under the spray. Her nipples brushed his chest but before he could do anything, she tipped her chin higher, went onto her tiptoes and pulled his head down for a deep kiss.

Alice hadn't made him think 'temptress' before. Sure, she was pretty and sexy and being around her made him want to pull her in for a kiss, but he'd never expected strength. Heat, sure, not power. The kiss surprised him, the unpredictability of it, so at odds with the invoice queen he'd gotten used to. Jay pushed his hands into her hair so he could change the angle of the kiss. Water pounded on his back as he took them deeper, pushing against her as she pushed back. Jay moved his leg in between hers, eased her against the wall of the shower, keeping them both under the spray so she didn't get cold – although there wasn't much chance of that with the heat between them.

'More,' Alice begged as she ran her hands through his hair, tugging it as he deepened the kiss. Jay slid his hands from her head to her shoulders, traced a finger down her back and felt her shiver as his hands cupped her bottom. Jay stroked her skin and she sighed, distracting him by moving expert fingers slowly over his shoulders, arms, hips and waist. He stopped them before they dipped lower by picking up her fingers and twining them with his, pinning them to her sides.

'Oh,' she purred as he ran his hands up her arms, leaving them pinned by nothing but her own unwillingness to let go.

'I've been waiting all day to do this, maybe since the first time I saw you on the beach looking bedraggled in that wetsuit.' Jay cupped her face, looking into her eyes, the desire he could see almost a tangible thing. 'Watching you move, swim, breathe and not being able to touch you, it's been driving me crazy.'

Before she could reply he brushed her lips again, kissing a path towards her ear. Alice reached for him as he began to move again kissing his way down her neck before peppering tiny kisses across her collarbone.

'Bed.' Jay whispered, moving upwards to nibble her ear. He ran his hands underneath her bottom and lifted; instinct must have made her wrap her legs around him. Jay got them out of the shower and picked up towels before heading towards his bedroom.

'Are you sure this is what you want?' Jay asked. He wasn't taking any chances because, as he spoke, he traced her lips with his tongue.

'Still deciding.' Alice teased.

Jay pulled back, his heart sinking. 'Second thoughts?'

Alice looked up at him and shook her head. 'No, just messing with you. It's the new me, I'm trying to lighten up.'

Jay laughed as he dropped to his knees and kissed her stomach, trailing kisses across the taught skin, taking time to explore her body. 'Funny.'

He nudged her gently until she fell onto the bed. She lay back for a minute, scanning his body slowly.

'What?'

'Nothing.' Alice blushed. 'You're beautiful.'

'Oh.' Touched, he moved towards her. 'Ditto, only you're better.'

Jay shifted until they lay facing each another. Alice reached out a hand to touch his chest, ran a fingernail from the dip in his neck downwards but he caught it before it got too low. She stretched out and he moved to touch a nipple, trailing his tongue around first one then the other while she moaned. His hand feathered from her waist, drawing lazy circles across her skin, and he was rewarded by goosebumps rising on her skin as her sensations heightened.

Jay moved lower, dipping a clever finger into the heart of her, and felt a strange flutter of pleasure when she jerked up to meet him. He caressed again, running the tip of his finger over the nub at her centre and she moaned.

'Hold that thought,' he whispered, kissing the tiny dip beneath her ear moving down to her stomach and lower still.

'What?' The word slid between her lips before she began to moan. 'Oh boy.' Her hands moved to fist through his hair as every inch of her body shuddered. Her hips jerked, moving in time with his tongue; teeth grazed and lips suckled, bringing her quickly to the edge.

'Oh.' Then she was gone.

Jay let her lay for a moment, enjoying the languor of her body, the warmth of her limbs, then moved to kiss her softly on the mouth. Alice trailed her tongue across his lips before kissing her way to his shoulder and pulling back. 'That was amazing, sorry I–'

'What?'

'… couldn't hold on.'

Jay leaned over to kiss her eyes, her cheeks. 'Good to hear, but I'm not finished with you yet.'

He bent to kiss her again, but she surprised him by pulling him towards her instead. Their skin brushed and she gently bit his lip as his body strained against her stomach, drifting her hands downwards she slowly eased him between her fingers.

And damn.

Jay looked into her face as she began to move her hands up and down, holding firm, exploring the hard, smooth skin. He groaned and his eyes drifted shut relaxing into pleasure. Gradually she trailed a finger upwards along the silky vein before circling a fingertip over the top, feeling the wet heat of his pleasure. He enjoyed the feel of her wrapped around him. She moved again and he met her, grasping her hands, pushing her down onto the bed underneath him until she was opening her thighs, welcoming him between.

'Protection.' He'd almost forgotten.

Alice gulped. 'Please tell me you have some.'

'In the bathroom.' Jay sprang up, ignoring the guilty niggle of what they'd almost done, grabbed some and headed back. He was inside her in a blink, stretching and filling. She sighed as he began to move, slowly at first, giving her time to build. Before she got swept up he increased the pace and felt her dig her nails into his back as she pushed herself upwards to meet him.

The climb didn't take long, but it was high. Jay stopped for a few moments on the edge waiting for her to join him. A sound tore from Alice's throat and he felt his muscles contract and suddenly he soared.

Later they lay side by side, Alice cuddled against his shoulder, a leg thrown across his thigh. Jay closed his eyes. This had been one of the best afternoons of his life. He felt relaxed and happy for the first time in forever – but with Alice determined to leave Castle Cove, he wondered how long it could last.

Chapter Twenty-Five

Alice giggled, and clasped Jay's hand tighter as they approached the fairground. She disconnected their fingers and pinched another hot chip from the open pack in his other hand.

'Thought you weren't hungry?' His voice rumbled in her ear, reminding her of earlier when he'd whispered a lot of sweet nothings in exactly that tone.

'I lied.' Alice grabbed another chip and ate it. Despite finishing off half the packet, her stomach grumbled.

'So you ready for your next heady adventure?' Jay drew them to a stop next to a queue snaking around boarding painted a garish pink and yellow that had turned almost luminous in the evening sunshine. Olly Murs pumped from nearby speakers, loud enough to pierce eardrums, although the screams of the passengers on the teacups outdid even that. Alice watched the twirling for a few moments and laughed.

'You were serious, this is our date?'

Jay shrugged, screwing up the empty chip packet and tossing it into a bin before grabbing her hand again. 'Teacups not exciting enough for you?'

'I think I can handle the change of pace, but I thought we were meant to have candyfloss,' she teased. Her stomach grumbled again reminding her she'd only eaten about fourteen chips between breakfast and now.

Jay grinned and scanned the stalls around them. 'Coming up, madam. Hold our place in the queue and I'll get some.'

'I'm fine, really.' Alice watched his retreating back, enjoying the way the denim of his jeans moulded his behind.

'Here.' Jay returned and thrust a stick in her hand. 'You'll need to eat that quick, not sure you'll be able to spin and hold onto it.'

'I dunno, you know I like to live dangerously.' Alice bit some off, licking her lips to mop up the sugar. 'Where's yours?'

'Here.' He bent and kissed her, making her insides swirl. 'Having fun?'

'Yes.'

The queue began to move and they followed, getting seated into a pink teacup. Jay paid and a frowning man confiscated the rest of her candyfloss, but not before Alice had taken another big bite.

'You'll need to hold on, these things can be dangerous.' Jay grinned and put his hands over hers on the wheel in the centre. 'Be ready, we're going to go fast.'

The music began to pump again. Alice didn't even know what it was because the bump and grind of the bass stopped her from being able to hear anything else, that and her laughter. She giggled as they span, feeling her insides open like a flower in sunshine. Her heart seemed to burst inside her and all the while she was watching Jay as his large hands worked the wheel, until he threw his head back as they span.

Jay looked so free, so happy, like something had lifted from his shoulders.

She blinked as the teacup sped up, as the lengthening queue and lights from other rides in the fairground flickered past. Faster. Alice smelled the sweet scent of the sea mixed with candyfloss and her stomach rolled and span, not unpleasantly, and not because of the ride. She could almost feel the emotions inside her release and expand, because she wasn't just hurtling somewhere, she'd already arrived.

The ride began to slow but her stomach continued to spin. Even as they left the teacup and headed into the crowds her head whirled with the implications of how she felt about Jay.

'Mate.' Shaun thumped his friend on the back, jerking her back to the present. He flickered his eyes across both of their faces before smiling. She didn't want to know what he'd read in their expressions but he looked amused.

'You not working?' Jay asked.

'Taking a quick break, I was meeting a girl.'

'Stood up?'

His eyes narrowed. 'We didn't really click. I bumped into your mum earlier.'

'Here?'

'Walking with a man. I know him from somewhere, but didn't catch his name.'

Shaun looked around, glaring at couples as they passed.

'Were they definitely together?' Jay asked.

'I was about to ask his intentions, but your mum gave me one of her looks and I chickened out,' Shaun joked, turning to Alice. 'You still okay to work tomorrow?'

'Looking forward to it.' Alice hadn't felt like that for the last few years when she'd been heading for a shift at the restaurant. 'You moved those soft drinks yet?'

Shaun flashed a smile. 'Waiting for your help.' He checked his watch. 'Ah, speaking of the Anglers, I'd better get back or someone's going to kill me. See you both.' Shaun patted Jay on the back but his friend didn't react.

They walked past a couple more stalls in silence.

'You worried about your mum?' Alice asked eventually.

Jay's forehead creased for a brief second before it smoothed out. 'Not really. She'll be fine, sounds like she's got a friend.'

'You want to look for her?'

'No.' His tone was sharp.

'I used to worry about my mum sometimes,' Alice said softly, wanting to recapture the closeness from earlier.

Jay remained silent as they wandered towards the big wheel and didn't take her hand, even when she let it brush against his. She bit her bottom lip.

'You want to go on anything else?' Jay pointed at the big wheel.

'No.' Fighting her gloomy mood she pointed to the North Star. 'Didn't think I'd see that so early in the day.'

'Home.' The corner of his mouth lifted.

'You ever think of leaving Castle Cove?'

'Why would I want to?'

Alice's heartbeat seemed to stall. Something seemed to have changed between them but she didn't understand what. She shook her head, confused. 'Oh, no reason, no reason at all.'

Chapter Twenty-Six

Alice had never seen the Anglers look so quiet. She leaned on the front of the bar and wiped the surface with a cloth, buffing a shine in the oak until her reflection appeared in the polish.

'I appreciate you working hard.' A door closed and Shaun came from the back room. 'But you're making me feel like a slave driver, and my customers tend to frown on me working the staff into an early grave.'

Shaun raised an eyebrow at the bar and scanned the rows of shiny pint glasses next to the sink. 'I'm going to have to start wearing sunglasses inside.' He knelt down and checked the front of the bar. 'And you moved all the soft drinks without me?'

'It's been quiet.' Alice avoided his eyes and placed a couple of glasses back on the shelving above the bar.

'There's a carnival down the coast tonight, I think all of my regulars are there.' Shaun looked around the room. 'It looks great in here, much more organised. Make sure you take a break soon.'

'I've only just got here.'

'Two hours ago.'

Alice turned to check the bar to see if she could find any customers but there was no-one waiting. 'I'll take one in a minute.'

Shaun watched her buff the oak again. 'You seen Jay yet, he normally pops in?'

'Nope.' Alice spotted a huge cobweb dangling from the ceiling above the till. 'Do you have a stepladder?'

Shaun followed her gaze. 'That can wait.'

'It's annoying.' Maybe she could pull up a chair and use the tea towel?

'He likes you,' Shaun muttered.

'What?'

'Jay.' Shaun looked uncomfortable. 'He likes you.'

'I—' Alice blushed. 'I don't know what to say to that, besides I'm not even sure you're right.'

'I'm telling you he does. He's pretty closed down, I'm seeing a new side to him when he's with you.'

'So?'

'It's odd he's not been in yet today, I know he's not on a shout. Have you guys had a fight?' Shaun gazed at her, his green eyes assessing. Alice liked him, she decided, there was a lot to be said for a man who stood up for his friends.

'Not that I know of.' Alice picked up a glass so she could get herself some water.

'He doesn't open himself up easily.'

'You warning me off?' Alice leaned a hip against the bar, sipping from the glass, fighting the urge to smile. Yes, she liked him a lot. 'I love that he brings out your protective streak, says a lot about a person if they do that.'

Shaun looked embarrassed. 'We've known each other a long time, and he's a good customer. I'll miss the sales if he stops coming to the pub, might even go under.'

Alice snorted.

The pub door swung open and Shaun frowned, his eyes darting towards the kitchen area.

'Hi,' Cath's voice sang as she headed for the bar.

'I've got stuff to do, see you later,' Shaun said, disappearing through the door into the back and slamming it shut behind him.

'He was in a hurry.' Cath pulled herself up on a bar stool looking unhappy. Her usually messy curls were pulled back in a ponytail and her face had that pinched look of someone who hadn't slept.

'He said he had things to do.' Alice stopped scanning her friend's face. 'Cath, you don't have to tell me but—' Her eyes darted towards the door.

'Shaun?' Cath pouted, the usual easy sparkle was definitely missing from her face. 'Can I have a red wine first please? I'm going to need alcohol for this conversation.'

'I've never seen you drink red.' Alice poured a merlot and put it on the bar.

'Dan says it's dull to always drink the same thing, my parents always do.' Cath picked up the glass and took a sip, trying to hide the grimace unsuccessfully. 'A pint of lager and a gin and tonic with one slice of lemon twice a week, on a Friday and Saturday, unless Christmas falls on a different day.'

'You and Shaun?' Alice reminded her. 'Why did you split up?'

'His idea.' Alice saw a raw flash of hurt on Cath's face before she hid it.

'Why's he so angry then?'

Cath rolled her eyes. 'He asked me to marry him.'

Alice waited.

'Marriage is… so middle aged.' Her face darkened. 'I never said I wanted that. We hadn't talked about it and he hadn't even bought a ring, said we'd wait for the sales,' Cath huffed.

'It was a shock?'

'Huge, it was huge. When I didn't jump up immediately and say yes, he got annoyed.'

'What happened?'

'We said a lot of things, I said things I probably shouldn't have and he stormed off.' Cath pushed her glass further away, almost hitting the edge of the bar. 'And that was that, the end of that great love affair, which doesn't say much for it considering how long we were together.' Her laugh was hollow. 'He didn't even fight for me, just walked out and never came back.'

'That's… I'm sorry.'

Cath fumed. 'People should be flexible in life, don't you think? Look at you, going out to conquer the world, nothing boring about you.'

'I–' Alice stalled. 'That's not true, I'm not sure I even want to go any more Cath, I like it here. You're the first person I've admitted that to and now I'm feeling guilty, my mum would be so disappointed.'

'Would she? If you're happy I'd say she'd be proud. I think you should stay, great thing about life, you get to choose. Lots of people here who'd like it if you changed your mind.'

'No. I promised myself I'd do it. I'd let more than Mum down if I don't go, I'll let myself down. I'm not going to have many adventures if I stay here for the rest of my life.' Alice picked up her cloth again.

'You sure about that?'

'Definitely.' Alice nodded as if she needed to prove it to herself. 'Want something else?' Cath's half-full glass was practically on the other side of the bar.

'Please, can I have white this time?'

Alice filled a new glass. 'Heard from Dan?'

'Mmmmm, he's stuck in Birmingham, leaking bath, would you believe, although I'm thinking it's just an excuse for another party.'

'Who's he staying with?' Alice asked, her tone idle.

'A mate, Archie something. We had a chat and he seemed nice, even gave me his mobile number in case I can't get in touch with Dan, his signal's patchy there apparently.'

'In Birmingham?'

'He'll be back this weekend, it's our ten-month anniversary soon. Why?'

'No reason.' Alice shook her head looking for an excuse. 'Might need some plumbing done, leaky tap.'

'I popped round earlier, I'd have offered to take a look. Not sure I'd be any help but I could at least fill Dan in on the problem.'

'I must have been out cycling.'

'Again? How's the training going?'

'Great, I'm there with the running, and the cycling is easier.' Now she'd conquered the swimming she'd definitely finish the triathlon without embarrassing herself. 'Were you looking for me?'

Cath avoided her eyes. 'Just thought I'd say hi.'

Music started on the jukebox, startling both of them.

'Gayle.' Cath turned and hopped from the bar stool, heading to greet a colourfully dressed woman about to take a seat in the corner of the pub. Aged somewhere in her fifties, she had greying hair, and looked oddly familiar.

Maybe they'd met in the Castle café?

A long floaty skirt swirled around her legs as she walked to greet Cath. Ben Campbell from Little Treasures hovered in the background looking uncomfortable.

'Hi Ben. Alice, have you met Jay's mum?' Cath headed back to the bar with the couple.

Ahhhh. 'No, I knew you looked familiar, you have the same colour eyes.'

'We do.' The woman smiled. 'I'm Gayle. I think I might have seen you before too, I work in the antique shop sometimes with Ben. Alice, isn't it?'

'Yes.' Hadn't Jay once told her his mother was awkward around new people? Confused, she checked for signs of shyness but couldn't find any. 'Can I get you something to drink?'

'Half a pint of Doombar and a white wine spritzer please,' Ben said.

Gayle studied Alice, a gentle smile playing on the edges of her mouth. 'I'm so pleased to meet you, Jay's told me absolutely nothing about you but I've known you were coming to Castle Cove for a while.'

'Oh?'

'She reads tea leaves.' Ben filled in before Alice could ask. 'It's good to see you again.' Ben held out a hand and Alice put the drinks she'd poured in front of him before shaking it. 'Gayle's been dying to take a look at you.'

'Why?' Flustered, Alice took the money, taking the opportunity to collect herself as she headed for the till.

'I wanted to meet you, I hoped we'd catch up the other night when Zeus went missing, but Jay said you had to get home?'

Alice felt her stomach slide into the floor. 'Yes, of course.' She reached for the cloth but stopped herself polishing the bar.

'You've got my son in a spin, not that he'd admit it.' Gayle's blue eyes pinned her in place.

'I'm… sorry?'

'Don't be silly.' His mother waved a hand. 'It's about time someone got to him, he's had it easy with women all his life.' Her expression darkened. 'Not so easy with everything else I suppose, but I like that you're making him work for you, that means he won't get bored.'

'I think you've misunderstood, he's helping me train for the triathlon.'

Gayle sipped her spritzer. 'You like Castle Cove?'

'Yes.' Alice relaxed a little and leaned against the bar as the music on the jukebox flipped to a Nina Simone track. 'I used to visit when I was younger, it hasn't changed much.'

Gayle smiled, her sharp blue eyes searching Alice's face. 'I expect it hasn't, and you're working here, and at the café too?'

Her cheeks warmed. 'Yes, Jay's talked about me?'

'I pick stuff up.'

'How about you, have you always lived around here?'

The older woman's face clouded. 'We moved here just before I had the boys, my husband… ' She paled. 'Jay's dad, loved the sea and wanted to settle near to it.'

Ben squeezed her shoulder. 'He left soon after Steve died.'

'Steve?'

'Jay's brother.'

'His brother?' Alice felt sick. 'I didn't know, I'm sorry.'

'No need to apologise, Jay doesn't like to talk about it.' Gayle looked resigned. 'Steve was three years younger.' Her eyes clouded and Alice thought she might say something else but the moment passed and she smiled suddenly. 'Are you coming to the beach on Sunday? I asked Ben to join us and I wondered if Jay had mentioned it?'

'Which beach?'

'Where Steve died. Jay likes to go every year on the anniversary.' Gayle's voice lowered. 'It's been ten years and it still feels like yesterday.' Her hand shook as she picked up her glass and took a sip.

'I'm not sure it gets easier,' Ben said.

'Ah, yes.' Gayle linked their fingers. 'Ben's wife died of cancer two years ago. We were friends, Mary asked me to look out for him, I think she knew.'

'Mary always liked you.'

'Dan was in the same class as Steve at school.' Cath joined in changing the subject. 'He says he had a wicked sense of humour.'

Gayle beamed. 'I always said he should have been on the stage, he was always so different from Jay, so much lighter.' Her expression darkened. 'Jay took too much on his shoulders, even as a boy. I used to think it was my fault, but I think it's just the way he's built, he feels guilty about Steve's death.'

Alice poured herself a glass of wine and took a couple of large gulps. 'Why?'

'Jay was meant to meet Steve that day. He arrived late.'

'What happened?' Cath asked. 'I never really knew.'

'His brother was messing around on the beach, jumping rocks, he fell, hit his head and—' She shrugged. 'Jay took it hard, he didn't talk for two weeks. Of course he found him, I could never get over how that must have been. That's not an image any seventeen-year-old should see.'

'Seventeen?' Alice sighed. 'No wonder he wants to save everybody.'

'Smart girl. You should come on Sunday, we're going to the beach, to walk, and remember him. Jay's booked a table here for lunch, maybe you could change the booking to four?'

'Ah—' Alice began to polish the bar. 'I think if Jay wanted me there, he'd invite me, we're just friends.' The lead weight in her chest proved it.

Gayle raised an eyebrow. 'I'm sure he'd love you to come.'

'I think the offer needs to come from him.'

Gayle studied her. 'Do you have any tea, dear?'

'Um, sure, there's some out back.' Alice pointed to the almost full spritzer. 'You want it now?'

'Not for me.' Gayle chuckled. 'I'd love to read your leaves.'

'Oh, I don't think—'

Behind her the door thumped making Alice jump. She turned as Shaun stumbled into the bar looking white and unsteady.

'Bugger, bugger, bugger,' Shaun said.

The blue tea towel wrapped around his hand was soaked with red, and drops of blood dripped and bounced on the floor. His jeans were stained red and even his shoes looked wet.

'What's wrong?' Alice took his arm. 'You need to sit, here. What did you do?'

She pushed him onto the floor and pressed a hand to his head feeling unsteady. 'Head between your knees, now, I did first aid training at the restaurant. Not much good at it though, blood makes me queasy.'

'Ow, tell me about it.' Shaun moved his hand out of the way as more blood dripped from the towel, but he let himself be guided downwards.

'What did you do?'

'How bad is it?' Cath dropped to her knees beside them.

'It's nothing.' Shaun's voice was gruff. 'I'm fine.'

Cath nudged Alice out of the way so she could see. 'It would serve you right if I let you bleed to death, lucky for you I'm far too nice a person to let that happen and unlike some, I don't hold a grudge, now show me.'

Cath unwrapped the tea towel gently, exposing a large, deep gash across Shaun's thumb, two fingers and palm. Blood leaked from the cut and dripped on the floor. 'What were you doing?'

'I went to the cellar to get some beer,' Shaun grumbled from between his legs. 'Fell over some broken glass I've been meaning to clear up, hit my head. I just need to sit for a while, there are plasters in the medicine cabinet.'

Cath snorted. 'This is too deep to treat with a plaster, you need to go to the hospital. How's the head?'

'I'm fine,' Shaun growled. 'Don't need anything.'

'Sure you are, you could probably hit that head with a sledge hammer and not make a dent, which is why I'm driving you to the hospital myself. Maybe one of the pretty nurses can knock some sense into you? Failing that, it'll make my Friday evening to watch them sew you up, maybe they'll do it without painkillers if I ask nicely.'

'Wouldn't put it past you,' Shaun grumbled but didn't say no.

'What can I do?' Alice asked.

'Stay here, lock up if I'm not back?' Shaun said. 'And if I don't come back, make sure you call the police and check I made it.'

'Sure you want to give her ideas?' Alice asked.

'Ignore him.' Cath put a hand on her shoulder. 'Blood always makes him grumpy, actually, scrub that.' She stood up. 'Everything makes him grumpy, it's part of his charm, or so he used to tell me, back when we were talking.' She rolled her eyes. 'I'm going to need to pop home. If I run, I'll be there and back in less than ten minutes. I'll fetch the car, good job I didn't drink any more of that wine. I'll check if there's another tea towel, or maybe a bandage out back first, I don't want him to bleed on the upholstery before I dump his body in the sea. Sharks are attracted to blood, right?'

'The sea around Castle Cove isn't warm enough for sharks. There's a medicine cabinet in the bathroom upstairs,' Shaun directed. 'Don't touch anything else.'

'If memory serves, I'd need a pair of rubber gloves if I wanted to touch anything in your house.'

'You say that now but that never stopped you from touching *me*.'

Cath blushed and disappeared through the door leaving an uncomfortable silence.

'We can drive?' Gayle said eventually. 'If you'd rather someone else took you, Shaun?'

'No.' Shaun shook his head looking unhappy. 'We can put up with each other for the length of time it takes to get to hospital. I was only joking about her doing away with me, that's not her style, she's more likely to nag me to death.'

Cath reappeared holding a medical box. 'Now you're giving me ideas, I can work with that.' She turned to Gayle. 'You don't need to ruin your date. I'll take Prince Charming to casualty, it won't take me long. Besides you two look like you've got better plans, mine were pretty non-existent.'

'Makes a change,' Shaun growled. 'You spend most of your time out these days.'

Cath sighed, kneeling down, grabbing his arm and gently unwrapping the tea towel again. 'It's called having fun, you should try it, we weren't all put on this earth to just work.' She wrenched open the top of the medicine tin and pulled out a pack of wipes, tore the packaging and yanked one out.

'Ow, ow, bugger, bloody hell woman.' Shaun tried to pull his hand back as she dabbed the cut.

'It's just an antibacterial wipe, it'll sting,' Cath's voice sang and the edge of her mouth curled.

'Thanks for the warning.'

'Seems neither of us is very good at those.' Cath narrowed her eyes. 'I'll apply some gauze and a bandage next so prepare yourself; that should hold until we get to the hospital, you really did a number on yourself.'

'It was an accident. Not that it's got anything to do with you.'

'I'll be the one letting them know what you did at the hospital if you faint from lack of blood. I wonder if they'll give you a tetanus?' Her voice held just the right amount of glee, but she continued to administer the gauze and bandage with gentle fingers, carefully wrapping it round his hand so she didn't hurt him. Shaun didn't even look up when she tied it off. 'Do you feel well enough to move while I get the car, or would you rather stay here on the floor?' Cath asked gently.

'Floor.' Shaun dropped his head to his knees again. 'Alice, can you call Jay, ask him to help you tonight?'

'Not sure I'll need it.'

'I don't like the idea of you here by yourself.'

'You fight it out while I'm gone.' Cath got up and brushed her knees with her hands. 'I won't be long.' She catapulted out from behind the bar, grabbed her bag from beside Gayle and ran through the door.

'Maybe we should make him some sweet tea, that's good for shock.' Gayle said.

'Bugger that, I'd rather have a beer, besides, I know you just want to read the leaves and I've told you a hundred times we're not getting back together.'

'We'll see, dear.' Gayle smiled.

'The bleeding seems to have stopped.' Alice bent to check the bandage. 'I'm not sure you should have anything to eat or drink if they're going to stitch you up, and I'd say they will, it looks deep.'

'Just a scratch, I've seen worse. I'll probably be in a cab back here in an hour.'

'I doubt Cath will leave you without a way of getting home.'

Shaun snorted. 'I'm sure she's got better things to do than wait for me, the boyfriend's probably got a party lined up.'

'He's in Birmingham,' Alice confided.

'Really?' Shaun perked up until he looked at his hand again. 'Stupid thing to do, I'm on call tomorrow.'

'I'm sure Jay can cover.'

Status Quo blasted out of the jukebox suddenly making Alice's ears ring. She scanned the pub but it was still empty.

'Can you turn that down please, my head's thumping. How long will she be?'

Alice switched off the music. 'It's not far and Cath was running.'

'That woman's never run anywhere in her life.'

Gayle's expression was filled with understanding. 'Anything you need?'

'Beer,' Shaun grumbled.

'Apart from that.'

Shaun sighed deeply. 'I'm getting an insight into life on the other side, I might be a bit more sympathetic next time I'm on a rescue.'

The pub door slammed and Cath reappeared looking red-faced and sweaty. 'Is he ready to leave or has he passed out?' She peered over the bar.

'Sorry to disappoint but I'm fine.' Shaun lifted his head. His skin looked pasty now, almost green and Cath paled.

'You were never good with blood,' she said. 'Or people, you're not great with them either.'

'Only certain people.' Shaun put his good hand on the floor to lever himself up.

'Are you two going to make it to the hospital without murdering each other?' Alice put her hands on her hips. 'Or do you need a chaperone?'

'We'll be fine.' Shaun said as she helped him to his feet. 'I promise not to murder her without calling you first, I'll need an alibi.'

'I won't give you one, neither will Jay.' Alice poked him in the chest. 'Sure you can make it to the car?'

'I'm parked outside on double yellow lines, you'd better move before I get a ticket.' Cath headed for the door.

'Stop fretting woman, I'll pay it if you do.'

'You think they'll be okay?' Ben said as the door slammed shut.

'They'll be fine. Young love,' Gayle sighed and put her hand over his. 'Don't you remember how much fun it was to argue?'

Ben smiled. 'Mary and I had some good fights.'

'Maybe we need to have a tiff, making up is fun?'

Ben blushed, then picked up his half and downed it. 'I'm hungry, are you hungry?'

'I could eat.' Gayle laughed. 'Of course, I'm sure if I try hard enough I'll find something wrong with the food.'

'Or the company, I can be boring.'

'Oh good.' Gayle hopped from the bar stool. 'Maybe you could tell me about the committee meeting at the golf club, that ought to do it. Alice dear, will you be okay on your own?'

'Of course.'

'You'll call Jay?' Gayle looked at her expectantly.

'Sure, if it gets busy, but I don't think I'm going to be rushed off my feet.'

Gayle fixed her with a blue-eyed stare. 'Call anyway, I'm sure he'd love the company, and don't forget about the beach, this Sunday at eleven o'clock.'

'I'll wait for Jay to ask me.'

Alice already knew he wouldn't.

Chapter Twenty-Seven

It wasn't every day you were greeted by a gold lamp. Alice had seen it as she'd approached her house, squinting her eyes under the dim street lights, but it wasn't until she'd hit the doorstep that she recognised it.

'My lamp.' Tears pricked her eyes as she approached.

Meow. The kitten jumped from behind a pot and wound itself around her legs like a Triffid.

'Did you see who left it?' she asked, lifting the tag hanging from the gold stem.

Because, sod romance,
every girl needs an ugly lamp in her life.
Love Cath xxx

'It's not ugly.' Alice giggled, opening the door before wrestling it inside. The stand banged against the door frame and walls, chipping out bits of paint she'd probably curse and then touch up later.

The kitten followed her into the sitting room as she shoved things aside and placed it to the right of the fireplace.

'There.' Alice stood back to admire it, feeling a curl of warmth in her belly. 'Perfect.' A tear tracked down her cheek but she didn't brush it away, instead she followed the kitten into the kitchen and fed it, then placed the dirty bowl in the sink, fighting the urge to wash it. Alice fished out her mobile and Cath answered on the second ring.

'Thanks for my present.' The words gushed out before she remembered her friend was probably still at the hospital. 'Sorry, how's it going?'

Cath laughed. 'As I predicted, Shaun needs stitches and we're waiting for someone to do it. I offered to bop him over the head with my handbag and do it myself but the nurse said it would be a shame to get blood on it.' Cath giggled.

'I told you not to wait.' Shaun grumbled in the background, making Alice grin.

'I told you I want to watch while they stitch you up, not often you get this kind of opportunity.'

Shaun snorted.

'Seriously, are you okay?' Alice asked.

'I'm fine.' Cath snickered, sounding like a teenager. 'I might be late to the café in the morning, depends on what time I get home.'

'I can handle it.'

'Is Jay with you?'

'No.' Alice headed for the front room and switched the lamp on and off, enjoying the soft light it threw across the room. It would be cosy here in the winter, she thought with a pang. 'It was quiet in the pub and I didn't want to bother him.'

'I don't think he'd have minded.' Cath's voice softened. Then Alice heard the sound of heels on the floor, before Cath spoke again, her voice lowered. 'I've moved so we've got some privacy from big ears, we both know where his loyalties lie, you all right?'

'Of course.'

'It's not what Gayle said, about Steve?'

'No.' Alice brightened her voice, 'I just didn't need to bother him.'

'You didn't know? I'm sorry, I never thought to tell you about Steve. I thought Jay would have.'

Alice leaned against the fireplace. 'He didn't tell me about his brother, but no reason why he would.' Even she could hear the hurt in her voice.

'Maybe he didn't want to share because you're leaving?'

Alice bit her lip. 'Not sure that's an excuse.'

'It's hard to get close to people you know you're going to lose.'

'You don't think I'm being fair?'

'Jay's a grown up, he knows the score, I just wonder if he's protecting himself from getting hurt?'

'That's ridiculous, he doesn't have feelings for me.' Alice let the words hang in the air.

'That's not what Shaun said.'

'You talking in between insults?'

'I'd forgotten how easy he is to talk to,' Cath admitted. 'I forgot myself a couple of times and we actually had a conversation without threatening to kill each other.'

'Novel.'

'We have a lot in common.' Cath's voice lowered. 'And he's funny, not as funny as Dan, or as much fun, but—'

'You're confused?'

'I don't know.'

'Having second thoughts?'

'No, of course not, I want to have fun, that's what makes me happy. I want Dan, Shaun was a lot of things but he wasn't fun.'

'You heard from Dan?'

'No, but he promised he'd be home by tomorrow, I'll hear before then.'

'Good.' Alice bit her lip.

'How did you get home?' Cath asked eventually.

'Walked, it's not far.'

'Jay would have a coronary if he knew you'd done that.'

'I'm in one piece, admiring my lamp and trying to figure out how I can get it into a backpack.'

Cath laughed. 'I think you might have to leave it behind.'

'Thank you.' There was a tremor in Alice's voice. 'I owe you.'

'Don't be a ninny. Honestly Ben couldn't wait for an offer, and Gayle helped me talk him down. He practically rugby tackled me when I threatened to leave without taking it off his hands, I got a total bargain.'

'I know you can't afford it.'

'Dan's working so much at the moment I'll be rolling in it soon. Hang on a sec, Shaun wants something.'

Alice waited while her friend walked back, she heard the crash of a trolley in the background and the rumble of voices.

'Where is she?' Alice heard him ask.

'Home.'

'With Jay?'

'She didn't call him.'

'Why not?' Shaun's voice raised above the rattle of trolleys in the background.

'I'm fine,' Alice promised. 'Seriously, tell Shaun I'm too tired for company and I've got my new lamp to ogle. You don't need to worry about what time you'll be home either. I can handle everything in the morning at the café, if anyone annoying comes in I've always got the ice cream.'

Cath chuckled.

'Thanks again for the lamp, it's probably the nicest present anyone's ever bought me, you're making it very hard to imagine life away from Castle Cove.'

The kitten jumped onto the sofa and sniffed her jeans before curling into a ball.

'Uh huh, looks like we're up.' Cath said suddenly. 'I'll text you later, let you know when I'll be in.'

The connection severed and Alice stroked the kitten and lay her head against the sofa ignoring the nagging ache in her chest. She must have dozed off, because it only felt like seconds later when she was woken by a hammering on the door. She stumbled to the hall rubbing her eyes and opened it.

'You didn't even know it was me,' Jay grumbled. 'Surely living in London taught you to check before you open the door, I could have been anyone.'

'I knew it was you,' Alice murmured, standing back as he swept inside and marched into the kitchen. 'No-one else in Castle Cove would be banging on my door after midnight, especially not so loudly.'

Jay stared at her, looking annoyed.

'You want a drink?'

'Sure, something soft please.'

Alice pulled a bottle of water from the fridge, and handed it to him.

'Shaun rang from the hospital.'

'Is he okay?'

'All stitched up.' Jay sipped the drink without looking at her. 'He asked you to call me so I could help lock up the pub?'

'I did it myself.'

His eyes narrowed. 'Something wrong?'

'Nope. Where's Zeus?' Alice kept expecting the dog to leap out and sniff her shoes.

'In the truck, I came to check on you.'

'Don't know why. I'm fine.'

His eyes leapt to the sink, then he put his water down and squirted washing-up liquid on the cat bowl and wiped it with a cloth under the tap. 'You sick?'

'No.' Alice grabbed the bowl from the counter and dried it. 'You don't need to do my washing up.'

'Is this because you're leaving?'

'No.'

'You regretting sleeping with me yesterday then?' His hand flexed as he picked up the bottle.

'Not at all.' Alice had to stop herself from putting a hand on his arm. 'You seemed a bit distracted at the fairground, I thought I'd give you some space.'

'Even if I was distracted, I still would have helped you shut the pub.'

Alice pulled open the dishwasher and began to unload it, wanting to keep her hands busy. 'I knew you'd come to my rescue if I needed it.'

Jay bent to help. Picking up a plate she was already holding, he looked into her eyes. 'Not just because you needed it, because I wanted to.' He stepped closer, removed the tea towel from her hand and put it on the kitchen counter before bending to kiss the side of her neck.

'Don't you need to take Zeus home?' Her voice came out husky.

Jay stepped backwards. 'You want me to leave?'

'No.' The force of her reaction surprised her. 'You can bring him in if you like?'

Jay disappeared from the kitchen without answering and she leaned against the counter and closed her eyes. This was a bad idea. A terrible idea. She was leaving in a few weeks and she'd already fallen for him, despite the fact that he'd kept so many secrets from her. One more night together would only cement her feelings and make leaving harder.

The front door slammed and within seconds Zeus hit the kitchen wagging his tail. As soon as he spotted the open back door he shot through it.

'So…' Jay stepped in front of her again. 'You were going to tell me what's wrong?'

'I'm fine, I realise this will come as a shock, but I don't need you to rescue me every night. I've been alone for a lot of years.'

'Redundant already.' Jay moved closer. 'I wonder if I can think of any other ways to be useful?'

Alice rolled her eyes, feeling the heat of his body down to her toes. 'The tap in the bathroom's leaking.'

His lips curled into a slow smile. 'I was thinking of something a little more… intimate.' Jay dipped his head and she could feel hot breath on her neck and her own caught.

Jay moved closer and his lips touched her collarbone and eased across to the centre before moving to the other side, making her heart hammer.

'You need to be taller,' Jay teased.

'I'm sure there are plenty of women – *whoa*.'

Jay picked her up and placed her on the kitchen counter before stepping in between her legs.

'That's better.' Jay moved until their noses almost touched. 'You going to tell me why you didn't call?'

Alice pursed her lips; his eyes dipped and caught on the movement. 'Nope.'

'Is it something to do with when we were at the fair?' His voice deepened. Could you conjure the taste and smell of chocolate with a sound? The man had skills.

'I don't think so.' Alice slid her eyes from his and focused on a smudge on the kitchen cupboard.

Jay ran his lips over hers, hijacking her attention again. 'You seem a little put out.'

'I – *ahhhhhh*.' He moved his mouth up to her ear and nibbled, making everything between her head and toes launch into the 'Hallelujah Chorus'.

'I'm thinking about when I leave.' Her voice squeaked as he continued working his way down under her neck. She tipped her head back then let out a low hum as he eased forwards inching her bottom closer to the edge of the worktop.

'You were frowning.' His hands moved under her t-shirt, stroking coarse fingers across soft skin, then he pushed it up and over her head before she had a chance to stop him.

'Ah, well.' Unable to stop herself, Alice slid her hands across the hard planes of his stomach, gliding them upwards across his chest. 'Travelling's a very serious business.' Her voice came out on a low whisper. 'You know, passports, money.'

'Condoms.'

'What?' Alice pulled back.

'In my pocket.'

'Oh.' Alice eased her fingers round and pulled one out setting it on the counter, before pushing his t-shirt over his head. 'Are those for me to pack?' She leaned back to admire his perfectly formed abs and the trail of dark hair that disappeared into his jeans.

'No.' Jay's voice sharpened as he pulled her forwards so their skin touched. 'Not a chance, have you considered staying?'

His hands moved across her back, sliding round to the clasp on her jeans, un-popping the button and zip. She countered by doing the same: at this rate they were going to be naked in seconds… he lifted her bottom and pulled down her underwear and jeans and pushed his way between her legs again, the rough denim rubbed in all the right places and she pushed closer. Okay, this wasn't going to plan at all.

'Staying?' Alice garbled the word feeling like an idiot, but at the same time something in her chest lifted.

Jay nodded. 'In Castle Cove?'

Alice pulled back, looking into his face. Jay's eyes had darkened to a deep blue reminding her of a stormy night.

She bit her lip. 'Why would I want to stay?'

'Because you're happy here?'

'I've got plans.' Her voice wobbled uncertainly.

'Plans can't change?'

'I suppose.' Her brain fought with her heart as she considered. 'Or you could come with me, at least for a while?'

Jay was shaking his head before she'd finished speaking. 'I can't leave.'

'Why?'

He moved back just a little, but she could feel the retreat. 'There's Zeus.'

'Right,' she agreed. 'Shaun or your mum couldn't have him for a few months?'

'There's my business, my mum, the lifeboat.' Jay frowned. 'I'm needed here.'

Alice fought the desire to tell him she needed him too. 'You're right, that's a lot to leave.'

'You could stay longer, see if you like it in Castle Cove?'

'I like it already.'

'Then stay.' Jay traced a finger across her lips, leaving a trail of fireworks.

'You make it hard to say no.'

'Then don't.' His fingers moved downwards to her collarbone again, fluttering further down her chest and she shivered.

'I've made a lot of promises to myself.' Her voice came out husky.

'You've made plenty of changes already, your life is nothing like it was a few months ago.'

Alice bit her lip. 'I hadn't thought of it like that.'

'Wasn't a lot of this about completing the triathlon, proving you could, doing it for your mum?' Jay continued, tipping her chin so he could look into her eyes.

'Yes, and travelling, having adventures.'

'Did your mum travel?'

Alice shook her head. 'Not after she had me. She did a lot of other things, filled her life.'

'Like you have here?'

Alice sighed, confused. 'I suppose.'

Jay watched her.

'I do want to stay,' Alice said eventually, feeling the truth of it as the words flooded out. 'I've been thinking about it for a while. I'd miss the kitten.' Her lips curled. 'And my new lamp.'

Jay smiled.

'And Zeus.' Alice joked. 'I'm still waiting for him to ditch that girlfriend.'

'Anything else you'll miss?' Jay leaned closer, kissed the top of her collarbone again making words flutter like confetti in her head.

'Ummm.'

Jay's lips feathered up her neck making her shiver. 'Anything at all?'

'There might be a certain lifeboat volunteer stroke superhero I've grown fond of.' Her voice came out on a groan as he began to nibble her ear.

'So stay?'

'Oh, wow,' Alice moaned as Jay pulled her closer. 'You're wearing too many clothes.'

Jay pushed his jeans down over his hips. 'Tell me you'll stay and I'll finish getting undressed.'

Alice couldn't stop her lips from curving. She reached out and tugged him closer, relishing the feel of his warm skin. 'I'll stay.' The words came out on a rush but she knew they were right, knew she'd been building up to them.

'Thank God,' Jay rumbled, hauling her closer just as his pager began to beep. He stepped back to answer it, leaving her sitting naked on the counter. Alice reached across for a towel and wrapped it round her stomach and legs.

'Sorry.' Jay looked up. 'I've got to go, but let's talk later? I'm glad you're staying.'

He leaned forwards and caught her mouth in a long, deep kiss and she closed her eyes, leaning into it. Then he stepped back and was out of the door with Zeus in seconds leaving her sitting on the counter. Alone.

Chapter Twenty-Eight

The café door rattled again. The place had been heaving since Alice had opened at eight and her feet were on fire. She quickly placed two mugs and a plate of biscuits on the tray and headed out from behind the counter.

'Table for two?' Alice flashed a smile, picked up menus and seated a couple in the morning sunshine by the window, then delivered the drinks and plate to Ted and Olive who sat beside the far wall with their heads together. They nodded and went back to their discussion. Then she stepped back and took a deep breath, checking her watch.

Ten-thirty, Cath would be arriving any minute. Alice picked up a cloth and wiped over a couple of clean tables, hovering ready to take more orders.

The bell above the door tinkled and Cath strode in, wearing a mix of vibrant blues and pinks. 'I'm here.' Her friend's eyes sparkled as she took in the café and headed for Alice. 'Looking good, but I can see you're tired.' Cath enveloped her in a waft of flowery perfume she hadn't smelled before.

Alice pulled back. 'Wearing make-up?'

'Covering up the bags under my eyes.'

'You look pretty.'

Cath flushed. 'Why don't you go out back and take a break, I can handle this.'

'Don't you want to change?'

'I can take an order wearing this old thing, I'll change in a minute. You look done in.' Cath looked at her closely. 'Get any sleep?'

'Not much.'

'Then go.' Cath shooed her out with her hands.

Alice headed for the kitchen, put the kettle on and cut herself a slice of chocolate cake, then sat, almost groaning as her feet got their first break of the day. 'I thought I was fit,' she grumbled, closing her eyes and leaning her head back.

Jay walked through the door and Alice tried to stand but he slung his workbag on the floor and held up a hand.

'Cath said if you try to get up, I have to threaten to superglue your feet to the floor again.'

'I've no plans to actually stand.' Alice looked at the kettle, wondering how she could make herself tea without moving.

'Want me to make you a cup?'

Alice grinned and nodded, then watched him work. 'My hero.' She sighed as he handed her the mug. 'How was last night?'

'Okay, we found the boat quickly. The crew's engine had blown, took a while to tug them into shore so I didn't come back, you wouldn't have got any sleep if I had.'

Alice flushed, remembering the undressed state he'd left her in. 'Maybe I wish you had, I didn't get much sleep anyway.'

'I'll remember that next time. I came to make a start on the shelving in the larder. Will I get in your way?'

'Not if you keep your tools off the floor.'

Jay grinned. 'No problem, they're even alphabetised, in case I need you to hand me something important.' He unpacked a tape measure and pad and placed them on the counter. 'Have you talked to Cath about Shaun?'

'No, why?'

'Don't know, I called him this morning to see if he was okay. He said Cath dropped him home in the early hours.'

'So?'

'He sounded... almost happy. It's been a while.'

'Cath said there were moments they actually talked.' Alice sipped her tea. 'She told me what happened.'

'The whole thing was crazy, it made no sense when they split.' Jay opened the larder door and got the tape measure out, his large fingers nimble and precise, making her think of how they'd felt on her skin last night.

'Shaun took it badly, but it's been getting worse since she started dating someone else. I'm not sure Shaun's ever seen life beyond Cath Lacey, but he's not very flexible. Wants everything his way.'

'Think I might know someone else like that,' Alice teased. 'Can I get up now, the dishwasher needs packing?'

'No. I'll do it in a minute. You planning on training later?'

'I need to sleep, I wanted to try swimming again on Sunday, you free?' She'd asked the question before she realised Jay was meant to be going to the beach with his mother.

Jay started to nod, then shook his head. 'I can do Monday if you like?'

'Doing anything nice?' Alice waited for him to explain about his brother.

'Just work stuff.'

Alice swallowed the hurt and tried to smile. 'I can cycle instead, it's meant to rain so I can test out my new lights. Monday's fine for swimming.'

The door opened and Cath entered carrying a tray piled with cups and plates. 'The customers have all left for now, Olive will be back later.' Cath nodded at Alice. 'I'm glad to see you sitting.'

Cath swept past and dumped the tray next to the sink.

'What time did you get home?' Alice asked.

'After two, then I stayed for a while. As much as Shaun says his hand didn't hurt, I could tell he was out of it and I didn't want to leave him.' Cath frowned. 'Did you hear my mobile? I left my bag by the dishwasher.'

'Nope.'

Cath's face dropped.

'Why?'

'Dan's supposed to be coming home today and I haven't heard from him.'

'You said the signal was a problem?'

'You're right.' Cath smiled but her eyes were dull in contrast to the glow she'd had minutes earlier. 'That's got to be it.'

'You tried his friend?'

'He's not answering, it's like everyone in Birmingham has disappeared into a black hole.'

Cath opened the dishwasher and began to load it badly, making Alice wince.

'You here to put those shelves in the larder? I think Alice is planning to build her own if you don't put them up soon, she keeps rearranging everything and it's driving me bonkers.'

'I'll do it today. Shaun might pop in to help.'

'Not sure he'll be able to do anything with that hand.'

Jay shrugged. 'He insisted.'

Cath shook her head. 'That's ridiculous, they told him to take it easy. I don't have time to take him back to the hospital.' She sighed as the bell in the front rang. 'You want to come out front and help me decorate some cakes?' She pointed to Alice. 'That way Jay can get on with the shelves without you distracting him.'

Alice picked up her tea and headed into the café. She pulled up a chair at the table next to the counter where Cath had already laid out twelve chocolate cupcakes. Her friend chatted to a couple who were just leaving the café.

'They wanted to know how to get to the castle gift shop,' she explained, pulling up a chair so she could sit opposite. She frowned at the cupcakes before picking up a tub of sweets and some catering gloves. 'Olive's bringing her grandsons in later, she wants us to spell out their names with sweets as a surprise.'

'What are they?' Alice pulled on some gloves.

'Ade, Ed and Charlie. It won't take long. I don't really need the help.' Cath looked up meeting Alice's eyes. 'I need someone here so I don't eat all the Smarties.'

Alice laughed. 'Who's going to stop me from eating them?' She opened a tube and poured them into a bowl quickly spelling out

Ed in blue and green sweets. 'They're boys so they're not going to want the pink Smarties.'

'Or the orange,' Cath giggled. She picked a pink sweet out of the bowl and pulled off her glove before popping it into her mouth, then she did the same for Alice. 'If Simon Wolf saw us now he'd dock our wages for eating the profits.'

Alice licked her lips. 'I'll keep my eye out for him. Are you okay?' She watched her friend carefully.

'Absolutely.' Cath nodded. 'I'm just tired after last night and worried about Dan, I'll be fine after a few more E numbers. I think Charlie's going to need two cakes or we won't fit his name on.'

'Lucky Charlie,' Alice chuckled.

Cath finished adding the Smarties and popped another orange one into her mouth, grinning just as the bell rang signalling another customer.

Shaun walked into the café, his hand bandaged to the wrist, and his eyes caught on Cath as she got up to greet him.

'Jay said you were coming to help. You're supposed to be resting that hand.' Cath sounded annoyed. 'The nurse told you to be careful.'

'I'm not planning on sawing it off.'

Cath headed to the kitchen without looking at him. Alice put the cakes into a container and followed.

Shaun had picked up Jay's tape measure from the counter.

'If you get up on a stool I won't be responsible for my actions,' Cath threatened.

Shaun smiled. 'Anyone would think you cared.'

Cath went crimson and disappeared into the front of the café again, slamming the door.

'I don't know why you get so much pleasure from winding her up,' Jay said, pulling trays out of the larder so Shaun could measure up.

'Don't you?'

Cath swept back in, ignoring everyone as she thumped a bowl on the side next to the dishwasher.

'I've forgotten the spirit level, I'm going to get it from my car,' Jay said with a half-smile. 'Do you want to come?' He raised an eyebrow at Alice.

'Sure.' Alice followed him slowly.

Jay waited for her outside the door. 'My car's parked at the station, I wanted to give them a few minutes alone while we walk there. I'm guessing they've got stuff they need to talk about.'

'Do we have things to talk about too?' The words were out before Alice could censor them, the thoughts had been sitting on the edge of her tongue.

Jay cleared his throat. 'Do you mean what you said last night, about staying?' He slowed so they could walk side by side. 'Because it's good,' he added before she could contradict him. 'Great actually. Now we've got even more time to get to know each other.'

Alice frowned. 'Don't think there's much more for you to learn about me, I'm an open book.' She waited for Jay to tell her about his brother, wanting so badly for him to share his feelings with her. They reached the car park and he opened the boot of his pickup without looking at her and bent to pull out the spirit level.

'Same here.' Jay's face was hidden so Alice couldn't see his expression, but she could hear the lie in his voice.

Why was he keeping things from her? All of a sudden Alice wondered if staying in Castle Cove was such a good idea after all.

Chapter Twenty-Nine

Jay picked up his mobile and dialled his mother's number for what felt like the twentieth time, gritting his teeth when it went straight to voicemail. She probably hadn't charged it again, but she usually answered her home phone and she hadn't done that, hadn't answered the doorbell either. Where was she?

Jay thumped a hand on the steering wheel of his truck wanting to kick something, hard. His mind wandered to Alice in the café, to her hurt expression when he said he wasn't free on Sunday, which didn't make any sense because she didn't know about this morning.

Where the hell was his mother? Jay checked his watch, ten o'clock, he'd told her to be ready at quarter to. The drive to the beach wasn't long, but he wanted to get there by eleven. That was the time they figured Steve had hit his head and so the timing was fitting.

A wreath of yellow roses sat wilting on the passenger seat. He'd felt a right idiot going into the florist and asking for them, but knew the gesture would make his mum feel good. She always liked to leave flowers on the rocks, it gave her something to focus on while she talked to her dead son.

Jay drummed his fingers on the dashboard. The keys to his mum's house were back at his house, he could pop by to pick them up.

Maybe she'd fallen? His heart thumped hard, he'd been too busy thinking she'd decided to avoid the whole day to consider whether she had a good reason not to be ready.

Jay started the engine but then his mobile buzzed with a number he didn't recognise and he picked it up. 'What?' He knew the greeting wasn't friendly, but he had a lot on his mind.

'Jay?'

'Mum?' He looked at the phone again and put it back against his ear. 'Where are you and whose number is this?'

'Sorry love, Ben said he'd drive me to the beach, we're sitting in the car park. My fault, I didn't charge my phone again and we had to call three people before I could find out your number.'

Jay's mind had stuck on the start of her sentence. 'Who the hell is Ben?'

'Ben Campbell, he was with me when Zeus went missing, remember? He owns Little Treasures. I think you did some work for him. He worked in London for a long time and moved back permanently just before his wife died so you probably haven't seen him around much. We've been – hanging out, I think you'd call it.'

'Right.' Jay wasn't sure if he liked the idea of his mum hanging out with anyone. 'So, why's he at the beach? I'd have driven you.'

'His house is closer and I stayed over last night.' The words hung in the silence.

'O-kay.' He'd have to talk to her later about going home with strange men. He ran a hand through his hair feeling out of his depth; when did he become the parent in this relationship? Jay sighed. 'I'll meet you at the beach. Tell Ben he doesn't have to wait, we're going to the pub after and then I can run you home.'

Gayle paused and suddenly he knew what she was going to say.

'Ben's coming too, I told him all about what happened with Steve, he said he'd like to stay and support me.'

'I thought that's what I was doing?' Jay knew he sounded angry again.

'I know, but I'd like Ben there too. Have you asked that nice girl you've been seeing? I mentioned it to her the other day.'

'You've met Alice?'

'In the pub.'

'And you told her about Steve?' Jay heard the bite in his words but didn't apologise. No wonder Alice had looked so upset when they'd been talking yesterday. She'd known all along.

'You didn't mention it?' Gayle sounded disappointed.

'I'll see you in fifteen,' Jay muttered, hanging up. He hadn't asked Alice what she was doing today; she wasn't working, she'd mentioned cycling but maybe if he swung by her house he could see if she was free after all?

But how crap would that look? I was in the area, and I thought I'd just check if you wanted to come to the beach to wish my dead brother well. You know the one I haven't told you about, oh, and would you like to meet my mother again, the one who blames me for his death?

Dammit.

Jay fired up the pickup and swung out of his mother's road, surprising himself by taking the turning to the right towards Alice's house, rather than the left towards the beach.

She'd be out if he called at her house, or she'd turn him down. It was unfair but he couldn't seem to stop himself from travelling in her direction.

Once there he parked and hopped down from the truck, heading for her front door with his hands gripped and his heart pounding.

Jay wasn't sure what he wanted to happen when he rang the bell. If Alice wasn't in he'd have nothing to regret, if she was he'd have so much explaining to do. The door opened and there she was, dressed in jeans and a soft grey t-shirt. Her hair was pulled up in a ponytail and she had a mark on her nose, like she'd been cleaning something and had wiped dirt across herself. He couldn't believe how much he wanted to reach over and rub it off.

'Jay.' Alice screwed up her face. 'I thought you were busy.' She dropped her eyes from his face, making him feel guilty.

'I am, I wondered... ' Jay stopped.

Alice leaned her hip against the door frame and looked up at him again, her grey eyes searching his face. 'Everything okay?'

'My brother died.' There. The words were out, but he didn't feel relief, more like stupidity. 'It was a long time ago, I don't talk about it... and I'm screwing this up.' Jay drew a long breath. 'Can I come in?'

'Sure, be warned, I'm cleaning the oven.' Alice stepped back, out of his way and watched him enter. The kitten came out of the front room and wound itself around his legs.

'Tiger, I'll feed you in a minute.'

'You named her?'

Alice shrugged. 'Since I'm staying I thought it sounded better than cat.'

'I'm glad you're staying,' Jay said, even though he knew the word *glad* was inadequate.

'You said that yesterday.' Alice nodded, acknowledging the words, hopefully sensing the feelings underneath. 'Your brother?'

'Steve died today, ten years ago. We're remembering it at the beach this morning and I wondered if you'd like to come, we're eating at the pub after.' The words came out in a rush. Alice stepped forwards suddenly and gave him a hug, holding him tight for a few seconds before stepping back. He wanted to grab her and hold on, but accepting comfort today didn't feel right.

'I know about the beach and your brother, your mum mentioned it. I assumed you wanted to go alone?' Alice kept her expression blank but he could see he'd hurt her.

'I changed my mind.' Jay waited for her answer, surprised at how tense he felt.

Alice searched his face, her expression warming. 'Of course I'll come, whatever you need. Will you give me a second so I can change into something more appropriate?' She glanced at her jeans and then his chinos. 'I'm guessing casual but smart?' Jay nodded, feeling relief flood through him. 'I can be ready in ten if that's okay?'

'Sure.'

'Make yourself a coffee and—' Alice blushed. 'Thank you for letting me be there for you. I know it wasn't easy to ask.'

'Ah,' Jay stumbled over his words, unsure of what to say. 'I'll feed the cat,' he offered. His voice sounded strange, so he headed for the kitchen and searched the cupboards for a bowl, keeping his hands busy so they wouldn't shake. That had been easier than he'd expected, hopefully the rest of today would turn out the same.

But he doubted it.

Chapter Thirty

'Your mum told me your brother got hurt on the beach?'

'Yep.' Jay hit the accelerator as they left Castle Cove. They weren't late, but he'd texted Ben's phone to say they were on their way.

'You don't like talking about it?' Alice looked out of the passenger window. Jay felt the distance immediately and wanted to fix it.

'I find it difficult. He was fourteen and I was older, I should have been watching him.'

'Fourteen's pretty grown up.' Alice stroked one of the yellow roses in her hand without looking at him.

'My parents didn't like us near the water alone. I guess that's what comes of growing up away from the sea, you never quite trust it.'

And if you grew up close to it and it took someone from you, you felt the same.

'I was seventeen, old enough to know better. I went to the arcade to meet a girl, told him I'd be along later, he was messing about jumping over rocks, he slipped and hit his head.'

'You found him?'

'You already know the story.' Jay gripped the steering wheel, feeling guilty all over again. 'I'll never forget walking along those cliffs searching, seeing the blue of his jumper. I didn't believe anything bad had happened until I was standing over him and—'

Feelings swamped him and he clamped his hands tighter on the wheel, concentrating on the road while he gathered his emotions close and stamped on them.

'Almost there.' His voice sounded gruff but he couldn't do anything about that.

'You hate this?' she said quietly.

'From the minute I get up.' Jay could feel it, the memories and constant nagging thoughts of what might have been.

Alice squeezed his arm trying to give comfort but he felt like shaking her off, he didn't deserve her pity.

Jay indicated right and drove down a narrow lane before pulling into a small car park overlooking the beach. It didn't look busy, rarely did, maybe because the sand was often covered with large beds of seaweed which tended to put any but the hardcore beachgoers off, and there wasn't much surf to speak of so mostly only walkers came here with their dogs.

His mother got out of a grey BMW parked to his right. He had to take a second look because she was wearing trousers and he found himself staring.

'Jay, I—' Gayle looked embarrassed. 'I thought these would work better on the beach.'

Last year her skirt had almost blown above her head in the wind and they'd had to leave early.

'You're right.' Jay said, fighting the wave of resentment that it was this year she'd decided to take the whole thing seriously because of her new boyfriend.

A man he recognised walked around from the driver's side of the BMW and stood beside his mother.

'Ah.' She went crimson. 'This is Ben Campbell. Ben, Jay, I think you two have met?'

Ben stepped forwards and they shook hands. 'Nice to see you again, Jay. You built a kitchen for me when I first moved back to Castle Cove full-time. I used to work away a lot.' He explained.

Now Jay remembered. 'Three years ago, I built it in maple. I remember the room, it was a good space. How's your daughter doing?'

'Great.' Ben's smile lit his face. 'Emily's working in Nepal with Doctors Without Borders.'

'That's amazing. Um, I was sorry to hear about your wife.'
Ben nodded.

How had this whole romance between Ben and his mother happened without him knowing anything about it?

'Alice, you made it.' His mother gave her a swift hug. 'Thanks for bringing the flowers.' She nodded at Jay and took the bouquet, turning towards the beach. She took Ben's hand and headed into the sand.

'I feel like a spare part.' Jay said to himself, following. Alice went in front, perhaps realising he needed time alone. She stopped as they reached the beach and turned back.

'You coming?' Alice offered a hand. 'If I can do anything, just say.'

They followed his mother and Ben as they marched towards a mismatched wall of rocks. There had been a few changes over the years but the rocks remained. Emotion blocked Jay's throat as they approached.

He remembered the flash of blue, the boy lying on the sand, the sea lapping at the body. Remembered the howl from his throat as he ran towards his brother, still half-believing everything would be all right. His coat had smelled of perfume from the girl he'd been kissing, his lips still tingled from the feel of her, he could remember that, but couldn't remember her name.

Jay could feel all the emotions swirling in his gut but focused his attention on moving his legs, on his mother laying the roses in the exact place Steve had been.

'She does remember.'

'You think she didn't?' Alice asked gently.

Jay frowned. 'She was there with my dad soon after me.'

'What did she do?'

'Hugged me, whispered in my ear, I don't know what else, I felt like I'd lost control of my senses.'

Jay watched his mother bend to speak to her son. He wanted to move away so he didn't hear her words but Alice held his hand, squeezing his fingers tightly, so he couldn't.

'I miss you.' His mum said softly to the flowers. 'I can't believe it's been ten years. I wake up sometimes wondering what you'd look like, would you be like Jay or your father?'

She sighed deeply and brushed a hand across her cheek. Jay didn't want to get closer to check in case there were tears. 'I want you to know I miss you every day but I'm so happy I had you for as long as I did. I want you to know how sorry I am that I let you go out on your own that day.'

Jay started to speak, to disagree, it hadn't been her responsibility to watch him, to be there, but Alice squeezed his fingers and shook her head. He tugged his hand and turned away, breathing deeply as he headed towards the sea, enjoying the feel of the wind on his face. This was the only place he felt right, the only place he didn't feel eaten up by guilt and emotion. He didn't want to hear any more, he had his own things to say, his own apologies to make and he needed to do those when he was alone.

What had his mother been thinking? Grieving wasn't supposed to be done in front of a crowd.

Jay heard soft footsteps beside him but didn't turn.

'I can't imagine how hard today must be for you,' Alice sympathised.

Jay shrugged, staring at the waves.

'I felt guilty about my mother.' Alice said suddenly.

'Why?'

'I wonder if someone had been there when she had the aneurysm we might have been able to help. Instead she called 999 and a stranger found her on the bathroom floor. By the time they got her to the hospital it was too late.'

'You were working?' Jay asked gently.

Alice nodded. 'Doing an extra shift over a hundred miles away. I'd promised to visit that weekend but I'd cancelled.' Disgust tinged her voice. 'I didn't know she was dead until my shift finished and I switched on my phone.'

'From what I know about these things there's nothing anyone can do.' Jay cleared his throat.

'I guess I know that deep down.' Hair blew into her face and she pushed it away. 'Sometimes guilt gnaws at you, even when it shouldn't.'

Alice focused on the sea, on the waves coming in and out and didn't say anything else. Jay did the same, watching the water roll over and over, feeling himself relax.

'Do you blame yourself?' Alice's words startled him and he didn't answer for a moment, couldn't wrap his head or mouth around the admission. 'I guess that would be a normal reaction.' She cleared her throat, 'I didn't mean to imply—'

'Yes.' The word came out too sharply. Jay knew that but couldn't look at her to see if it'd made an impact. 'If I'd have joined him instead of kissing a girl I hardly knew, he'd still be here. I've always wondered how one fairly innocent, selfish act could lead to one so devastating. How many times I've wished I could go back in time and change everything.'

'Maybe it would have happened anyway?' Alice whispered. 'Don't you ever think things are just mapped out?'

Wind blew off the sea, mussing his hair. 'I think that's a cop out; we're all responsible for our actions and the effect they have on other people. Drop a pin on the floor, it's bound to hurt somebody.'

'Which makes you responsible for everyone else's tragedies if you happen to be in the vicinity. Isn't that a bit egotistical?'

Alice turned to him. He could feel the warmth of her body as she moved closer but he still didn't look at her, instead he focused on the sky. The clouds were getting darker, a sign of a storm coming, even the waves seemed rougher. Jay looked back at the beach. His mother was still bent over the flowers, talking, with Ben stood over her like a palace guard.

'I had a responsibility, I failed, simple as that.' He felt the bite of the words, the pain of the truth.

'That's bullshit.' Alice stepped closer and he smelled chocolate again and wanted to lean into the innocence of the scent.

'Even you said you felt guilty.'

'I know that's irrational. Same as I knew my fear of swimming was irrational, and you've helped me to overcome that.'

'My guilt isn't irrational.' His stomach squeezed. 'Even my parents blamed me for what I did.' His hands started to go numb and he uncurled them.

'Your mother?'

Jay shook his head. 'She's a good woman, she'd never say it.'

'Then how do you know?'

The question was reasonable but Jay still resented it. 'Because I feel it, it's in everything she doesn't say. It was in every look from my father during the months after. No-one talked about Steve, especially not him.'

'You said he left?

The waves swept into the shore, reminding him of the time his dad had taken him and Steve to the beach to bounce pebbles off the water. After that there was nothing. 'One day he was gone without a word, and we haven't heard anything since. If that doesn't tell you anything, what does?'

'It tells me he wasn't worth having in your life,' she told him. 'Seems to me you take too much on your shoulders.' Alice stepped closer and put an arm around his waist. He didn't pull back but he didn't accept the comfort either, somehow doing that felt wrong, like he was acknowledging he deserved it.

So, he let her hug him as he stared into the sea, watching the dark clouds gather in the sky and move closer to the shore. He felt the rain and wind in the air before the shower started and when it did he took Alice's hand and headed back towards the car, stopping briefly by the flowers to give his own silent apology to his brother.

'Pub,' Jay said to his mother.

'We'll see you there.' Ben replied, making Jay's temper flare even though he knew the feelings were unfair.

Jay tugged Alice's hand and they ran towards his truck as the rain got harder, beating down on both of them like a bad feeling you couldn't shake off.

Chapter Thirty-One

The pub was heaving when they entered, tables rattled under the weight of wet coats and bags and everything smelled of damp and rain. It was a dreary end to what had been a gorgeous few weeks, but the weather had perfectly captured the emotions of the day. Alice followed Jay inside, wiping drips of water from her face. They hadn't been able to park nearby so they had needed to run when they got out of the car as well, but even Superman couldn't outrun this weather.

'Raining?' Shaun greeted them near the door and led them inside. Music played on the jukebox and the room was filled with the low hum of conversation, a welcome relief after all the emotion outside.

'How did you guess?' Alice smiled as water dripped down her face. 'You look good, less pale.' She studied him, noting the rough smattering of stubble across his jawline. 'How's the hand?'

'Can't shave.' Shaun ran a finger over his cheek. 'But better, Cath checked it for me this morning.'

'Oh?' Alice raised an eyebrow but he ignored it. 'Did it hurt?'

Shaun smiled. 'A little, I swear she enjoys it. That's a whole side of her I didn't know about.'

'But you like?' Alice cocked her head.

'Ah.' Shaun shook his, smiling. 'I'm not giving secrets away to the enemy, I know you're on her side.'

'I think I'm on both of your sides.' Alice put her hands on her hips.

Shaun seemed to mull the statement over. 'Then tell me, what does she do for fun these days?'

Alice considered the question. 'Honestly, she talks about parties and Dan, but I've only ever seen her in here. She likes the bands, walking on the beach, a decent cup of coffee, all the normal things.'

Shaun looked confused. 'All the things we used to do together, I don't understand anything any more.' He sighed as they weaved in and out of people heading towards the back of the pub where Alice knew the tables were most private.

'It's set for four?' Jay looked surprised.

'Your mum called this morning.' Shaun admitted. 'I guess she is psychic after all?'

Shaun turned to Alice. 'You were on the beach too, I didn't think you were going?'

'Mum took her *friend* Ben.' Irritation dripped from Jay's voice. 'So Alice came with me for moral support.'

'And because you needed a friend,' Alice added.

Shaun gathered a bundle of menus and handed them over. 'I'm going to have to get behind the bar, I'll come and take your orders when everyone else arrives.'

Jay stared at the table with a dark expression. 'It's the first time I've persuaded my mother to come for lunch after the beach and I'm not going to get the chance to talk with her.'

'I guess four's a crowd?' Alice knotted her hands.

'You should sit, I don't know how long they're going to be and we might as well have a drink.'

'I don't need to stay.'

Jay shook his head and pulled out a chair for her. 'I'd rather you did, I'm not fond of playing gooseberry. Sorry, I know this isn't fun for you.'

'I'm not feeling awkward, I'm here for you and I like your mum.' Alice sat and watched him do the same. 'You should talk to her.'

'Who?' Jay lifted one of the menus and buried his head in it.

Alice pursed her lips. 'Gayle.'

'About what?'

Alice sighed, considering the choices on the white card. 'The goat's cheese pastry looks good.'

Jay snorted. 'Does it come with lamb?' He glared at the door. 'Where *are* they? Maybe they got lost, he looked the type.'

'Ben was here the other night so I think he'll find his way, maybe your mum wanted to stay a bit longer?'

'It was raining.'

'She's a grown woman.'

Jay huffed and looked at the menu again.

'Do you go there every year?'

'I do, Mum isn't always up to it. She says she prefers to grieve in private, at least she has until today.'

'I think sometimes it's easier for people to just forget about things rather than remember them,' Alice said.

'You wouldn't forget.'

'Well, no, but I guess we all deal with things in different ways. Perhaps my dad getting on that plane to Thailand was the only way he could deal with the divorce?' The words resonated, it might have been the first time she'd really understood.

'Does he mind that you're not planning on travelling any more?'

Guilt made her grimace. 'I haven't told him. I might pop over to visit for a week as I have enough money saved for a plane ticket, I'd love to see him.'

Jay looked towards the door again and scowled. 'They're here, and they're soaked.' He got up and went to his mother, frowning at her wet hair before leading her to the table. 'Shaun said you changed the booking?'

Gayle smiled gently, her eyes bright. 'I thought we'd all be hungry, Shaun said it was no problem.' She sat and looked at Jay, a familiar crease appearing in her forehead. 'Is that okay?'

'Yes,' Jay muttered, taking a seat beside her, leaving Ben to sit the other side. 'You were gone a while.'

'I guess I had a lot to say this time. It was a good idea, I'm sorry I've missed it so many times.' Gayle squeezed Jay's shoulder, leaving him speechless.

'What's good here?' Ben asked, trying to lighten the mood.

'The goat's cheese pastry apparently,' Jay said.

'I like the sound of that,' Gayle agreed, her voice light.

Ben grimaced. 'I'd prefer the lamb.'

Alice tried not to smile.

'Did you get a chance to say what you needed?' Gayle asked Jay.

Jay nodded without looking up. Alice didn't remember him saying anything, just staring at the sea like he wanted to thump something. She could see his knuckles whiten as he clenched the menu. Gayle's eyes flickered to his hands too and her brow puckered before she picked up her napkin and unfolded it.

'Shall we order a bottle of wine, so we can toast Steve?' she asked.

'I'm driving,' Jay said too quickly.

'I'll have one,' said Ben.

'So will I.' Alice felt grateful suddenly for the reassuring presence of Ben.

Shaun appeared at the table holding a pad and pen. He bent to kiss Gayle on both cheeks. 'So do you guys know what you want?'

Conversation was stilted during dinner, both men polished off their lamb but Gayle ate very little of her pastry, and even the toast to Steve fell flat.

Gayle sighed and shook her head when both men headed for the bar to pay the bill. 'Think they'll fight over it?' she joked, her blue eyes assessing.

'No, but I'm not sure who I'd put my money on if they did.' Alice straightened her cutlery on the empty plate.

'I hoped they'd get on.' Gayle sounded wistful. 'I know Jay likes taking care of me, but it's nice to have company of my own age.'

'I think he's just being overprotective,' Alice admitted. 'And I got the impression he wanted to share this day with just you.' Her cheeks heated. 'I don't mean you did anything wrong.'

Gayle patted her hand. 'I know what you meant and you're right, but I wanted to try something different this time. I didn't want Jay to focus all his attention on me and how I was feeling. I hoped bringing other people might give him a chance to open up.'

'Ah.'

'I take it he didn't?'

'A little, but I get the feeling he doesn't like talking about his brother. This must be a hard day for you?'

Gayle played with her napkin, folding it and unfolding it as she talked. 'Actually, it feels better than it has in years. Jay has always tried to get me to face up to what happened, but I found it easier to bury how I felt. Somehow, when Ben said I ought to do it for myself and Jay, it made me realise I'd been unfair.'

'It's not always easy to face death.' Alice stared at her plate.

'It's funny, while Jay's always been so keen to face it, to acknowledge it each year, I feel like he's the one who's moved on least.' Wrinkles formed around the corners of Gayle's eyes as she considered her son.

Alice squeezed her bottom lip between her teeth. 'Maybe you should talk to him about it?'

'I'm not sure he'd appreciate it.'

'Perhaps he'll surprise you, do you think there are things he wouldn't want to hear?'

'I—' Gayle looked surprised. 'Like what? I have to admit I've always preferred to avoid the subject. Sometimes I can make it difficult, but if there was something he wanted to know, he'd only need to ask.'

'Maybe he's scared of what he might hear?'

'What do you mean?' Gayle asked.

Alice paused. 'Do you think he blames himself?'

'To an extent, we all do, Steve was the baby of the family. It's hard not to feel guilt, but Jay has no reason to feel he's to blame, it was just a stupid accident. I used to wish we'd never moved near the sea, but something might have happened if we'd stayed in Edinburgh.' Gayle twisted the napkin round her finger. 'It's no-one's fault.'

'Jay was meant to be watching him?' So, this was what walking on eggshells felt like.

'They were supposed to meet up, it wasn't a firm arrangement, he was always so good with his brother.' Gayle's brow wrinkled, reminding Alice of Jay. 'So responsible. I always said he needed to let his hair down, but he never has. If anyone was meant to be watching Steve, it was his dad, he'd promised to take him for a cycle ride but he'd forgotten and disappeared somewhere.'

'Does Jay know that?'

The line in Gayle's forehead deepened as she thought back. 'I've no idea, yes, probably. I don't remember discussing it but his dad often let them down, it's just the way he was.'

Someone laughed at another table and Alice looked round, making sure Jay wasn't on his way back, but he was standing at the bar, chatting. 'Sometimes people can be dense, I mean.' What did she mean? 'They read things into other things. You perhaps need to spell things out.'

'Things?' Gayle looked confused.

'Done.' Ben arrived, clapping his hands behind them, making Alice jump. 'Jay's chatting with Shaun, you fancy heading home, it's been a long morning?' Ben rested a hand on Gayle's shoulder as she nodded.

'I'm a little tired, let me give my son a hug and we can head off. Thank you for joining us Alice.' Gayle stood. 'It's great to see him with someone who understands how he ticks, I think you're good for him.'

'Oh well.' Alice's cheeks flamed as his mother pulled her into an unexpected hug. 'I was happy to come, Jay's done so much for me.'

'He's a good man, he deserves some happiness.' Gayle kissed Alice on both cheeks before picking up her bag and heading towards the bar.

Alice's mobile buzzed and she picked it up quickly.

'Cath?'

'I'm sorry, I know you're busy.'

'Something's wrong?'

'Not sure.' The phone went quiet. 'I talked to Dan last night, he said he'd smashed his phone so couldn't get in touch with me over the last few days. He said he couldn't make it back yesterday but was supposed to get here this morning, but he hasn't turned up again. We're supposed to be going out.'

'Have you tried phoning him?'

'A hundred times. I know he's unpredictable, that's one of the things I love about him, but—'

'You wish he wasn't always like that?' Alice guessed.

Cath sighed. 'I feel disloyal, but I've got to talk to someone about it, Alice… And he owes me money for rent.'

Alice waited.

'I can pay, but I'm eating into my savings and every time I mention it he makes me feel… boring.'

'Sometimes boring is just another word for sensible.' Alice stopped, knowing she was holding back but Cath might not want to hear it all.

'Or stable and middle-aged,' Cath grumbled. 'I'm being silly, he'll be back in a minute, he's probably got distracted coming home. He's like a magpie, flicking from one shiny thing to the next.'

'As long as you're not one of those shiny things.' Alice paused, biting her lip. She knew she'd said too much. 'Let me know if you don't hear from him, and don't worry, I'm sure you're right and he's just got sidetracked on the way home.'

Alice just hoped whatever had distracted him, was prepared to let him go.

☆

'Thanks for coming.' Jay fired up the engine of his truck but didn't take the handbrake off. 'I'm sorry it took me so long to invite you.'

'That's okay.' Alice looked out of the window at the promenade, waiting for him to move the pickup and take her home. She could finish cleaning the oven, maybe go for that cycle.

'Do you want to come to mine?'

Alice shook her head reluctantly. 'Cath might be coming over later, you could come to mine?' She knew he'd say no before he opened his mouth, his mood seemed off.

'Maybe later, I need to feed and walk Zeus, maybe see if my mum's free, make sure she got back okay.'

'I think Ben will look after her.'

Jay's mouth turned down. 'He shouldn't have to.'

Alice twisted her fingers in her lap, feeling torn between wanting to get involved and wanting to shut up. 'He seems to make her happy.'

Jay snorted.

'You didn't like that he was here today?' Cars began to move in the car park but Jay sat staring out of the windscreen.

'Today was fine.'

'You didn't get a chance to chat with her alone, and your mum said she wanted you to talk to Steve but I know you didn't.'

Jay took the handbrake off and began to reverse the car. 'I said what I needed to, so did she.'

'You didn't say anything to each other.'

'Nothing to say,' he said gruffly as he headed out of the car park, towards her house. They didn't speak even as he parked outside and hopped out coming around to open her door. It was a relief when she got to the porch and little Tiger trotted round to greet her.

Alice bent to stroke the kitten's soft head. 'You could ask your mother if she blames you?' The words left her mouth quickly, but she knew straight away that saying them was a mistake. 'I'm sorry, it's none of my business.'

'Is this what you were talking to her about in the pub?' Jay looked annoyed.

'I'd never break a confidence. But she openly told me Steve was meant to be meeting your dad that day but he forgot, he must have felt guilty about not being there.' Emotions she couldn't read flitted across Jay's face before he blanked. 'Did you know?'

'I don't remember.' Jay ran a hand through his hair, looking lost. 'I probably did, the whole thing's become a blur.'

'Maybe you should ask?'

Jay shook his head. 'In my experience, some things are best left unsaid. I've got to go.' He bent to kiss Alice on the cheek before heading to the street to pick up his car.

Alice watched him go before opening the front door. 'In my experience, not talking about things makes them far worse,' she said, knowing he couldn't hear. She headed for the kitchen and put the kettle on.

Jay was hurting, so was Cath. And whatever happened, Alice would do whatever she could to help the people she loved in Castle Cove.

Chapter Thirty-Two

The windows rattled as a large gust of wind caught them in its grip, and rain hammered on the ground outside as the storm whipped itself into a frenzy.

Wow, sometimes the weather was bad by the sea. When Alice had first moved to Castle Cove she hadn't been expecting the contrast of good and bad, of hot and cold. In some ways, she enjoyed the unpredictability of it but another side of her found the constant change unsettling.

Alice wrapped herself in her fluffy red blanket and curled onto the sofa next to the kitten, closing her eyes at the same instant the doorbell rang.

'Damn.' Alice leapt up, heart hammering, because she was dressed in her oldest clothes and it was probably Jay, hopefully here to talk because he needed her.

'Cath, I thought you weren't coming, didn't Dan turn up?'

Her friend stood on the doorstep, dribbling rainwater onto the mat. Her hair hung limply around her shoulders in a mass of wet curls and her expression drooped, matching it.

'Where's your coat?' Alice pulled her inside and picked up the small wet bag she'd dropped in the porch. Clothes were poking out the top along with makeup and a hairdryer proving she'd packed in a rush.

'Forgot it.' Cath's voice was flat and her face pale. Mascara ran down her cheeks, darkening the skin under her eyes.

'What happened?' Alice took her hand and pulled her into the sitting room, slamming the front door on the storm. 'You're freezing, I'll get you a towel.' Alice ran upstairs and got one from the airing cupboard and gave it to Cath who wiped the worst of the weather from her hair.

The fire flickered in the grate but Alice popped on a couple more logs to make sure it didn't dim. It might be July, but the temperature had dropped at least ten degrees today. Cath started to shiver so Alice picked up the red blanket and wrapped it round her shoulders, guiding her onto the sofa.

'Do you need a bath to warm up?'

Her friend stared at the floor but didn't answer.

'How about a wine, I've got some white in the fridge with your name on it?'

After a few seconds Cath nodded, so Alice rushed into the kitchen and poured them both a large glass, gulping a couple of mouthfuls before heading back.

Alice nudged herself onto the sofa and handed Cath the drink. She took a small sip, mumbling a thank you.

'Is it Dan?'

'Yes.' The word came out on a hiss.

'Did he come home? Has he done something?' Alice could guess by Cath's expression what it was.

'I might be the most stupid person ever to walk the earth. I found a G-string in his pocket,' she murmured, her voice clear but sad. 'When I put on a wash after he came back.'

'Ah.' Alice took another couple of gulps deciding what to say. 'Definitely not his?'

Cath frowned.

'I'm not making a joke of this… He loves parties, he might have bought it as a prank, to put them on his head, you said he liked to mess around?'

Cath drank her wine again, almost finishing the glass. 'Nope, they belonged to a girl.'

'Ah.' Alice paused, waiting for Cath to fill the silence, instead she held out her already empty glass for a refill.

'I'll get the bottle,' Alice said, fetching it and topping up both of their glasses.

'Where did he meet her?'

Cath glugged some wine. 'Doesn't matter, you know he had the cheek to tell me it happened because our relationship was *boring*?'

'Boring how?'

Cath lifted her shoulders. 'Perhaps it's the way I pay our rent, or do the washing, maybe it's because there's always food in the fridge?'

'He said that?' Alice had a sudden urge to punch him.

'Pretty much. He accused me of being middle-aged, me!' Cath put the glass on the coffee table with a slam. 'Maybe now I under-stand how Shaun felt, which makes me a cow as well as an idiot.'

'You're neither, Cath.' Alice gave her friend a gentle hug. 'What else did he say?' She tucked her legs up onto the sofa, making herself more comfortable just as Cath's mobile rang.

'It's in my bag.' Cath narrowed her eyes at the offending article dripping on the floor. 'Ignore it, it'll be Dan, he's been ringing since I stormed out. Luckily, he goes to so many parties, he's not been around in Castle Cove long enough to know where you live.'

'We won't answer the door, just in case.' Alice pushed the shutters closed so no-one could see inside. 'What else did he say?'

Cath pursed her lips; her nose had turned an unbecoming shade of red and her eyes watered. 'He said I was special, that he cared for me, but that people like us weren't meant to follow rules, that fidelity was as outdated as marriage.'

'How convenient.' Alice snorted. 'I wonder if he'd feel the same if it was the other way around?'

'Stupid thing is it could have been… Shaun tried to kiss me the other night and I wanted to kiss him back, but maybe I'm too middle-aged and boring to cheat.'

'I guess being boring isn't so bad after all then?' Alice suggested quietly, sipping from her glass.

Cath pulled her legs underneath herself and draped the blanket over her feet. 'Maybe, but this isn't about Shaun, it's about Dan, and me. It's about what I want.'

'So what do you want?' Alice asked gently.

Cath screwed up her face. 'I honestly don't know.' She looked into her empty wine glass. 'I'll start with another one of these.'

Alice chuckled, picking up the bottle and refilling both of their glasses. 'Don't you think wine is a lot less complicated than men?'

Cath pulled a tissue out of her pocket and blew her nose. Her expression brightened. 'You're right. Plus, there's loads in the supermarket – Italian, Spanish, German, French – I can choose a different nationality every night of the week if I want.' She checked the label on the bottle on the table. 'Yes, a nice crisp glass of Italian white beats Dan Bates any day.'

'I'll drink to that.' Alice smiled, lifting her glass and tapping it against Cath's.

Chapter Thirty-Three

Waves roared, throwing themselves against the boat, spraying water inside and soaking all of the crew as they headed out to sea. Jay squinted into the distance but visibility was awful. Cloud covered most of the moon and the stars were barely visible, even the North Star had been put out of action.

'What did the coastguard say?' Shaun shouted from beside him, his voice tense. The boat seemed to bounce and another wave bashed against them, making everyone brace. Freezing water sprayed into their faces and Jay had to fight to get a breath.

'Small sail boat, went out early this morning. They got a distress call at five o'clock to say it was taking on water. Three people on board, a man and woman, both in their fifties plus a teenage boy. They're experienced, all the right equipment.' Jay fired out the words like bullets, hoping Shaun could keep up.

'If they're experienced, what the hell are they doing out in this?' Shaun grunted, sounding annoyed. Another wave crashed on the side of the boat bringing with it a waterfall of water. 'Anything coming up on the SAT?'

Jay shook his head, feeling the familiar sickness low in his stomach, maybe a leftover from today on the beach?

The waves were in danger of dwarfing the small craft, God knows what they'd do to the boat if the family were still in it. If it wasn't already upside down, holding them under the waves. Was everyone an idiot these days?

'Is everyone an idiot?' Shaun echoed as they continued to bounce into the darkness, led only by a couple of lights on the front of the boat and their own desire to beat the weather and save the day.

'Dammit, wind's picking up.'

The waves were too. Jay steered into them feeling the bump of the boat as it hit them. His stomach rolled, imagining what it would feel like to be stranded in this.

'Coastguard's found them, but they'll need our help picking them up, they've no idea if there are survivors, no-one's answering the radio.' Shaun reeled off the co-ordinates and Jay quickly changed direction and accelerated.

They'd be there in less than twenty minutes.

None of the crew spoke as they travelled. It was hard to joke or to talk about normal things when you weren't sure if you were about to be greeted by dead bodies. They saw the helicopter and lights as they approached, a beacon of hope in the darkness.

The boat was listing to the side as waves battered it from the left and right, wind howled, shouting and screaming as if the whole thing were a giant toy it was fighting over.

Jay quickly assessed the scene. The sail looked torn, and the boom had broken in half and was partially submerged, so getting on there would be tricky. The constant waves and rain wouldn't help.

'No-one's been found,' Shaun reported. 'They want to know if one of us can get aboard to take a look?'

Jay pulled the lifeboat alongside, facing into the wind, trying to avoid the worst of the waves. Freezing water sprayed in his face as he checked the scene.

'We need to be quick, I'm not sure how long that boat's going to last in these waves. Jenny.' Jay chose the smallest member of the team. Even though it killed him to ask someone else to put their lives in danger, if he wasn't prepared to he wasn't up to the job. 'I'd like you in there first, you're the lightest. If there are survivors, Mark will join you.'

At twenty-three, Jenny was the youngest member of the crew, but her dad had worked on the lifeboats for over twenty-five years so she'd been born and bred to do it. She nodded without questioning him and began to get ready.

Shaun helped, hooking her up to a line so they could keep her linked to the boat – in this type of weather one stray wave would wash someone out to sea in a heartbeat.

Jay hated this, hated his crew risking their lives. He wanted to be the one out there, in the waves facing death, but as coxswain he was in charge of steering the boat.

He held everything steady as Jenny stepped out onto the bow, steadying herself as another wave hit. Moments like this had them all holding their breath, but when she stood and nodded she was okay they let out a collective sigh of relief.

The boat rocked as waves battered back and forth, back and forth, wind whistled around them squealing.

The coastguard's helicopter held steady, shining a light on the water. It would help with the search, especially inside the boat and if anyone was alive, it could get the casualties to safety more quickly.

The downside was that spray from the blades made visibility almost impossible.

Jay stopped breathing as Jenny edged carefully along the boat, easing herself along inch by painful inch. She waited long enough to check her passage was safe, before inching closer still, stopping each time a wave crashed to brace. They waited and watched as Jenny moved gingerly down to look inside the boat, then everyone seemed to relax a little bit as she raised a white thumb, indicating at least one person was alive, then another two.

As soon as the casualties were confirmed, Mark followed the same path, manoeuvring himself gently onto the boat. There was a moment when the vessel rocked and they thought he'd gone overboard, but when the water cleared, he was still there hanging on tight.

After that it was all hands on deck. Both Jenny and Mark secured the passengers as the others worked to get them to safety.

The first member of the crew to be saved was a woman, who limped out supported by Jenny. Even from a distance Jay could see her arm was probably broken. A medic swung down from the helicopter, checked her over and nodded, indicting she could travel back with the lifeboat crew. Mark guided her to a safe place on the boat as they waited for the next passenger.

A man came out of the cabin and stumbled a few times up the stairs, even with Mark helping. Jay could see red on his life jacket and the top of his head. The medics would be on him in seconds once they got in the helicopter, head injuries could turn bad fast.

Finally, the teenage boy was pulled out of the cabin on a stretcher. They'd usually have secured him first, but Jay knew from experience the limited space down below would have made manoeuvring him out impossible. Jay could only imagine how tricky it had been to strap him in and move him out of the tiny space without knocking his head or body. He could see blood on the boy's coat and it was obvious he was unconscious. Jay's breath caught in his throat, but they'd learn more once he reached the hospital.

Jenny stayed with the boat, helping to guide the stretcher up as the man and boy were winched into the sky and the helicopter took off. Jay kept the boat steady until Jenny and Mark guided the woman back to the lifeboat. They wrapped her carefully in a blanket, and gave each other and the rest of the crew high fives as they got settled.

As they did, the boat took one final hit from the sea and turned on its side, disappearing into the inky depths in seconds. They heard the suck of the water over the roar of the waves and rain. The woman gasped and paled, closing her eyes. Then the boat was gone, leaving the lifeboat bobbing alone in the darkness.

'Good work,' Jay shouted as he turned and steered them to safety.

Thirty minutes later, the woman had been taken away by an ambulance and the crew had showered and were back at base drinking tea.

'You think the boy will be okay?' Shaun came up behind Jay, his mug half-full.

'I hope so.' The alternative wasn't worth contemplating. Jay drank his hot drink down in one, ignoring the burn in his chest.

As he fired up the truck, Jay contemplated going to see Alice, thinking about how it would feel to lie in her bed, but he had Zeus to get back to and his thoughts were jumbled.

But, when he turned out of the lifeboat station, he found himself heading in her direction anyway. It was still raining and the drips were falling down his face as he headed up her road. Would she be in? Probably.

Jay checked his watch, it was already eleven forty. Even as he reached her door and knocked, he knew he was making a big mistake.

Chapter Thirty-Four

Jay stood on the doorstep as rain thundered down on his head but it was his eyes that stopped Alice in her tracks.

'What's wrong?' Alice pulled him into the hallway, wanting to offer comfort. Instead Jay gently grabbed her hand and closed the door, then manoeuvred her against the wall pulling his jacket off and dropping it. Droplets fell from his hair onto Alice's t-shirt giving her goosebumps.

'You're cold,' Alice murmured as her heart pitched up a notch. She'd never seen Jay like this, his eyes were hot but his expression was serious.

'I need you,' Jay growled as he moved closer to brush a kiss across her cheek. Wanting to offer comfort, Alice wound her arms around his neck and pulled him closer. She could feel his heart racing through his clothes.

'Bad night?' Alice asked, softly.

'Don't want to talk about it now.' Jay moved his lips across her collarbone, leaving tingles in their pathway.

Alice pulled his wet t-shirt out of his trousers and let her hands wander slowly over his back, his skin felt cold. 'Do you need a towel?'

'Not now.'

'Cath's asleep upstairs,' Alice whispered.

'Then we'll have to be quiet,' Jay said, reaching down to pull Alice's cotton jumper over her head and to unclip her bra before throwing them on the floor. Before she could comment he spun her into the sitting room and closed the door.

'I need you,' Jay repeated.

'I need you too.' Alice heard the words and knew the truth of them, so pulled his t-shirt off too. She began to fold it but Jay grabbed it from her hands and dropped it, then stepped back to look in her eyes.

'I—'Jay stopped.

'Had a bad day, I know.' Alice's voice softened and she pulled his head down and kissed him deeply. For all the darkness she could see inside him, she knew Jay needed connection right now, and knew she could give it to him. She ran her hands over his shoulders and arms, easing them down to the crease at his elbows, to his tattoo. She pulled back.

'The date. It's when Steve died?'

Jay dipped his chin, his eyes dark and unhappy. He began to pop the buttons on her jeans and edged them down along with her pants so her bare bottom was pressed against the wood panelling of the door.

'You're cold,' she murmured, pulling him closer and biting on his earlobe.

'Not any more.' Jay didn't wait, instead he shoved the rest of her clothes off and followed with his own. He drew back to look at her, his eyes hot and questioning.

'Now,' Alice agreed. This wasn't about slow kisses or taking time, Jay needed her and she was ready. The windows rattled as wind and rain hammered on the glass and the room was cast into dark shadows as clouds moved across the house.

As they did, Jay picked Alice up, pressing her against the door and eased himself inside of her. She gasped and held onto his shoulders, wrapping her legs around him as they began to move, slowly at first but the power built, like the storm battering the windows outside. Alice could feel herself building, could feel heat from Jay as they rocked. Her breathing hitched as he pulled back so he could take her mouth into a long, deep kiss. Their tongues twirled and fought as Alice held on tighter.

Jay's fingers bit into her bottom as they moved, but it felt good, almost like he needed to hold onto her. Alice could feel anger in him, the burn of rage and wanted to help him let it go. Whatever had happened tonight, he had to be able to live with it and this time, perhaps she could help.

They rocked, faster and faster, as the storm built howling and swirling inside and outside of the room. Alice was on fire, emotions built as sensation surged, then suddenly they both fell, hard and fast with a sigh.

Out of breath, Jay let Alice slide to the floor.

'I'm sorry.' Jay said after a short silence. 'I didn't come here for that.'

Alice pressed her hands against her hot cheeks, feeling her heartbeat ease. 'I know but the last thing I want is an apology. That was… incredible.'

'It was.' Jay jerked his chin looking unsure. 'Thank you for understanding, for knowing what I needed.' He pulled her to him and gave her a hot kiss.

'Maybe I needed it too.' Alice picked up her knickers and trousers and tugged them on without looking at him, knowing he was doing the same, then pulled the door open to retrieve her bra and jumper.

'You want a coffee, tea?' Alice could feel Jay's need for normality and wanted to give it to him. Whatever had happened tonight he needed the space to share. Her eyes flickered upstairs. 'Perhaps we should go in the kitchen before we wake Cath?'

'She okay?' Jay tensed.

Alice's lips curved. 'I love that you've had a bad day but still worry about other people. She's fine, she's just got some stuff to figure out.'

'Shaun?'

'Partly.' Alice led him through the hall.

'Got any beer? It's been a long night.' His voice sounded tired. 'You sure you're okay?' He touched a hand to her cheek and she nodded.

They entered the kitchen and she pulled out a chair and watched him sink into it. He'd pulled his black t-shirt and trousers back on but they were still soaked and clinging to muscles she now knew intimately.

Water dripped onto the tiled floor and she went into the downstairs bathroom and got him a towel, then handed him a drink. 'I got some in specially. You want to tell me what's wrong?'

Jay looked at the bottle in surprise like he'd forgotten he'd asked for it. 'Nothing.'

Alice poured herself a glass of water and sat opposite, watching as he dried himself. Her eyes followed a path from his hands along the muscles on his arms, stopping on the small tattoo. The memory of his brother, the feelings he couldn't or wouldn't let go of. There were goosebumps everywhere but he wasn't shivering, it was almost like he'd forgotten how.

'Bad rescue,' Jay said eventually, taking a long sip from the bottle. The kitten wandered into the kitchen and wound itself around his leg. Jay bent to rub its head, letting out a long sigh.

'Tell me about it.'

Jay took a while to begin, she could see the emotion on his face and knew it wouldn't be good news before he'd even started. 'Capsized boat, not sure what the hell they were doing out in this.' He waved a hand at the window as if that said it all. 'Two walked off, one is badly hurt.' His lips pursed as he took another long sip. 'A teenage boy, only just fourteen.'

Alice winced. 'How badly?'

Tension etched a path across his forehead, into the creases at the edges of his eyes.

'I need to call Shaun, I was going to do it in the car.' Jay popped into the hall and picked up his jacket from the floor then checked the pocket for his mobile. 'Crap.' He put it on the table, the screen was blank. 'Must have forgotten to charge it.' Jay slammed the empty beer bottle next to it and closed his eyes.

'Use mine.'

He took the phone and dialled.

'It's me.' Jay paused. 'Forgot to charge my phone, what's the latest?' His fingers whitened. 'Crap.'

Jay stood and whipped round, staring out of the kitchen door with his back to her. She watched the muscles in his shoulders flex under the wet material and ached to comfort him but knew she couldn't. He held himself too far apart.

'Any idea what they were doing out in this?' Jay barked. 'Well he wasn't as experienced as he thought.'

His back straightened.

'I'll be at home. I need to charge my phone and Zeus is with Peter, best if I don't leave him all night, right. Just keep in touch.'

Jay hung up and handed the phone back, not looking at her. 'I need to head off.'

'What happened?'

Alice didn't think he was going to answer for a minute.

'They don't think the boy's going to make it, he has hypothermia, and a bad head injury. His mum and step-dad are fine.' He ground the last word between gritted teeth. 'I need to go.'

Alice touched a hand to his arm feeling rigid muscles underneath. 'Can't you stay here and dry off, I can make you a sandwich and call a cab to take you home later?'

Jay frowned at her hand, so white against his tanned skin. 'I don't think you should do it.'

'What?'

'The triathlon.'

'It's going to be fine,' Alice whispered. 'And you're going to be with me the whole time.'

Jay shook his head. 'I don't think I can. What if you have another dream about your mother and panic while we're swimming? There are so many people I might lose you in the crowd? I know you think you're okay now, but the whole thing could kick off again at any time, some phobias are like that.'

Alice kept her voice low, trying to stay calm. 'Don't you think you're overreacting?'

Jay pulled his arm away. 'When you watch a teenager being pulled from a boat, practically dead, you'll understand about over-reacting. I can't be part of this.' He headed for the door.

'You don't think I can do it?' Alice's hands shook as she followed him.

'I'm not prepared to be the one to pull your body out of the sea. I've had my fill of death, there are plenty of other places to find adventure, it doesn't need to be that.'

'You think this is just about adventure?'

'I know it's about your mother, but she wouldn't want you putting yourself in danger.' His voice was firm.

'She wouldn't want me to hide from it either.' Tears of exaspera-tion pricked her eyes. 'I've spent too many years hiding from life, I won't go back to being that person.'

'I like her just fine.'

'You don't know her, I'm different here, braver. I run, swim, cycle, zip wire, I'm beginning to have a life.'

Jay stepped closer, his eyes were dark and unhappy. 'And you do invoices and books, you organise cupboards like you were born to it, make friends who care for you. You're not defined by the amount of excitement you can pack into your life Alice, or by the number of challenges you set yourself.'

'I know that,' Alice said, exasperated.

'I don't want to be part of anything bad happening to you.'

'So you'll wrap me in cotton wool, stand in my way when I want to do something you don't consider safe?'

'I took you on the zip wire,' Jay snapped.

'An adventure you could control.' Alice could feel the temper rising, making her skin tingle and her teeth grind. She clenched her fists, trying to fight the words climbing up her throat. 'Don't get me wrong, I loved it, I've loved everything we've done together but I can't live a life that someone else controls. I do enough of that myself, why do you think I love organising things so much?' She looked around the kitchen. 'Why nothing's ever out of place? On some level I need it. But if I give into it in every corner of my life I won't have one, and I definitely won't if you start controlling everything I do.'

Jay ran a hand through his hair, leaving it standing on end like he'd just been shocked. 'That's not what I'm trying to do.'

'Isn't it?' Alice cocked her head. 'Do you know you're not defined by the number of people you rescue? Or that no matter how many times you save someone you're never going to bring your brother back?'

'That's not what I'm doing.'

'Isn't it?' Alice stepped aside and opened the door, as tears pricked her eyes. 'I know you want to help, I know you want to save everybody Jay, but sometimes you've got to let people save themselves.'

☆

Cath shut the door with a sigh as the last couple left the café and turned to survey the mess.

'Another day in paradise,' she muttered, locking it after them. 'You going to stop moping?'

'Nope.' Alice flopped on a chair as tears welled up in her eyes, they'd been doing that a lot.

Cath picked up a tray and started piling plates and mugs onto it haphazardly. 'I'm worried about you, you've practically gone a whole day without reorganising something. Do you want to have a look in my handbag, it's a mess?'

Alice tried to smile, but the edges of her mouth seem to be frozen downwards. 'I've an urge to do something about the plates on that tray, but I can't seem to muster the energy.'

'Jay hasn't called?' Cath didn't wait for an answer, instead she disappeared through the door into the kitchen, returning a few minutes later with an empty tray which she began to pile up again. Plates, cups, saucers and a couple of vases quickly stacked up.

'I'm sorry.' Alice gathered a salt and pepper shaker and piled it on.

'Sit, I'm fine. You normally do twice the work of anyone else, I can manage. Have you called him?'

'Once, two days ago, but I didn't know what to say so I hung up. I don't know what to do.' Alice put her head in her hands and stared at the table. 'Castle Cove isn't the same without him.'

Cath sighed. Leaving the tray, she sat opposite. 'I know how you feel.'

'Dan?'

'He keeps calling.'

'You miss him?'

Cath shook her head. 'Not sure why.'

'So it's Shaun?'

Her friend's cheeks pinked. 'I've been thinking about him a lot over the last few days. He'd never cheat. I'm not sure I ever appreciated how good it felt to be with someone you could trust so completely.'

'Maybe not so boring?'

'Maybe.' Cath tapped a finger on the table.

'Have you called him?'

Cath narrowed her eyes. 'We weren't talking about me. What are you going to do?'

'I don't know.'

'This adventure of yours was never meant to be about a man, or a relationship, Jay was just supposed to be a bit of fun remember?'

'He's more than that.'

'You love him?'

Alice nodded. 'But when I think back to my mum, all those promises I made to myself, I can't give them up.'

'So maybe you shouldn't?'

'What do you mean?'

Cath shrugged. 'Maybe you should still do the triathlon, go on your trip. You know I don't want you to go, but maybe if you don't, you'll regret it.'

'I can't do the triathlon without Jay. It wouldn't feel right.' Standing at the start, knowing he wasn't there. Alice felt empty just thinking about it.

'So don't do it.' Cath said firmly.

'As easy as that?'

'Why not. It's okay to run away sometimes Alice. God knows I've wanted to. You've got somewhere to go. If being here's too painful, start your adventures early.' Cath looked around the room. 'It won't be the same here, but Alice, all you've talked about since you arrived is going to Thailand, maybe you'll regret it if you don't go?'

Alice knotted her fingers, twisting them this way and that, mimicking the turmoil in her head. 'I don't know what to do.'

Someone tapped on one of the panes of glass in the door and Alice got up and went to look through the window. 'It's Dan. You didn't turn the sign, it says we're still open.'

'Bugger.' Cath came to join her. 'I guess I couldn't avoid him forever.' She opened the door and stood out of the way as Dan barrelled inside.

'More new jeans?' Cath folded her arms.

'Could you give us some privacy please?' Dan waved a hand in Alice's direction.

'Please don't.' Cath left the door open but flicked the sign to closed. 'I'm not sure you've got anything to say to me Alice can't hear.'

Dan brushed his hands on his starched pink shirt looking less confident. 'Whatever you want babe. I'm sorry, I messed up. Cath, I know it's a cliché, but she didn't mean anything.'

'She did to me.' Cath picked up a cup and saucer from one of the tables and added it to the increasing pile on the tray. 'She made me think about what I want.'

Dan looked confused. 'We want the same things.'

'I'm not sure we do.'

'We have fun together,' Dan said. 'That's all that's important.'

'Nope.' Cath's curls bounced as she shook her head. 'Last night I was trying to remember the last time we went out.'

'We're always out.'

'No, I remember you being out, I remember lending you money, I remember working or having to stay in because I had an early shift. Last time I went out was with Alice, time before that too.'

'So we'll go out.' Dan stretched his arms as if to hug her but she stepped back.

'I think you're right Dan, I'm boring.'

His forehead creased and he dropped his arms. 'Babe, you're not.'

'I am, but I like being boring and maybe I am on my way to becoming middle-aged, but I like that too.' Cath widened her eyes as if she was seeing something for the first time.

'You're not boring.'

'How do you know? I'm not sure you know anything about me. Do you know I like to eat chocolate cake, drink tea and watch the telly in the evenings because I'm tired?'

Dan looked surprised but didn't say anything.

'Do you know I don't like going out at night or meeting new people, people I don't care about and who won't remember my name the next time we have a conversation?' Cath smiled. 'No, you didn't know that either, and damn, it's good to finally be honest.' Cath fluffed her hair with her hands. 'Do you know a few months ago, I watched a programme on knitting and decided I wanted to try it, only I didn't.' She looked annoyed. 'Because of you.'

'I never said you couldn't knit,' Dan exclaimed.

'No.' Cath blew out a long breath. 'I did, and how stupid does that make me? Sitting in alone, not knitting, while you were out doing who knows what with who knows who.'

Dan opened his mouth and closed it reminding Alice of a goldfish. 'You're making no sense.'

'I'm not, am I?' Cath grinned suddenly. 'How very middle-aged of me. I'm sorry Dan, but I think I'm over this. I want stability and honesty, I want someone to stay in with, and it's not you.'

'You want to knit?'

'I do.'

'I don't understand.' Dan ran a hand through his red hair looking exasperated.

'No, but I do.' Shaun said appearing in the doorway, his eyes fixed on Cath, his expression unreadable.

'You do?' Cath's eyes widened as he nodded and stepped inside the café.

'I know you love coffee and chocolate cake, sometimes for break-fast. I know you enjoy warm baths on dark nights and sometimes you like it if someone scrubs your back.'

Dan's mouth dropped open but Cath's eyes stayed firmly fixed on Shaun's face. He stepped closer, ignoring everyone else in the room. It was like they'd entered a vortex where the whole world spun around the two of them and Alice couldn't look away.

'I know all of your favourite TV programmes, I've been recording them in case you came back, even though I've been too angry to ask you, or to apologise for being such a stupid ass.' Shaun's voice deepened.

'You have?' Cath's voice wobbled.

Shaun nodded. 'You were right Cath. I took you for granted and I'm sorry. You don't have to marry me, just be with me. Life is too short, people die and all that matters in the end is that you fill your world with the people you love, keep them close, and make them happy.'

'You make me happy,' Cath murmured.

Shaun nodded. 'You make me happy too. I knew you'd want to take up knitting before you did. Before we split up, I'd bought you some needles and wool.'

A tear tracked down Cath's face. 'You did?'

Shaun nodded.

Cath smiled, her eyes luminous. 'I could knit you a jumper.'

Shaun laughed. 'The wool's pink, but what the hell. I'll wear anything you make for me, because all I want is you.' He took another step and suddenly they were in each other's arms hugging and kissing. Shaun picked Cath up and spun her around as Dan shook his head and disappeared out of the café door.

Alice watched them for a while, her heart swollen with a strange mixture of love and sadness. She was so happy for her friends, but watching Cath and Shaun reminded her of the argument with Jay, and how they'd never be together.

Alice stood and removed her apron and put it on one of the tables. 'You know you're right Cath, all the time I've been listening to you, I've been thinking about what I want and need.' The couple stopped embracing and faced her. Shaun's arm was slung over Cath's shoulder and she leaned into the hug, her face glowing. 'I'm so sorry, but I can't work tonight because I'll be packing. Watching you both has made me realise that I want what you have and I'm not going to find it in Castle Cove. I think it's time I went to Thailand like I planned.' Alice blew a kiss at Cath. 'I'm so happy for you, I love you, and I'll be in touch as soon as I land.'

Chapter Thirty-Five

Alice stretched. Her back ached from last night's shift in Tom Yum – the restaurant she'd worked in since arriving in Phuket two weeks earlier. Who knew such a small place could feed so many people, or how much the tourists' capacity for eating spicy green curry really was endless? Alice only had a couple of hours before she needed to get back to work.

She surveyed the deck of her father's boat. He'd gone to buy supplies with Beth, leaving all the mess from the last diving expedition. He'd told her to leave it, to lie on the beach and enjoy the heat, but she couldn't. She picked up the stray plastic cups that had been left behind and headed for the shed where they kept the equipment.

Alice just needed to hose down the wetsuits and hang them up, check the tanks and wash the bits and pieces they'd used for lunch. She put a kettle on to heat some water so she could add it to a bowl they used as a makeshift sink, then opened the cupboard underneath it. A couple of cleaning products fell onto the floor and she dropped to her knees and pulled everything else out – a small chipped cup, yellow, blue and green bowls, a couple of rags and some washing-up liquid, the same brand they'd used in the café in Castle Cove. She sighed and hugged it to her chest as tears pricked her eyes. 'You think if I pulled this off the wall, Jay would come and fix it?'

'I thought you'd still be here.' Her father's deep voice echoed behind her.

'I thought you'd gone shopping?' Alice twisted on her knees to face him.

'Beth said she'd go ahead, I wanted to talk to you.' He turned a large plastic barrel onto its side and sat.

Alice hadn't seen her dad for five years, aside from a few snaps on WhatsApp, and when she'd arrived at the airport, she'd almost walked past him. He looked younger, his beard had gotten silvery and the deep tan on his legs and arms made him look fit and healthy, proving living in Thailand suited him. Just looking at him made her feel warm.

Alice leaned back. 'What do you want to talk about?'

'I wondered if you'd like to go out on the boat tomorrow, just the two of us, I could take you diving?'

'I've got to work at Tom Yum.'

'Again?' He looked annoyed. 'I thought you were working tonight?'

'I offered, they were short-staffed.' It would keep her busy too.

'They always are, because they work everyone too hard and they leave,' he explained. 'See if you can swap your shift?'

'I'm not sure.' Alice picked up a rag from the cupboard and wiped around the sink.

'Alice.' Her dad touched her arm, held it. 'Can you stop just for a minute?'

Alice sank to the floor, putting her knees up in front of her so she could hug them, feeling like a little girl.

'You've been here for two weeks and you haven't changed colour.' Her dad pointed to her pale legs.

'I've been busy.'

'Working, I know.' He paused. 'I love having you here.'

'I love being here,' Alice said. 'You think I'm working too hard?'

'I know that's not what you came here for. You told me you came for adventure, and unless your adventure consists of working until dawn in a Thai restaurant, collapsing on a bed until lunchtime and then helping us to clean up after our guests, you're not having one.'

'Not everyone's idea of adventure is the same.'

'Sure you're not just using work as an excuse?' His forehead creased.

'For what?' Alice knew what he was getting at but didn't want to face it.

He reached out and took her hand. 'To stay busy so you forget? You sounded happy in Castle Cove, I thought you'd met someone?'

'We were looking for different things.' Alice turned her face away as her eyes misted.

'So, the man didn't work out, you've still got a chance to do something with your life here. I admire your work ethic, but you haven't had a day at the beach, or made any friends since you came, it's not like you.' He squeezed her hand.

Alice pulled it away. 'How do you know?'

He looked surprised.

'Sorry, I wasn't criticising, but it's exactly like me.' Alice bit her lip. 'I'm just like Mum, I like being busy.'

'She'd have found time to put her feet up, gone diving. She'd probably have signed herself up for a race by now. She wouldn't have been hiding away in here.'

'Maybe I'm not like her?'

'You're exactly like your mum. Except when she was unhappy she went out instead of burying herself away.'

'Why did you divorce?' Alice asked suddenly.

Her dad shrugged. 'Nothing sinister. We grew apart. Your mum wanted passion, excitement and challenges and I didn't give that to her.'

'The divorce was her idea?'

'We were happier in the end. We never meant to hurt you. It took us a while until we realised we had. I think your mother hoped by getting you to Castle Cove she could help you find yourself again.'

Alice nodded. Maybe she had.

Her dad leaned forwards, his expression intense. 'Call in sick, come out on the boat this afternoon.'

'Maybe tomorrow.'

'Promise?' Her dad brightened.

'Sure.' Alice couldn't say no. 'Tomorrow.'

Chapter Thirty-Six

'She's miserable.' Jay's mother looked inside his empty cup and swirled the tea leaves. 'And she misses you.'

Jay sighed and glanced at Ben who grimaced and took another sip of the black tea. Jay had to hand it to the guy, he wasn't complaining, maybe he was a smitten as his mother seemed to be?

'I doubt that.'

'Cath says she's working all the time.'

Cath hadn't told him anything.

'Can't you take some time off?' His mother put the kettle on, he'd have to make an excuse before he got subjected to yet another cup of tea.

'Not sure why I would,' Jay grumbled.

'To get some sun?'

'There's plenty of sunshine here, besides, what about my job? I've got months of work lined up, and I'm on call.'

'I think your clients could wait an extra week.' His mother took his cup and rinsed the tealeaves down the sink. 'And I'm sure the others would cover for you.'

'I don't want another one.' Jay pointed to the empty cup.

His mum pulled out her box of tea leaves and opened the fridge. 'Ben dear, I don't suppose you could get me some milk?'

'You've got some.'

She cleared her throat. 'You're mistaken, I could do with a couple of pints and maybe a pack of cat food?'

'Oh.' Ben looked between them and Jay tried not to laugh. Ben was growing on him. Even if he wasn't ready to accept a new man in his mother's life, he could see how much she'd changed. Since the day at the beach, his mother had transformed back into the vibrant woman he remembered from his childhood.

'No problem.' Ben gave his mother a peck on the cheek, and a backwards, apologetic glance at Jay before disappearing.

'You wanted to talk to me?' Jay wasn't going to let her skirt around it. Far too many years had been spent avoiding things.

'I think you might want to talk.' His mum pulled up a chair and sat, and a cat wound itself around her ankles. 'Do you want to ask me anything, Jay?'

Jay reached for the mug and was surprised when he didn't find it. Where was his cup of tea leaves to bury his face in when he needed it?

'You want me to guess what you want to ask?' His mother smiled, her eyes creasing in the corners.

'It all feels so long ago.'

'Just because time passes, it doesn't make things mean any less. I know you want to ask me about your brother.' Her eyes misted. 'I find it difficult to talk about him too. I know you've always tried to get me to open up but I found it easier to ignore.' She looked guilty. 'I thought it was best for both of us, now I wonder who I thought I was helping. I hurt you.'

The admission surprised him. 'No.'

'Alice said you blamed yourself, I've always known that on some level, but now I wonder if you thought I blamed you too?'

Damn this was hard. Maybe talking about it all wasn't such a good idea, burying the whole thing felt—

'It was never your fault, you know that?'

Jay agreed without looking at her. 'Can I have some tea?' He needed something to focus on so he bent to stroke the top of the cat's head.

His mum put the kettle on. 'Your dad and I were having problems.' She looked out of the window. 'I tried to keep it from you both but I think Steve had an inkling. He'd heard us arguing one afternoon when he got home from school.'

Jay avoided looking at her. 'Everyone has problems at some point, Steve wouldn't have taken it to heart.' If he had, surely he'd have said something?

'Don't be silly, you wanted me to be honest and I am.' His mother tapped his hand sharply. 'He asked some questions. We tried to compensate and pretend everything was okay afterwards, then when... it happened, I guess your dad felt like he had no reason to stay.'

'He never contacted you? I always wondered.'

'I think he found it easier to just move on. I know he met someone soon after, although she could have been on the scene before.' She screwed up her face. 'You never knew with your father.' Jay knew the shock must have shown on his face because his mother blushed. 'And that's more than you needed to know.'

'I thought... ' This was more than he could take in.

'I let you. I didn't want to spoil your memories, perhaps that was another mistake? Steve was a happy boy, you were the serious one. You looked after me right from the start. I still remember you insisting I put my feet up when I was pregnant with him.' She laughed. 'You were only three, you sat on my feet so I rested.' The smile fell. 'You've always taken too much on.'

'I like being responsible, I know I can take it too far.'

'It's important to let your hair down sometimes, to be irresponsible.'

'I did that once,' Jay murmured. 'I ditched Steve to kiss a girl I hardly knew, and look what happened.' The words burned in his stomach, the acid reflux of memory. Damn, if he could go back and change that day he would.

'Your father was meant to take him for a cycle ride, he forgot. If he hadn't, you'd have been the one getting ditched.'

'Two wrongs don't make a right.'

'Taking on guilt when it isn't yours to shoulder isn't right either.'

She paused long enough to make him another cup of tea. He grabbed the thin china mug and wrapped his fingers round it like a drowning man clinging to a life raft.

'I never thought you'd think I blamed you.'

Jay couldn't deny that's what he'd believed, all this time. Hearing her say she didn't, made him feel strangely light. 'I learned to live with that.'

'You shouldn't have, I never blamed you, neither did your dad.'

Jay shook his head. 'Things changed so much after. No-one wanted to talk about it, especially not to me.'

'We were grieving, fighting, I guess we thought not talking about it would make things more normal. God.' She ran a hand through her hair. 'Neither of us knew what we were doing. I lost my head for a long time after, I could hardly bring myself to get out of bed.'

'I remember.'

The blue of her eyes shone with unshed tears. 'I never meant to make you feel guilty, or to shut you out. It's taken me a long time to face what happened, and to accept my part in it. I stayed in a marriage that was wrong. I put up with a man who didn't give my children the time or attention they deserved. If anyone's responsible for Steve's death it's me.' A single tear slid down her face.

'You're not to blame.'

'Neither are you,' she said gently. 'It's time you accepted that and pushed that weight of responsibility off your shoulders. Live a little, let yourself go mad, be irresponsible. Stop trying to save everyone,' she pleaded. 'I can't believe I'm saying this, it's the opposite of what most parents want, but I guess I think it's time you let yourself be young. You've spent far too much time being a grown up, let someone else do it for a while.'

The front door banged and they both looked up. 'I could get him to go and buy some chocolate biscuits?' His mother's eyes crinkled at the joke and he put a hand over hers.

'I'm glad you've got him, it'll take me a while to get used to the idea, but I can see he makes you happy.'

'He's helped me see things… differently.'

Some people did that.

'I think you should go after her.' She gave him the mother look.

'She's where she wants to be,' Jay said a little too sharply. Ben walked into the kitchen with a couple of bags.

'I got biscuits.' Ben dropped them by the fridge and shrugged when they laughed. 'You're talking, I'll put it away later.' He backed away and left the room.

'You sure she's where she wants to be?' His mother watched Ben retreat. 'Maybe she's like the rest of us and doesn't have a clue?'

'She didn't even stay for the triathlon, she wanted to leave so badly.'

'You could go and bring her back?'

'Why would I?' Jay drank the tea in one, just avoiding choking by leaving a small swamp of leaves in the bottom. 'I've got to go.'

'Stay for dinner, apparently, we have biscuits.' His mum smiled.

'I've got stuff to do.'

Jay was meant to be singing in the pub later, and Zeus needed to be walked. Somehow, he couldn't work up the enthusiasm for either but he'd go through the motions because it was what he did.

Zeus barked and wagged his tail when Jay opened the door of the house. Peter headed out of the kitchen with his backpack. Peter was fifteen, lanky, with a dark fringe that covered most of his face. His skin was clear, aside from a couple of spots on his forehead.

'Bad day?' the boy asked.

'Usual,' Jay grumbled.

Peter nodded, no explanation necessary. 'I've fed Zeus and I walked him earlier.'

'Sure.' Jay nodded. 'How's your mum?' he added, more out of courtesy than interest. He wanted to be alone.

'Keeping to the parks.' The boy answered, heading for the door. 'I still don't understand how she managed to get herself stuck on those rocks.'

Jay shrugged. 'Easily done. The tides come in quickly at certain times of the year. She's not the first and won't be the last.'

Peter flashed a smile. 'Thanks again for saving her. You're basically a god in our house. I think Mum's got a bit of a crush on you to be honest. Dad's not best pleased.'

'Ah, well.' Jay opened the door. Usually the thought of a rescue filled him with warmth, but today he felt empty. He handed Peter a couple of notes. 'Thanks for dog sitting. I'll call when I need you again.'

'Sure.'

Jay closed the door and headed back into the kitchen. A pile of mail sat on the counter and he flicked through it, pausing at an envelope with his address scrawled in unreadable handwriting, postmarked Castle Cove.

Ripping it open he pulled out a pack of information about the triathlon.

He chucked the pack on the counter and pulled a beer from the fridge, then took a long sip, ignoring Zeus padding around his legs.

He headed for the deck and stood just inside the large windows staring at the sea. The waves were calm today but the sky looked cloudy. What time would it be in Thailand? Would Alice be swimming? Damn, he hoped not, what happened if there was no-one around to help if she got into trouble?

That wasn't his problem any more.

Jay glanced at his bookshelf. Steve stared at him from the silver picture frame. The picture had been taken a year before he died, they were standing over their bikes, smiling. It had been a good day on the beach, cycling between dunes. His dad hadn't turned up, he remembered that now, he'd promised to join them and had pulled out at the last minute. His stomach squeezed. His mum had laughed but it had sounded false and even then, he'd known something was wrong, he'd never thought to ask what.

Steve had been happy though, he remembered that. He'd been fearless too, always getting into scrapes, and for as far back as Jay remembered, Steve had expected him to dig them both out of any problems he'd managed to get them into.

And Jay had.

He shook his head, and picked up the frame in one hand staring into his brother's eyes. If he was here now, what would he say?

That you're a bloody idiot.

Jay put the frame down, turning from his perfectly alphabetized bookshelf and headed for the door.

'Zeus.' He knew the dog would be at his heels before he got outside. He'd rearrange those books when he got home, he didn't need any more reminders of Alice.

The air smelled fresh as Jay headed towards the beach. Zeus ran ahead, tracing the path they'd been taking every night since Alice had left. Along the sea front and promenade, up Fisherman's Road and then through town, out the other side, up Sunny Lane, left at Albert Street, right onto Regents Road, past her house and then up again onto the cliffs. He walked quickly with his hands in his pockets, ignoring the ache in his chest as he passed Alice's house. The lights shone above the shutters so Cath was obviously living there at the moment and Shaun's car was parked in a space just outside. He sped up.

The air felt cooler on the cliffs but he welcomed the way the cold burned his skin. Stars flickered as the sun began to set and still Jay walked, pushing Alice, his mum, Steve and the boy in hospital from his mind. Maybe if he walked all night he'd be able to forget them? He travelled further, ignoring the dark as it surrounded him. He had a torch somewhere at home. If Alice was here, she'd have pulled one out of her backpack by now, along with a couple of cheese sandwiches and a blanket. God, he missed her.

Jay found a bench and sat, searching for the North Star. Usually the sound of the sea and the wind calmed him, but today everything felt off.

Zeus sniffed the grass around his feet and he leaned down and picked up a stick and threw it. The dog bounded after it.

Jay wondered what Alice would be doing right now? Could she be miserable? Could the great adventure not be all she'd hoped for? If he hadn't tried to stop her competing in the triathlon, would she still be here? He breathed in deep and let the air out slowly searching for the North Star, remembering the day he'd first pointed it out to Alice.

He missed her more than he thought possible. He hadn't felt this lonely when Mel had left, somehow life had continued, as if a wave had flooded his life erasing his feelings and memories. No wave had come this time, instead there was an empty space where his heart used to be.

Zeus put his head on Jay's knee as he continued to search for the star. Maybe if he found it he'd know what to do?

Chapter Thirty-Seven

Sun wasn't all it was cracked up to be, Alice decided as she lay in the sand, squeezing some between her fingers. She'd been lying in the same place for almost twenty minutes and was already restless. She watched tourists play in the sea, throwing water over each other; a couple headed into the waves kitted out in flippers and snorkels, on the hunt for fish all colours of the rainbow.

Stupid, but she couldn't get excited about any of it. Her dad had tried to get her out on the boat again but she couldn't summon the enthusiasm. She hadn't been into the sea for a swim either, somehow being in there without Jay didn't feel right, like he'd become necessary to her happiness.

Alice picked up her *Lonely Planet* and pad. She'd been making a list of the places she wanted to visit while she was in Thailand, only she hadn't got far beyond the airport. There was so much to do here, but every time she imagined herself zip wiring, or trekking through jungles Jay's voice rang in her head, telling her to be careful.

The temperature must have notched up another twenty degrees since she'd been sitting here. She might as well have been slathered in factor two million and five, but a swim would help her cool off. She surveyed the waves through narrowed eyes, maybe a paddle?

The water felt cool, not cold like Castle Cove where the temperature seeped right into your bones. She took another step, allowing the waves to wash over her knee, bringing a wave of sadness with it.

Why did men have to be such idiots? She walked further in and looking closely under the waves she could see schools of fish darting back and forth commuting between her legs. People were splashing around her, shouting and laughing, Alice sighed and moved in deeper, enjoying the sensation as the ocean hit her waist and then shoulders, wiping out the burning heat.

Strange how all of the fear had gone, like a dark cloud had evaporated. She had Jay to thank for that, without him she'd still be sitting on the beach, counting grains of sand. She stood looking forwards at the horizon, the sky shone blue and there were no clouds. What would Castle Cove be like today? Would the sun be shining? She swallowed a surge of what felt like homesickness.

The café would be busy if the weather was good and Cath, Lily or Anya would be manic. Maybe Olive would be in there now in her too-large coat, chatting with Ted about the letters he'd delivered?

Alice had exchanged emails with Cath a few times since she'd arrived and knew Lily and Anya were covering her job at the café between them, but it was only temporary. Cath still hoped she'd come back. God, she missed it, the pub too, and Tiger.

Alice waded in deeper, until the water hit her neck.

'You not swimming?' The voice was so familiar yet so out of context Alice didn't recognise it at first. She spun around to find Jay stood about a foot away, dressed in swimming trunks, with water at his waist lapping his flat stomach.

Alice blinked a few times but he didn't disappear.

Jay waded further until they were standing toe to toe. She couldn't take her eyes off his face, drinking in every contour and line.

'Why are you here?'

He studied her. 'Fancied a swim.'

'In Thailand?'

His eyes scanned her face, resting on her mouth and her stomach did that dippy thing again. 'I missed you,' Jay said eventually.

'I don't understand.' The waves pushed Alice forwards and she leaned into his chest. She could smell sea again and she wanted to touch him badly, but stayed put. 'Tell me why you're here?' Her heartbeat picked up speed as she watched him, exploring his body with her eyes.

'I'm sorry I tried to stop you doing the triathlon. I was wrong and scared.' Jay paused, but she didn't say anything.

'I shut you out, wouldn't let you get close because I was afraid you'd be taken from me.' He frowned. 'And all I succeeded in doing was to push you away myself. I know you need this. You've got places to see, things to do, I would never stand in the way of that, no matter how much I wanted to.'

'You want to?'

'I've been thinking maybe I need adventure too.' Jay grinned. 'If you can wait, I could rent my place, come and join you?'

'Oh.' The smile built inside her but she knew it hadn't reached her face because he still looked unhappy. 'What about Zeus?'

'My mum said she'd have him.' His frown deepened.

'And the lifeboat?'

'I can take some time off, I've checked, they'll get cover.'

'And your mum?'

Jay shook his head. 'She doesn't really need me, especially now Ben's on the scene.'

'I like him.'

'Me too.' Jay nodded. 'So it's all lined up, I can join you... if you want me?'

'I'm not sure... '

Jay's frown deepened further and Alice put a hand on his chest, relishing the feel of his skin after their weeks apart.

'... that Thailand's where I want to be. All I've been thinking about since I arrived is how much I miss Castle Cove.'

'Oh.' Jay didn't smile but something sparkled behind his eyes and he took a step closer. 'Go on.' His voice deepened.

'I miss the café and the pub, I miss the sea, even though it's cold.'

'And?'

'I miss running on the cliffs and looking for the North Star. Did you know you can't see it here?'

'Anything else?' Jay stepped closer.

'Zeus.' Alice stopped herself from smiling, but could feel the shimmer of tears in her eyes. 'Is he single yet?'

His mouth twitched.

'And,' Alice put her arms around his waist and pulled herself closer, 'I miss you Jay O'Donnell. All I've been able to think about since I arrived is how much I wish you were here. I haven't been able to bring myself to swim because you aren't swimming with me.'

Jay smiled. 'I went walking a few nights ago on the cliffs, I've been going every night since you left and when I looked for the North Star I couldn't find it. I lost my anchor when you left, I lost my home and my mind. I don't care where I live, it just needs to be with you. I've spent so long feeling tied to a place, because I felt guilty, I guess maybe I've realised without guilt, I'm tied to nothing, except you.'

'Well.' Alice rested her head against his chest. 'I think I'd prefer to be in Castle Cove. I love Thailand, it's beautiful and it's been amazing to see my dad, but I miss what I had. Being here feels like a holiday, not a life. I want to run and to sit on the cliffs looking for the North Star, with you. I've realised adventure isn't about a place, it's about who you're with and what you do every day, it's about finding time to live as well as work.'

'What if I try and rescue you again?'

Alice reached up to kiss his mouth. 'Isn't that what you're doing now? I needed you and you've come. If that's not what a superhero does, I don't know what is.'

☆

'Are you ready?' Jay paused in front of the Anglers and pulled Alice into his chest for a quick hug as she shivered. The sun was still high and warm, even at seven o'clock in the evening, but the temperature had dropped a good ten degrees from what she'd been used to in Thailand.

'I'm nervous,' Alice whispered into Jay's t-shirt, pulling him closer so she could breathe him in. 'What if they've forgotten me?'

'No-one's forgotten you.' Jay opened the door as everyone in the pub began to clap.

'Woo hoo!' Cath shrieked, launching herself at Alice and dragging her inside. The place looked packed and all the tables were filled with faces she recognised from the café. There were balloons strung over the bar with a welcome home banner and Shaun stood behind it wearing a pink knitted jumper that stretched across his chest. He beamed at Cath as she walked into the crowd with Alice and blew her a kiss.

'Thank God Jay dragged you back home, you've no idea what it's been like here without you organising us all.' Cath said, her eyes shining. 'Someone's already un-alphabetised the soft drinks. When I went to pick up a lemonade tonight I got cola and the café is a shambles. Castle Cove's falling apart without you.'

'It's true,' Ted shouted from a table next to the bar. 'Even the coffee tastes different.' He pulled a face; next to him Olive nodded and Lily chuckled.

To the left of the bar, beside a couple of café regulars, Alice spotted Simon. His jaw looked more angular than normal and his mouth had set into a grim line. He sat glaring at Marta from the gallery, who chatted with Anya, oblivious.

'Don't ask,' Cath muttered in her ear. 'I thought they'd made up, but every time Marta comes near the castle I think Simon's going to push her into the wine cellar and lock the door.'

Alice laughed as Gayle swept over to give her a warm hug. 'I'm pleased you decided to come back,' she said. 'I knew you would but I wasn't sure how long it would take. This one,' Gayle nodded at Jay with an indulgent smile, 'has been moping since you left. Honestly, I thought if I gave him enough of my tea it would make him leave the country, but it took more cups than I expected.'

'I agree, he's been a nightmare.' Shaun came to give her a big bear hug. 'Me and the guys were thinking of taking him to Thailand in the lifeboat, only we decided we couldn't risk it because we'd probably push him out half way there. Welcome back, when can you start work?' Shaun joked, squeezing her shoulder as he stepped back.

Alice grabbed hold of Jay's hand, her eyes shining. 'I can't believe I ever left. Thank you for this.' She looked around the room, feeling her heart overflow. 'I missed you, more than I expected.'

'We missed you too,' Cath said as Shaun popped a couple of bottles of prosecco and began to pour it into glasses. Anya, Lily and Cath helped and in a few minutes the whole room had a drink. 'To Alice, thank you for coming back to us, the place hasn't been the same without you. We promise to keep your life filled with adventures so big, you'll never think of leaving us again.' Cath continued.

'Hear, hear.' The crowd chorused and Alice sipped her bubbles as Jay leaned down to murmur into her ear.

'I never did show you my etchings, did I?'

Alice laughed. 'You can show me them later.'

'I'll hold you to that.' Jay murmured. He tipped Alice's chin and leaned in for a long deep, kiss.

☆

The sun beat down on Alice as she stood at the triathlon starting line. After six months of training the day had finally arrived and she was ready for it. Her wetsuit felt tight again – maybe she'd been eating too much since she'd been back from Thailand? But that's what happened when you were happy.

The sea looked dark but the waves were gentle and inviting. Alice took a deep breath, feeling nervous. Butterflies fluttered inside her stomach but she didn't feel afraid. She turned towards the crowd gathered on the beach. In the background Cove Castle rose up into the sky, its grey stone glinting in the sunshine. A red flag on one of the castle turrets waved in the gentle wind and Alice knew that Simon had got someone to put it up this morning, especially to cheer them on.

Olive, Ted, Shaun, Lily, Anya, Gayle and Ben beamed at them from the beach and Cath held up a banner reading *Go Alice*.

'You ready?' Jay put an arm round Alice's shoulder and moved closer.

'Sure.' She turned and tugged him closer, putting her arms around his neck so she could kiss him firmly on the lips, letting herself linger until someone shouted at them to get ready.

'And later we'll get our tattoos?'

'Of the North Star, so we can always find our way home.' Jay nodded.

'Remember I'll be there every step of the way today.'

Alice smiled. 'I'm counting on it.'

The whistle went off and Alice grabbed Jay's hand and ran towards her next adventure.

A Letter from Donna

I want to say a huge thank you for choosing to read *Summer at the Castle Café*. If you enjoyed it (and I really hope you did), and want to keep up-to-date with all my latest releases, please sign up at the following link. Your email address will never be shared and you can unsubscribe at any time.

www.bookouture.com/donnaashcroft

Summer at the Castle Café was such a joy to write and I'm so excited that I've been able to share it with you. Did you fall in love with Jay as much as I did? Did the romance between Jay and Alice make you laugh, cry and crave a delicious slice of chocolate cake like the one served in the Castle Café? Did you enjoy visiting Castle Cove in the summertime? If you did, it would be wonderful if you could please leave a short review. Not only do I want to know what you thought, it might encourage a new reader to pick up my book for the first time.

I really love hearing from my readers – so please get in touch on my Facebook page, through Twitter, Goodreads or my website.

Thank you,
Donna x

www.facebook.com/DonnaAshcroftAuthor

@Donnashc

www.donna-writes.co.uk

Acknowledgements

Writing a book is a team sport. I might provide the words, but they wouldn't be half as good, or even make it onto the page in the first place, without the amazing team of people who have helped and supported me over the years. I'd like to say a huge thank you to all of them.

Firstly, to my own hero Chris and gorgeous children Erren and Charlie – you've lived through the highs, lows, and hastily thrown together meals (or cooked them for me). Thank you for putting up with me!

To Natasha Harding, I'm so appreciative that you loved my writing and have given me this chance to be published. Thank you from the bottom of my heart, I love working with you and the rest of the incredible Bookouture team and can't wait to continue.

Katie Fforde – a huge thank you for awarding me the joint Katie Fforde Bursary in 2017. You are pure magic, and I will be eternally grateful for the incredible boost to my confidence.

To the RNA and New Writers' Scheme – I'm so proud to be part of such an incredible and supportive organisation. A big thanks to the readers and the whole team behind it.

To all of my writing buddies – Jules for your support, cheerleading and kick up the bum when I've wanted to give up. The Prosecco Writers – Anita, Liz and Jules – we've had some wonderful and productive weekends, one of which helped to birth this story. To the Tring Writers, especially Sue, Katy, Moira, Jude, Indra and Nick – joining you over ten years ago was definitely the first step in my journey to publication.

To Jackie and Julie, a lucky star was looking down on me when you came into my life. You've kept me sane, believed in me when I didn't, and have helped to make me the writer I am today.

To my work colleagues, especially Gemma, Ben and Kay. Thanks for giving me the time to write and for being so fantastic to work with. Good work days definitely help to make better stories.

Finally, to Mum, Dad, Peter, Christelle, Tanya, Lynda, Louis, Philip and the rest of my family. I'm so lucky to have you all.